CURIOUSER AND CURIOUSER . . .

skulked up four dim flights—each step threatening to squeal—until I saw light sort of oozing out an open door. I paused on the stairs.

There were two voices: Laszlo's overfamiliar mush and an odd, somehow pedantic voice, a low baritone, that spoke in a strange accent involving clicks on every consonant, like a professor of philosophy accompanying himself on castanets.

More stealthily than the cats of Queen Berúthiel, I made my way to the door and peered in ever so cautiously. I was lucky: they had their backs to me, and I got a good, long look.

My mind very carefully boggled.

The other voice belonged to a six-foot-tall, deep blue lobster. This was getting more interesting than I really liked.

THE
BUTTERFLY
KID

THE
BUTTERFLY
KID

THE GREENWICH VILLAGE TRILOGY
BOOK ONE

CHESTER ANDERSON

With a Foreword by Peter S. Beagle

DOVER PUBLICATIONS, INC.
MINEOLA, NEW YORK

For Lee and Toni Lamb, sine quibus non

FOREWORD

Robin Williams is supposed to be the guy who first said, "If you can remember the sixties, you weren't there." It's a perfectly good line, and as accurate as most such good lines. I've heard it attributed to a number of people; any number of aging stoners of my acquaintance still claim it as original, even when they have some difficulty remembering their street addresses. Personally, I usually go with a considerably older Italian saying: *"Si non e vero, e ben trovato."* (If it isn't true, it ought to be.)

Me, I have real trouble with the sixties myself. And I was there.

I already was living and raising a family in the hills of Santa Cruz, California, by 1967, when Chester Anderson published *The Butterfly Kid*. As Donald Trump is forever declaring, "Most people don't know" that it is the first installment—for lack of a more exact term—of a legendary epic called in toto the Greenwich Village Trilogy, written in three sections by three different writers: Anderson; my truly ancient friend Michael Kurland completed the second part, *The Unicorn Girl*, the following year; and T. A. Waters finished off the whole unique opus with *The Probability Pad* in 1969. *The Butterfly Kid* itself was nominated in 1968 for a Hugo Award. Unfortunately, that was the year Roger Zelazny came out with *Lord of Light*. Timing is everything.

I knew Greenwich Village well in those more-or-less innocent pre-acid days. To quote the great jazz poet Dave Frishberg, "I was hip when it was hip to be hep." (In my memory, by the way, to call someone a "hippy" then meant that he or she was faking the style without ever getting it quite right.) One of my several painter uncles had a studio deep in the Village, and my buddy Phil Sigunick and I used to pose for him on a regular basis. He paid us five dollars each, and back then you could get some serious mileage out of ten dollars in Greenwich Village on a sunny afternoon. Our Bronx was as boring as home always is. But, oh, there were golden people hanging around MacDougal Street in our time, Sonny—as, of course, there were in Edna St. Vincent Millay's time and Charlie Parker's time and Delmore Schwartz's time. I know that I saw Lenny Bruce then (still in the process of becoming Lenny Bruce), and Woody Allen doing stand-up a couple of times, and any number of folk and blues singers you might want to mention. Dave van Ronk, naturally, and Brownie McGhee and Sonny Terry; Larry Adler, the great harmonica player, and the tap dancer Paul Draper (both of them run out of the country in the fifties for signing the wrong petition or hanging with the wrong friends). Phil and I were more than once struck silent to spy our hero Josh White walking the street like a natural man. (What? Actually *talk* to him?) Hedy West . . . Judy Collins . . . Ramblin' Jack Elliot . . . that grubby little kid everyone who caught him at Gerde's Folk City called "Lockjaw Dylan." It was that time, and we were that young. Everybody was young.

As are Chester (author and charming, candid narrator of *The Butterfly Kid*) and Mike (doughty, if chronically drowsy, sidekick). The time is some way beyond the sixties—though clearly not *that* far removed—and there's this amiable, innocent kid named Sean. He's just arrived from Fort Worth, Texas, and he's a lead guitarist, and he makes butterflies. They're increasingly big, increasingly numerous, increasingly beautiful butterflies out of nowhere—and he has absolutely no idea how he creates them. Nor do Chester and Mike. Nor does Sativa, Sean's instant groupie. Nor, really, does anyone else in a Village turned even zanier than usual, more than usually populated by what had just better be walking fever dreams and more or less sweet hallucinations. It's all very much as though all of New York City, south of the mystic region where *Hew*-ston Street becomes *How*-ston, has gone on the collective Trip of Trips.

The villain of the piece—and a truly grubby, slovenly, treacherous, pathetic piece he definitely is—turns out to be one Laszlo Scott, currently the purveyor of something he calls Reality Pills, which he scatters freely throughout the Village as the representative of an invasion of six-foot-tall blue lobsters. They're quite courteous, immensely intelligent, and utterly nonviolent—though they have absolutely no objection to violence employed by another species, when it serves their purpose. Their purpose—with the willing assistance of pitiful Laszlo Scott (everyone in the Village, except for friendly blue extraterrestrials, despises Laszlo, and he knows it)—is to test out the reality-distorting Reality Pills on an audience of distortion-tolerant stoners, all as eager for the treat as Mr. Carroll's oysters. If the results are as satisfying as the blue lobsters plainly expect them to be, the next step will be to introduce billions of gallons of "reality" into the New York City water supply, which will inevitably lead to utterly peaceful, utterly remorseless conquest of the entire planet, which, with any luck at all, might not even be noticed.

And the heroes of this epic? The true cavalry riding to the rescue in the nick of time, bugles a-blare and banners a-snap in the wild wind of triumph?

Well . . . there are fourteen of them, counting Chester and Mike, racketing up to the New Croton Reservoir—and directly into it, courtesy of the legendary all-purpose Tripsmobile (courtesy, in turn, of the Merry Pranksters' equally legendary bus *Furthur*). They are more or less called the MacDougal Street Commandos. Many are musicians of one discipline or another—if *discipline* is quite the word I want—often playing at their beloved Garden of Eden coffeeshop, under Chester's *direction* (which may not be the right word either). And as a group they are generally too stoned to be much afraid (thank goodness!). They say "groovy" a lot.

Okay. This is a silly story. It starts out silly, with all those butterflies and all those "groovies," and it unquestionably gets sillier and sillier, what with the blue lobsters ruthlessly torturing the captive Chester by forcing his helpless mind to visualize the complete adventures of Donald Duck: ". . . 3V, wide screen, with full sensory participation. Fine. I've always enjoyed the classics." But the lobsters are only warming up, and it gets worse.

Mind you, it's not a perfect story. (Nobody in the entire development of human speech has ever sounded remotely like poor Laszlo Scott, to start with.) The entire geological epoch has, of course, dated notably itself over half a century. I can testify (being quite nearly as old as Michael Kurland) that "hippy" flourished best and longest in the year-round Greek-myth climate of Northern California and withered early on in the cold, dirty sidewalks of New York City. Then, too, it's impossible for me not to notice the lack of African American persons in the entire novel, since both Phil and I knew so many in the Village, even in those dear, dim days. As I've said, "Timing is everything."

Given these caveats, what we do have is a very nearly pure delight. Each of the successor books takes off in a slightly different direction, but the three stories fit together like pieces in a cosmic jigsaw puzzle and re-create a time that perhaps never was. And without benefit of Reality Pills.

—Peter S. Beagle
El Cerrito, California
October 2019

PREFACE

always feel vaguely cheated by first-person novels wherein the name of the narrator is not the name of the author. This is irrational, but there it is. I never claimed to be particularly rational.

Therefore, I made myself a character in this book, using my own real name (with, of course, my permission). Having gone thus far, I modeled the character of my friend, roommate and manager on my real-life friend, roommate, and (quondam) manager Michael Kurland (with whom I collaborated on *Ten Years to Doomsday*—advt.), using, with his permission, his real name.

Both of these characters, however, are purely fictitious. They are only *based* on us; they are not in reality us.

All other persons, all places, situations and events, are 100 percent fictitious (would you believe 95 percent?), and any resemblance to real persons, places et cetera is both coincidental and ridiculous.

This is especially true of Greenwich Village, where most of this story happens. Do not be deceived: there is no Greenwich Village. Never was. Pure fiction, all of it. Ask anyone who's lived there.

1

The trouble with most warlocks is that they talk too much. That's how I happened to notice the kid in Washington Square: he wasn't saying anything. He just sat there, quietly making tropical butterflies, while the teenyboppers rippled past, unnoticing.

Okay, I thought, I'll play your silly game. I parked myself on the bench across the walk from his and elaborately ignored him, which wasn't all that easy.

He was a pretty ordinary-type kid, by Greenwich Village standards: yellow hair, darker eyebrows, longish face not quite finished yet, blue unbelieving eyes—a sufficiently good-looking kid, but most Village kids are good-looking. The eyebrows gave him a touch of distinction, but there were already three or five other kids making the two-tone scene that summer, so he was going to have to find himself some other trademark. Those butterflies, I thought, would probably do it for him. They were vulgar butterflies, too big and too flashy, but good taste doesn't matter much in miracles, and anyhow, he'd learn.

I still couldn't see how he was doing it. He'd clench his fist, then open it, and off'd go another butterfly. Whatever he was doing, he was doing it very smoothly.

The kid looked to be about two weeks late for a haircut, and his clothes were nearly clean. Check. But he was so fair I couldn't tell whether or not he was growing a . . . Yep, he was growing a beard. When he turned to watch a particularly garish butterfly veer off toward Fifth Avenue, the new sun hit his face at just the right angle to show he'd recently quit shaving.

He was obviously new to the Village then, but he didn't look around to catch reactions to his butterfly routine, which was unusual. I was mildly fascinated.

Finally he reached into his shirt pocket, found nothing, and didn't bother to explore his other pockets. His face looked immaturely rueful. Right. I lit a cigarette as ostentatiously as possible and did not smile.

"Do you have another one of those?" in a light tenor drawl. He was being casual so hard it almost glittered.

"Huh?" The object was to keep him on the offensive, let him write the script. I was very curious about those butterflies.

He said it again, more expressively, and conjured up a small, gray moth.

I said yes and held out my pack, he crossed the path and parked himself beside me, and the crowd remained the crowd. He tore the filter off the cigarette I gave him, but I forgave him for the sake of those lepidoptera.

The kid had a problem. Every time he tried to strike a match, a red and yellow butterfly got in the way. After three butterflies I shrugged my shoulders and gave him a light.

"Thanks, man."

We sat there for a while. The butterflies got better, more imaginatively colored, and I nodded quiet approval at some of them. Just before he was ready to throw the cigarette butt away, I said, "Pretty good butterflies."

"Yeah." He smiled a few watts and generated a large butterfly that had "Pretty Good Butterflies," gold on brown, printed across its wings. If the trick was still so new to him that he could openly admire it, I figured, he must've learned it in the Village, which would be interesting. Of course, he might've picked it up at the Bicentennial Exposition, but that could be interesting, too.

"How do You do it?" I stressed the you a bit, ever so gently, so he wouldn't think I was trying to steal his secret. Forestalling someone else's paranoia is a basic Village survival technique.

"I dunno," he said, smiling mysteriously. "I just . . . Well, I . . ." He closed his left hand and opened it to emit an iridescent green beauty with a pattern of crossed question marks in gold across its back. Pretty good, for an amateur.

"It just, like, kinda *happened*. You know?" he went on. "I mean," he gestured colorfully, "I was at this Party." He boosted his smile by a few more candlepower and leaned back. He wasn't exactly smug about it, but he liked it.

"Pretty good butterflies," I repeated. Then we were both silent for a while. A female teenybopper, blonde or so, in white pants just too tight enough, enjoyed our unanimous total attention for as long as it took her to strut down the path and out of sight, whereupon the kid produced a huge chromatic butterfly of pornographic implications.

"Would you believe," I invited, "that the term *teenybopper* was invented sometime prior to 1962 by Lee Lamb?" which I thought might interest him.

I was being inordinately cool, not rushing the kid or frightening him, but generating just as hard as I could the feeling that it'd be lots of fun for him to tell Uncle Chester all about it. After a while, a short one, I could see that I was beginning to get to him. He filled the air with color for a few minutes and then said, "You know, it's kinda funny . . ."

"Good morning!" quacked Michael the Theodore Bear in his favorite comic voice. The kid twitched.

"Oh, good Lord!" I tried to sound genial, but it wasn't easy. "This is Mike Kurland," I explained. "He's my Roommate." I didn't know quite how, but I was sure Mike was going to scare the kid away. He's sometimes hard to take if you're not used to him. Of course, so am I, but . . .

Mike stuck out a hand for shaking, being a professionally genial sort. The kid'd had his hand closed, so naturally a butterfly popped out when he made to accept Mike's paw.

"Howdy. My name's . . . Shawn. S-e-a-n. You know, like . . ."

It didn't work. The butterfly was blue on one side and green on the other, and Michael, face frozen at the start of whatever he'd been about to say, watched after it until it had blended into the new summer foliage and a little longer, all the while shaking hands reflexively. He looked more comical than he'd ever looked on purpose, but I was too bugged to enjoy the show.

"Quack?" he said plaintively. "Quack?"

Mike turned back to us and, completely deadpan, sat down. He used to be something of a spy—our side, of course, during the Second Cambodian Crisis—and took just pride in his utter unflappability. "That was a butterfly." He said it like a line of print, which showed that he was pretty shaken by it all.

"Yeah," the kid explained. "I've got these Butterflies." He demonstrated.

"Hmm. So I see. Yass." He sounded like W. C. Fields, a very bad omen.

"What's happenin', Mike?" I burbled in alarm. That's an ancient Village greeting, full of implicit hipness and signifying nothing. Mike was in the habit of satirizing this with a blatantly absurd program of events, and I was willing to endure anything to prevent a battle of cools between him and the kid. Cooler-than-thou contests are never informative, and I was starving for information. But it didn't work. I began to think nothing was going to work.

"*Butterflies*, you say?" Mike had now said four complete sentences, using a different voice for each, and the kid was growing nervous, very carefully keeping both hands open and fingers widely separated.

"Hey," I blurted, "that's right! I haven't even introduced myself yet." It was a clumsy *non sequitur*, but it just might turn the tone back toward casual and comfortable conversation, I hoped. "My name's Chester," I drove on. "You," an enormous concession, "can call me Chet." We shook hands formally. "Where are you from?"

The butterfly that fluttered where our hands had met was extravagantly baroque, and Mike, his cool now wholly blown, overtly goggled.

"Howdy, Mister Dillon," the kid drawled. Every Chester in America hates that line. Usually when I hear it, I deliver a short prepared speech on the evils of TV and memorized wit, but I had other fish to fry at the moment, so I let it pass.

"Yeah," I sighed. "*Where* did you say you're from?"

The ornate handshake butterfly was perversely circling Mike's head, he swiveling pompously about to keep it in view, and I hoped it'd go away and he'd follow it. From the look on his face, if it did he would.

"I'm from Fort Worth," said the kid, forgetting about Mike. "I just got here Saturday, last Saturday. I'm a lead guitar player."

Fine. A bull teenybopper with butterflies. Just what the Village always needed. Great.

"How do you like the Village?" I asked politely. Mike was still occupied with that butterfly, and his antics (twirling about like a dignified top to keep it safely in front of him) were attracting some attention. A small herd of tourists was developing about us. I tried to keep the kid from noticing.

"It's funny," he said. "I mean, well, the people are kinda funny. You know, strange." The herd was increasing, but the kid went on. "I mean, well, I went to this Party last night and, well . . ." He made a sweeping gesture and the air was thick with butterflies.

That's when it hit him. He gaped at the butterflies and the crowd, dropped his jaw, then turned back toward me with panic in his eyes: precisely what I'd been trying to avoid.

People don't make butterflies! It was a truth so basic it had never needed stating, and now Sean's universe was crumbling in lepidoptera.

"And what else can you do?" breathed Mike at this worst of all possible moments.

And all the stunned while, the sentence Sean had been working on, impelled by its own momentum, dribbled out one word at a time. "I went to this Party and they gave me this Pill . . ."

Phuip! Where he'd been was just a kid-shaped heap of butterflies.

There was scattered light applause. Somebody threw us a copper quarter. Then the butterflies and tourists drifted off. A mixed bag of teenyboppers wafted past us unawares. In the distance a Good Humor man plaintively cried his wares.

"Hmm." Mike stared at me with his very best hurt look. A plaid butterfly landed on his knee and he slapped at it petulantly. I hate to see grown men petulantly slapping innocent plaid butterflies.

"Coffee?" I suggested. No response. I stood up, rescued the debased quarter from an approaching wino, and started toward MacDougal Street. Michael came along, still looking hurt.

Whenever a butterfly approached, he ducked. He seemed to be dancing *Swan Lake*.

At last, "You gave me your Solemn Word," he said earnestly, "that you weren't going to doctor my orange juice anymore. In fact, you Promised."

So that's what was bothering him. "No, Mike," I swore. "That was all real. Honest."

"That kid? And all those . . ."

"The whole bit, baby." My public image at the time involved a cultivated smattering of hip jargon, which I undertook to speak with a distinctly Liverpudlian accent. The tourists expected it.

Mike brooded a little. Then, "No LSD?" he asked.

Just once I'd spiked his orange juice, just once.

"Not a bit."

"You really saw it, too?"

"Everybody saw it. Honestly, Mike, it really happened."

But he wasn't convinced until he overheard two nuns talking about the strange butterflies and one ancient chess player named David explaining how freak air currents sometimes blew migratory butterflies off course, and even then he had reservations. I'd played a regrettable series of complicated jokes on Mike a few years back, and he wouldn't put it past me to be in collusion with a brace of nuns and old David.

However, as we strolled down MacDougal toward West Third, Mike's expression moved slowly back to the bland malevolence that passed for normal with him. By the time we reached the Garden of Eden, the coffeehouse our people frequented that year, he was chattering animatedly about an elaborate joint deception we were working on.

We peered past the awful paintings in the foggy plate glass window to see who was there. Everybody does this—even the Law—even though he'll be inside in a few seconds.

Moving toward the door, Mike said, in total explanation, "Contact high?"

"Right."

"Obviously."

It had been that kind of summer.

2

Contact high!

We heard those words at least ten times before Bonnie-Sue, the day girl, brought our coffee. Ever since last May, when an anonymous philanthropist had distributed magic mushrooms free to everyone in the Village who'd accept them, imposing on Lower Manhattan a whole week of psychedelic fun and chaos . . . ever since then, *contact high* had been the standard explanation for all impossibilities, and the impossible had lately grown common in the Village.

Not that this explained very much. A contact high was only the subjective response to someone else's real high, and we had no proof that there actually was such a thing. No matter. We were able to make do with precious little explanation in those days.

". . . and then man (dig it) this cat starts whistlin' *Bach*, man! Like, I'm thinkin', 'da Di—pa-ba Diddilly . . .' you dig? An' this cat's inside my *Head*, man. An' he's got this like Orchestra! Oh WoW!" Little Micky was on the customary verge of hysteria.

"Contact high," M. T. Bear and I chanted in jagged unison, and Little Micky donned his shades and said Oh WoW again and split. We'd met him at the door.

The Garden of Eden was a long, dark, ostentatiously air-conditioned cave with black walls, and our group's table was the big round one halfway to the rear. We greeted Joe at the cash register ("Hey, you know what? Guess who had one of them contact highs last night. Me! Yeah, me. Honest to God! I musta been outta my skull: givin' everybody free coffee onna house! Nin'y t'ree dollars 'n' change, Christ!") and journeyed tableward from greeting to greeting, eavesdropped here and there en route

("I had the nicest contact high last night and I don't even know who it was!"), moving with all the cozy pomp of celebrities in a gathering of celebrities. The Garden of Eden, as a *Gestalt*, treated everyone like a celebrity that year, which might as well explain its popularity. The trip from door to table was wearying but wondrously flattering, a potent drug on which we'd neither of us admit to being hooked.

"I'm getting tired of this place," Michael muttered as we sat down.

"Yeah," I agreed. "Same old faces, same old talk." We were lying.

We were the first members of our circle there that morning, so Mike pulled a paperback mystery out of his right hip pocket, I took a spiral-bound notebook out of my briefcase, and we settled down to kill a little time. Neither of us mentioned butterflies.

All around us The Garden of Eden hummed like any garden. Since the place had no entertainment and was located in the throbbing left ventricle of the Village's entertainment district, most of the patrons were entertainers and such— rock 'n' rollies, superannuated folkniks, assorted groupies, plus a smattering of teenyboppers (teenage rock fanatics) who managed to sneak in past Joe's cerebean glower. This made for liveliness, in a superhip and nervous sort of way. Geetar cases littered the aisle like a herd of leatherette dinosaurs, and the raucous Kallikak box was OD'd on all kinds of electrified git-fiddle music. Almost every regular Gardener had at least one record on the box, but the unwritten rule against playing one's own records kept The Garden relatively bearable.

"Hello there."

Ah. That oddly bassoon-like sound came from Andrew Blake, one of our group's more shining lights, who would normally spend the whole afternoon explaining that he could only stay a few minutes because he had a deadline coming up (professional writer of paperback dirties) and besides he just couldn't take Saturday in the Village anymore. So Mike said Hi and I said Howdy and Andy sat down.

"I'm beginning to think," he claimed, "that the whole damned world is just somebody else's contact high."

"In the beginning," I intoned, "God created the heavens and the earth."

"In July?" Mike said, referring mainly to Andy's habitual black suit and gold brocade vest.

To Mike: "It matches my beard." To me: "Sure, and the earth was without form, and void. Oh wow!" Then back to Mike: "And why not? The whole world's air-conditioned now.

"Summer, winter," shrug, "I never used to catch colds. I was more the humiliating-accident type. You know, whenever all the snow decided to slide off some roof, I was always the kid it was waiting to land on. I was sixteen before I learned that zippers aren't supposed to gape open when girls are watching. It was like living in a comic strip, sort of, but at least I never caught colds. Now look!"

Mike: "So what else is new?"

"Ninety-five outside and sixty-five in here. If I don't wear a suit, bubie, I'm dead." He sounded like a melancholy woodwind.

Meanwhile, a small Black-Haired Chick I'd been noticing around lately was sitting by herself across the aisle and staring at us. With her unfashionably healthy face and lorn waif eyes, she looked like a kid outside a toyshop. A collector of sorts, I decided, checking to make sure I had all my sorts about me.

Just now she was watching us with what looked to be pure reverence, perhaps. Most likely she'd just found out who we were—you know, real live authors she'd almost read books by, and I a long-haired minor rock 'n' roll celebrity as well.

I wasn't alone in noticing the chick, but then, I never am.

Mike said, "That makes sense." Though he was ostensibly talking to Andy, he was using his invitation-to-overhear tone for the chick's benefit. "You hang out here to beat the heat, so you have to wear a suit to keep from freezing. Sure. Tell me more."

"What can I tell you?" Blake performed his famous Yiddish shrug. "So I'm without form, and void." *His* open-letter voice was now in operation. The Black-Haired Chick was getting the full treatment.

I refused to participate in this foolish charade. I was a working entertainer, among other things, onstage every night. I'd be damned, so to speak, if I was going to stage a private showing for his hero-worshipping adolescent matriarch, this antique teenybopper who was clearly all of seventeen. Nay, sir, not I.

"Not quite," I stated firmly and sonorously. "What it is, Andy, is that Contact High routine again." Blake groaned and the chick leaned eagerly toward us. "And darkness," I explained, "was upon the face of the waters." I sat back, smiling proudly.

While Andy's face was arranging its well-known That's-It! grin, Mike chuckled in quick appreciation of the joke, and the chick looked vaguely puzzled. Frankly, I agreed with the chick. I didn't know what was funny about it either, only that Mike would surely laugh and Andy would certainly explain, giving the chick a clear choice among Mike the Clever, Andrew the Understanding, and Chester the Profound Humorist. It's nice to have friends.

"That's it!" Grinning, Blake clenched his right fist in front of its shoulder and stuck the index finger out at shirt-pocket level to emphasize the point—a gesture I felt to be unfairly phallic and subliminal. "Of course. This is all somebody else's hallucination and," he paused to let the understanding index finger take effect, "I keep stumbling in the darkness."

I was disappointed—he generally does much better by me—but the chick seemed satisfied, and yes, that out-thrust finger business was decidedly unfair.

Ranting on, Andy said, "I just wish to God whoever's running this show would move on to the next verse."

Whereupon all three of us declaimed in loud, clear unison, "And God said, 'Let there be light!'"

By now, of course, everyone was staring at us. That's what they were supposed to do, and they always did it. Once you've been famous in the Village, no other fame can wholly satisfy you. The chick looked sinfully idolatrous. A few trained cynics near the door applauded. Then everyone said OH!, for Behold, there was light!

The Garden of Eden was a sudden deep pit of silence, and Andrew Blake, renowned author of *Love Pusher*, *Virgin for Eight Hours* (". . . enthralling reexamination of progressive education . . ." Appaloosa *Post-Chronicle*), and *Sex, Incorporated*, good old Andy, sat across the table from me swathed head to sole in what could only be called a halo.

It was baby blue and it pulsed.

I was appalled. I remember thinking that somebody had pulled a monumentally unfair trick, and even wondering to whom it was unfair, during that long, frozen stillness; but then there was an unusually sincere scream and Little Micky, who'd come back, left the coffeehouse again, this time through the front window, and ran noisily off toward the East Side. It was a lovely exit, and I was irrationally glad he'd had the opportunity to make it.

Blake looked undecided, as though he and I were maybe thinking the same thing. *Saint Andrew the Pornographer?* Mike looked heavily put upon. I've no idea how I looked, and wouldn't care to know, but the Black-Haired Chick was smiling like Christmas all year long.

"Pardon me," Saint Andrew bleated with grave courtesy as he rose slowly to his feet. "I feel, ah, unwell. I think I will go Home now. Thank you. Yes?"

What was there to say? Mike nodded, I gawked, and Good Saint Andy walked slowly toward the door, his path made perfectly visible by halo shine. He looked like a dignified, contemplative, thickly bearded will-o'-the-wisp (but he cast fuzzy violet shadows, alas), and everyone he passed shrank from contact with the pale blue-white light he shed. Joe even let him leave without paying his check, an event almost as unprecedented as the halo itself.

Other than Andy, nobody moved but the Black-Haired Chick. She followed him at three yards' careful distance through The Garden of Eden and out to the street.

For a long time after they were gone, the unnatural silence did not break.

As soon as I could, I asked Mike, "Contact High?"

"I . . . ah, I . . . think the butterflies were prettier."

3

Home was several billion butterflies distant, on St. Mark's Place in the mysterious east. We walked there through a contemplative silence broken only by distant screams we carefully ignored. It was an amazing walk. Michael hummed classical rock songs out of tune, I wondered if the butterflies'd hurt that night's business, and neither of us thought at all.

Nobody spoke to us. Not even the panhandlers and tourists were talking to us that afternoon, which felt very curious. We were both a little up tight by the time we got through Washington Square.

The world seemed to be blaming us for the Andrew Blake affair. Mike insisted that even the pigeons were avoiding us, but he's always had this artistic leaning toward paranoia. It comes of having been a spy. The pigeons were merely afraid of the butterflies, that's all, but I didn't try to explain this to Mike. Go reason with a paranoid counterspy.

When we got home, we found Sandi Heller pressing desperately against our front door, pounding on it with both fists. Great natural sense of rhythm. We could also hear the phone whistling inside.

"Hi there," Michael chirruped.

She spun around as only a dancer should, yelping, "Oh good Lord! You're all right!" She pressed her shoulders against the door and cried or something—it was hard to tell—saying, "Oh," gasp, "Good Heavens." The phone was still whistling.

I was confused, but M. T. Bear penetrated to the heart of the matter at once. "I deny everything," he explained. "Categorically."

"It was on the radio!" Twenty watts of frantic contralto. "Wings! I thought you were dead or something."

Oh. That explained something. It also brought me down like a pail of cold water. Wings indeed. And Butterflies. Right.

"Sandi?" I said. She was still doing whatever it was that she was doing against our door. "Sandi, why didn't you go in and wait for us? It's never locked."

She fell silent, looked stunned (Stanislavsky # 31-a), groped for the doorsnap behind her, pushed it, tottered into the living room, regained her balance brilliantly, tripped over a footstool, and fell plomp on her dignity beside my harpsichord.

It turned out to be one of those Busy afternoons when nothing gets done. To begin with, Mike and I spent at least an hour coaxing Sandi out of her hysteria. This was pretty fair time, really, considering the rumors she'd managed to invent concerning Andy's halo, plus her innate fondness for psychodrama. I'd rather have spent the time practicing, or writing, or loafing, or doing other such creative things.

When Sandi wept, Mike comforted her, proving by glorious syllogisms that everything was perfectly all right, honestly it was. I've always been helpless with crying women.

When she laughed, it was my turn. I solemnly reminded her that we had no idea yet just how serious the situation was and that there was no telling what was going to come of it all. Mike, who is an ursine mountain of stability when that's what's needed, couldn't cope with Sandi's laughter, mainly because he was having much the same problem himself. I, on the other hand, worry gracefully.

Finally Sandi recovered and brewed a pot of maté. Then we talked about what had actually happened—Andy's awkward aura and all that—and she said, "Is *that* all it was? My God, you people do *that* every day," which I thought was a bit unkind.

Then it was five o'clock and I remembered that I ought to get some-practicing done. I played amplified harpsichord in a rock 'n' roll ménage, called Sativa and the Tripouts, a complex vice of which I've since been cured. Anyhow, while I ran through changes, fiddle tunes, and baroque riffs, Sandi and Mike cleaned up the maté things and rehashed Andrew Blake's adventures as a lover, literary agent, raconteur, stand-up comic, and, most recently, saint.

"Oh!" Sandi yelped. "Oh my! Oh good Lord! Oh my!" I leaped up, ready to stem off another laughing jag, but she just sputtered, "Phone! I mean, the vidiphone. Listen!"

It was still whistling at us, its pathetic little view screen flashing off and on red. Mike and I looked appropriately sheepish, and I picked up the mouthpiece. "Howdy," I said, and, "Hello? Hello there? Speak up, baby, it's your quarter." Then I hung up. "No one there."

"Oh my! I have to go home. Right now." Sandi whirled through the place like a ponytailed butterfly (alas), with Mike and me trailing along behind her, being ponderously reasonable.

"You don't understand," she insisted, quite accurately. "I'm all right, really I am. Only, when I heard about it, you know, I tried to call you, but you didn't answer, so I had to come over here, and I forgot to . . . Oh my God, whatever will Leo say?"

Ah, it was all so beautifully normal. And when Sandi was gone (saying, as always, or quoting, "I *trust* everything will work out all right," at the door), I wandered through the pad, lazily dressing for work—tight black pants, suede boots, and a gold silk paisley shirt—singing classical Beatles tunes with the day's events for texts, chuckling inanely, and grinning till my face hurt all over me.

All this euphoria stopped when Mike said, "You know something? I'm worried."

He was standing at the living-room windows, staring down into the courtyard. In fact, I recalled with a start, he'd *been* staring out the windows for the past half hour or so. This was significant. I'd learned years before that whenever Mike spends as much as ten minutes in silent thought, for my own protection I'd best take his conclusions seriously.

"Explain?" I mourned.

"Look." He pointed down toward the courtyard, a grubby red-brick and tin-can oasis temporarily bathed in glory.

"Oh," I said after an incredulous while. "That's a Butterfly, isn't it?"

"Right."

There was no question whose butterfly it was, for it was mainly yellow, but fluorescent, with a wingspan upward of a yard. Sean'd evidently realized that the absurd size of the thing might cause confusion: when it spread its wings it displayed a pattern in glowing sable running from tip to tip that looked like this:

$$\mathfrak{BUTERFLY}$$

"He's getting good," I breathed.
"Yeah. Good."
Later, "So?"
"So wait."
We didn't have to wait long.
"Hey," I wondered, "I hear trumpets." And I did, too, a blatant horn call that knew the price of everything, coming, approaching, from somewhere above the building.
"Yeah." I could tell Mike was impressed by the unemotional flatness of his voice. "Look."
I suppose it was another butterfly. I'll never know how, but it was obviously making its own music—gaudy fanfares from the fool's-gold days of Hollywood—and the day-glo polyethylene-extruded fanfares were perfectly apt.
"God." I wasn't swearing.
"Wait."
It landed in the courtyard with an audible thud (an awkward butterfly?) and waddled about to the accompaniment of a hidden symphony orchestra, mainly horns and strings, not quite in tune but much concerned with the importance of the occasion. I was far too awed to comment, which was just as well, for, with a loud orchestral sweep, it spread its polychrome wings to their full ten-foot span. So, a wide-screen butterfly. Groovy.
The colors skittered and glowed, changing in a rigid order just beyond comprehension. Almost subliminal patterns of psychedelic urgency swept erotic eddies across the wings in deep tides of hypnotic rhythm, making me uncomfortably conscious of the heavy July heat; and over all this, in a living red that seemed to strike directly into my brain without passing through my eyes, bruising words succeeded each other, became one another, intersected each other like virtuoso drill teams in competition:

I'MportANT

significant   eSTABliSHEd

rESPecTABle

f

a

m

O.

U.

SEAN!

over again and over, always the same idea but nothing else the same, while the music screamed BELIEVE THIS like a hundred 3V pitchmen pushing soap.

Mike and I backed slowly away from the window, thoroughly unnerved. "Hey," one of us breathed, "he's getting good!" and then that footstool caught us from behind and we fell loudly to the floor. I still have that footstool.

We felt better the moment we landed.

"Yeah. Worried." I wasn't about to admit I was scared.

"What," asked Michael in a skinny voice, "what do *you* make of it?"

Night had already taken place. While I tried to think of some kind of answer for Mike, glibly colored light from Sean's superlepidopteran rippled across the ceiling.

"Joke?" I suggested.

"Yeah, joke." Doubtful.

"Sense of humor," I urged.

"Yeah," he jibed. "Humor."

"I mean, it's a very good sign, you know?"

"Good. Sure." Mike isn't always the most comfortable kind of roommate to have around.

The lights on the ceiling grew brighter, crisper, more primary, and the music tasted like pure tent show. That seemed encouraging, somehow. "How old is he?" I asked.

Mike thought about it while the music sprouted piccolos. "Oh," he drawled, "would you believe seventeen?"

"Thereabouts," I agreed. "And therefore more brilliant than subtle, right?" I liked kids.

"Oh yeah?"

"Okay then, clever. Spoilsport. What do you want from the kid? Anyhow, the odds are in our favor."

So we said it together: "A Butterflybynight!" and I went on: "But I sure wish we had better odds." For no sensible reason, this seemed to mollify Michael.

The thing flew off then in an exuberance of calliopes, and we, dazed, finished getting ready for the evening's entertainment.

A famous proto-hipster* once said, "It requires a very unusual mind to undertake the analysis of the obvious." Michael the Theodore Bear, my beloved roommate and manager, has precisely this odd twist of mind, and he's always producing shattering surprises with it. Being Mike, he has a special voice he uses only for pointing out momentous obvieties everybody else has failed to notice: a dry, insouciant, malty tone I can't at all describe. When, just before we were ready to split, he, said, "You know what?" in just that voice, I stopped whatever I was doing, shook myself gingerly, stood at parade rest, and held my breath.

"Swell," I drawled nasally. "No, Michael, what?"

"You know," he repeated, dragging it out, "I've been thinking. That kid's been making butterflies since sometime before eleven o'clock this morning. Lots of butterflies."

Silence.

I grabbed my briefcase and scuttled toward the door. Mike followed, whistling a happy little monotone.

I was in a hurry, latish, so we took the stairs instead of waiting for the elevator. I tried to estimate how many butterflies a young rock 'n' rolly from Fort Worth could generate in nine or ten hours, and just before we reached the street door I stopped short, turned to confront Mike (beaming blandly), and said, "Thanks a lot, baby."

I didn't sound sincere.

---

* Alfred North Whitehead

4

Washington Square was an armed camp. Two huge searchlights, one by the fountain and the other in the chess circle near MacDougal, reared fluttering cones of illuminated moths boiling toward the sky. Nervous, heat-gun-toting GI's stood guard almost everywhere, swatting moths and cursing brilliantly. Moths. I was charmed by the kid's adaptability.

Tourists and chastened teenyboppers, shielding their faces with outstretched hands and/or autographed straw hats, moved sluggishly through the park, herded by the sweaty soldiers. Photographers played fast and loose with flashbulbs, giving the whole area a strobe-lighted, discothequeish feeling. Hardened Villagers openly gawked.

The shiny NYU library showed battle scars. One friendly old oak near the park *pissoir* had been truncated by somebodys skitterish heat gun. Everyone who didn't look confused looked terrified. I hadn't seen anything like it since the famous beatnik riots in the sixties.

"Michael," I shouted, the militia being rackety, "this could become rather serious."

"Serious? I think it's hilarious."

"That's what makes it so damn serious." We had a private convention that summer: when in doubt, philosophize.

If the park was frantic, MacDougal Street was worse. Ancient Italians chanted clackety Rosaries. US Army vehicles of strange shapes, and even odder functions (known only to Michael) swarmed up and down the street, making jaywalking hazardous. Fuzz stood puzzled on the corners and pointed uneasily at things. Panicky teenyboppers stampeded in tight

18

circles, shrieking, "Dig it! Dig it! Dig it!" and knocking unwary tourists off their feet. Jittery reporters loudly interviewed jittery businessmen. Moths and untimely butterflies abounded.

Mike and I, habitually cool, cautiously pretended nothing much was happening, but we were both a bit stunned. At the corner of Third and MacDougal we bowed gravely to each other (one more private ritual), said "ciao" in unison, and parted, I to the left and workward, he to the right and The Garden of Eden.

I watched him bumble his way through the confusion, thinking sadly, Yonder goes what may well be my last link with reality, which was a hell of a thing to think about someone like Mike. By then, however, I was used to bidding my last link with reality farewell, so I squared my shoulders and loped off toward The Mess on MacDougal Street, flailing my briefcase before me to clear the path of lepidoptera and things that go boomp in the night

Chaz Wainright's Mess on MacDougal Street, actually on Third Street two blocks away, was already crowded, despite or because of the Army and the butterfly plague, but nothing was happening onstage yet.

"Good evening, Chester Anderson!" Charley trumpeted with false and boisterous formality. Thanks to the day's events and incidental publicity, every head in the house turned its empty face toward me. Appalling, but that's just what Chaz'd bellowed for. He was a native showman, and I was part of the show. Far, far be it from Charles J. Wainright to let free publicity go to waste.

"Howdy, Chaz," I trumpeted back, because I *was* part of the show. "Read any good butterflies lately?"

One of the customers tittered hysterically, a terrifying sound, but Charley performed a saving belly laugh, and the whole house crashed into hilarity like surf on old rocks. All at once I felt great. Hurrah! The laughter of a hundred happy strangers was too strong a high for *me* to kick, and—butterflies be damned!—I knew it was going to be a swinging night.

Stu, Pat, Kevin and Sativa were waiting in the back room. Stewart Fiske (a chortly, mustachioed drummer from the distant wilds of outer Milwaukee), Patrick Gerstein (a perpetual Bucks Count teen-ager who looked like a black-haired baseball hero but was really our lead guitarist), Kevin Anderson (a warmly chocolate-toned MIT dropout who preferred rythm guitar and lead singing to the aesthetic rigors of quantum physics), Rosemary Schwartz (i.e., Sativa, a svelte, suede chick who did nothing but sing and practice sex appeal and Subud), and I, your friendly neighborhood harpsichordist, had banded together a few months before as Sativa and The Tripouts. We played a kind of music of our own invention that we called, when we *had* to call it something, either Baroque and Roll or Raga Rock, as the fancy took us. McLuhan music, as it were. It never really caught on, but it was more fun than working, and it paid better, too. Michael was our manager, so to speak.

"Wow," said Pat as usual. "How 'bout them bugs?"

"Butterflies," I answered, and Stu amended, "Moths." Kevin seldom had anything to say. Now he just grinned. He and Sativa were holding hands, this being his week or something.

"Sure," Pat veered. His conversation was generally erratic. "Let's warm up."

We retired to the alley behind The Mess and, dodging inquisitive moths *et al.,* smoked a few pipefuls of marijuana, which was still illegal in those days. We firmly believed it improved our playing, and perhaps it did.

When we were properly stoked, we wandered onstage and started tuning. We had among us some 120 strings (most of them mine) to put in order, and tuning could be a fairly poignant experience. To keep our audience happy, we made a more or less comedy routine out of tuning, an ad-lib blend of topical jokes and hip ambiguities, from which we broke without warning into our most popular song, "I'm in Love with a Girl Called Alice Dee," carrying everyone within earshot along with us. What the hell is earshot?

That got the evening started, and for a long while I was too busy with keys, dials, and switches to notice anything else. It was during Patrick's solo, while Stu and Kevin were scanning the house for new soft young round ones and Sativa was staging a private latihan, and I was counting noses (each nose representing one four-dollar cover charge, of which we Tripouts were entitled to one-third—which is sixty-six point six cents per nostril, if you like to think along such lines) . . . It was during this that I noticed our boy Sean, the Butterfly Kid himself, sitting in the front row at a table all alone.

Right.

Sean wasn't making butterflies, thank God, just sitting with his hands in his pockets, which was something of an accomplishment, looking slightly hypnotized, like all the rest of our audience. I wondered what'd happen if he tried to applaud after the set, then decided not to worry about it.

I drew a yellow index card from my right cheek pocket, wrote on it in red, "butterfly boy here Grab Him!" and propped it up on my console. The Tripouts' warm-up routine made it necessary for me to write down anything I wanted to remember.

Pat's solo ended in a burst of ethnic gaudies, and before the house could gather itself to applaud, we segued into "Green Sleeves and Yellow Hair," one of my tunes, ending the set with a proper bang. We liked to run a good tight show.

The kid clapped a total of two golden moths, and then restorted to tapping the tabletop hipply with his right index finger like the rest of the audience. Before the frantic clicking had a chance to fade, we went off stage and Al Mamlet, a very funny man, was on and running through his first riffs.

I grabbed the kid by a handy shoulder (inadvertently traumatizing him), whispered, "C'mon, baby," and half-dragged him into the back room.

My colleagues had already split. Our schedule allowed for ninety minutes between sets, and they liked to spend the time hanging out on the Street. It's fun to be even a little bit famous.

"Okay, Sean." I was firm and comforting, like a pastor or slightly older uncle—somebody wholly unlikely to administer a spanking. "First question: where did you go?"

"Go?" Still scared.

"Yeah, go. I was talking to you in the park and then you disappeared. I saw you. Or rather, I *didn't* see you. Where did you go?"

He looked slowly around at the back room, hunting for eavesdroppers maybe, but finding only cobwebs and poorly stacked old lumber. This gave him confidence. "Oh yeah," he mumbled, "I went home."

"Dallas?"

"*Dallas?* Hell no, man: Fort Worth!"

"That's boss. How?"

"How?" Oi. If Sean was going to make a habit of repeating everything I said, I might easily go bald before I got any information out of him. "How?" he redoubled. "Well . . . To tell you the truth, man, I don't rightly know." He threatened to sniffle.

"Hey, baby, don't cry! There's nothing to . . . I mean, just . . . Oh shit." I gave him my only clean handkerchief, red silk, and he noisily blew his nose. Emotional people embarrass me.

"Anything wrong back here?" That was Charley. Sometimes he worried. He was afraid somebody might break a law or something on his premises.

"All clear, Chaz," I guaranteed. "Just talkin' to an ol' buddy of mine from Texas." The whole truth seemed uncalled for.

Charley looked dubious—one of his better looks—but went peacefully away. Meanwhile the kid stopped sniffling.

He half smiled. "Hey, y'all play *Good*."

"Thanks. Now what . . ."

"What do you call that thing?"

"*What* thing?" Interruptions!

"That piano thing you was playin'. What'd you *call* that?"

"That's an amplified harpsichord."

He opened his mouth to launch another question, but I beat him to it. "I'll explain later," I promised. "What were you thinkin' about just before you went home?"

"Huh? Oh yeah. I dunno. I was just a tad bit homesick, like. You know."

"Okay, I'll buy that. You were homesick. Maybe you had butterflies in your stomach." We winced. "But why did you come back?"

"Man, I *hate* Fort Worth!"

"Oh."

We were silent long enough to hear Mamlet, out front, yell, "And then they told me what it was *For!*" while the audience broke up gloriously. Al is a very funny man.

I, meanwhile, was scheming as hard as I could under the circumstances, hunting for some way to open this kid up. Those butterflies of his were bugging me.

Then, "Where are you stayin'?" I remembered my own Village puppyhood.

"Me? Here 'n' there. I dunno," meaning the kid was up tight for a pad. Right. Now we were back where we'd started in the park, upward of too many hours ago.

"Need," I insinuated, "a place to crash?" Playing it slow.

"Well . . ." Yes.

"You're welcome to use my Guest Room for a while, if you want to, until you can find a place of your own." I was hard pressed to keep a note of pride from marring the precisely nonchalant tone in which I performed this ritual incantation. Guest Rooms are scarcer in the Village than gold-plated diaphragms.

"Gee thanks!" Pause. "I mean, ah, if like you don't mind . . . I mean . . ."

I explained that of course I didn't mind and delivered a small but polished lecture on Village mores and the tribal custom of the pallet on the floor. Within, I exulted. There wasn't much in the world that I wanted more than any old explanation for those damned butterflies.

Then, "You *do* look kind of beat," I recited, strictly from memory.

"Um."

Right. "When did you sleep last?"

"Oh man, sleep? I dunno. Thursday?"

"Oh *yeah?* C'mon."

I still had half an hour before the next set, so I led Sean tenderly out through the dark auditorium, pausing to collect his guitar and put him on my tab, and on out to the street. There we encountered Mad John, the spherical pride of New Orleans, lewdly eyeing an anthology of tourists from Ohio.

"Greetings," he offered. He was wearing gaudily trimmed green lederhosen and an Alpine cap with a pigeon's tail feather hanging from its band, his standard Village tour guide outfit, but he didn't have his usual cash-and-carry following tagging along.

"Howdy, Swamprat," I sang out. This was meant to make him sputteringly furious, a most engaging spectacle, and usually worked, but not tonight.

"Look around," he said with word and gesture.

I looked. "So?"

"They're gone."

So they were. No moths! The only nearby reminder of the plague was a clutch of wibberly GI's wearing uneasy expressions.

"You're right!" I rejoiced. "Wow! Later."

I hauled Sean away before Mad John could start rapping, and we practically ran down West Third Street. "What," I panted, "happened to the," gasping, "butterflies?"

"I came down."

Oh.

At the Garden of Eden ("Hey, baby, like, ah, What Happened?"), we found Mike at the family table surrounded by Harriet, Gary the Frog, several people called David (that having been a big summer for Davids), and the usual three or four total strangers who knew all about us, so to speak: our admirers.

Whilst everyone talked at once, I explained the situation to Michael in my firmest *sotto voce*. "So take him home Now," I finished. "Feed 'im, put 'im to bed, tuck 'im in, and for Christ's sake, don't let him get away."

Mike, the kid, and I pushed through a swarm of questions to the street.

"How come you call him Michael the Theodore Bear?" the kid wondered as we wove a path back to The Mess. The Street was Saturday-packed, but we seemed to be the only moving bodies. Everyone else just stood there, still and gape-mouthed, staring at everyone else.

"Because he's much too dignified for nicknames," I explained, "and Pooh had already been used."

We parted at The Mess's door under Charley's most paternal eye—the left one, possibly glass—they to feed and bed the Butterfly Kid and I somehow to work.

"Wow," Sativa whispered in the alley as we warmed up for the second set. "What happened to the butterflies? Pretty?"

"The kid who invented 'em came down." By them I didn't care *what* I said.

Sativa took it calmly—being that kind of chick—but Stu choked and coughed, maybe because of the smoke. The explanation seemed to satisfy Patrick, though. But then, most things satisfied Patrick.

Sativa sighed. "I *liked* them," exhaling clouds of solemn blue smoke. "Pretty."

Chaz insists I gave the best performance of my life that night, but I didn't notice. My head was busy.

The kid came down.

Sure.

Oh wow.

5

I woke up at seven thirty and instantly repented. The sun was blaring in my face and a so-help-me monarch butterfly was clinging to the outside, praise God, of my window screen. These were clearly Bad Omens, and if I'd had as much faith in omens as I thought I did, I'd've stood the day in bed, missing out on everything and looking like a total ass.

I couldn't remember why yet, being still two-thirds asleep, but the sight of that innocent, battered monarch languidly pulsing its wings outside my sunrise window bothered me. I threw a critical slipper at the screen and fell, exhausted, back against the pillow. The butterfly was unimpressed.

By eight o'clock I was reconciled to being up, and I'd recalled what happened to my lifelong fondness for butterflies, too, all of which left me with no decent reason to stay in bed. Ah well. I pulled on a light bathrobe and pattered into the living room.

No one else was up yet. The pad felt crowded and empty at the same time, like a well-stocked haunted house. Then one of Mike's more ambitious snores pushed through his door, and in that broken hush of a moment I was thoroughly at home in the present again after all night's dreaming, irrevocably awake. Michael's snores are nothing if not real.

Obviously Mike was still asleep. The guest-room door was open, and I could see that Sean was sleeping, too. He was bent and twisted into an improbable position he couldn't've held for a minute wide awake.

Spurred by a pint of orange juice and some of the muddiest thinking on the Upper East Coast, I set out for church fully and properly dressed and in plenty of time for the ten o'clock Mass.

The ten o'clock turned out to be a supersolemn High Mass of sorts, somebody's daring new liturgical experiment horribly sung to the accompaniment of nothing but percussion instruments: a real piety tester. Therefore I didn't get home with my nineteen pounds of Sunday *Times* until quarter of twelve, almost.

They were still sleeping, and Sean had developed an even more elaborate and unlikely position. I wondered idly if yoga were popular in Texas and shed a little surplus pity for the poor girl Sean'd someday marry, wondering how she was going to react the first time she saw her brand-new husband turn into a topological whimsy in his sleep. But maybe Sean's luck'd mate him to a young female contortionist.

The Times was full of yesterday. So was I. Things had certainly happened. The butterflies'd been so thick they'd stopped traffic. Charming. Not a wheel had turned between Fourteenth Street and Canal after 3:00 p.m. They'd even stopped the subways for a while, until the City sent four guys down with Army surplus flamethrowers to clear out the West Fourth Street station.

It'd been a funny day, in its own quaint way. An old wino was smothered under a pile of burgundy butterflies. Plate glass windows were shattered by the things. Governor Kennedy had declared the Village an official New York State Disaster Area, Class III, and called out the whole National Guard. Forty-seven tons of government surplus DDT was scattered over the neighborhood. The coffee would doubtless taste foul for a week.

And it wasn't just the butterflies. There was a coyly retouched photo of some vaguely familiar little blonde teenybopper from Long Island who'd walked all the way from West Eighth to MacDougal and Bleecker mother-naked and twelve feet up in the air. Yes, quaint.

A grove of gaudy orange palm trees popped up right in the middle of Sixth Avenue and then, poof, vanished just before the men with the flamethrowers got there.

It'd been a very busy day. No wonder I was tired. A bright spot was that Andy's halo wasn't even mentioned. I'd been worried about that.

Three cups of maté and *The Times* kept me happy till one or so, when, "Enough will do," I quipped and sat down at the harpsichord. Naturally, the phone chose that time to whistle at me.

"Yes?" I don't like phones, with or without color screens.

"Chester?" A strange, thin, possibly strained through cheesecloth and certainly unhappy voice. Vision squelched.

"Speaking."

"Help me! Please!" Absolutely tragic, and not a quiver of it faked. Nevertheless:

"Who's this?"

"It's *me,* Andy! Andrew Blake. You've got to help me, Chester. I haven't slept all night!"

Now that he'd identified himself and set the mood he wanted, he let his voice resume its basic double-reeded plaintiveness, like an orphaned English horn. In the background something possibly giggled.

"Andy?" I said. "What seems to be the trouble?"

"I can't sleep."

"It's Sunday afternoon."

"I couldn't sleep last night, either."

"Why on earth not?"

"The light gets in my eyes."

"So turn if off or pull the shades down or something."

"I can't turn it off, it's my . . . that is . . . ah, it's . . ."

"Oh! Your halo?"

"Please don't call it that." Pause. "Yes." most dejectedly.

Now here was a thing or two. Somehow I'd tacitly expected the aura to go away when the butterflies did. I said this.

"Well, it didn't." Petulance. "It didn't go away at all. It's been getting *brighter!"* Again that giggle in the background. "And this Girl . . ."

"Yes? What gir . . . Oh, *that* girl!"

"She's sitting in the dinette laughing at me."

This went on for some time, because, no matter how he happens to be feeling, Andy dearly loves the vidiphone. It proves that he's in touch, that people actually like him, that he might even be real. It's his only true addiction, and he takes the same kind of pride in a four-hundred-dollar phone bill that a shopworn junky takes in a fifty-dollar habit.

Finally, when I'd established that no real information was currently available from Andy or to be had from That Girl, I suggested that he might try blindfolding himself. This he hadn't thought of, he confessed, but it sounded good and he promised to try it and let me know. Hurrah. We said goodbye for several minutes and hung up.

The chat had lasted more than half an hour, and I *still* didn't like the phone. It made me feel vaguely like property. Pfui.

I poured myself another slug of maté and returned to the harpsichord. After making the electronic and mechanical adjustments needed for a really impressive racket, I plunged massively into *The Carman's Whistle,* an Elizabethan treasure I hope to live to master.

It worked. By the last chord they were both sitting in the living room, looking all bushy and bemused and mightily put upon.

"Good morning," I announced. "We have a lot to do this lovely morning, don't we?" Michael groaned.

During brunch we milked young Sean.

"My name, it ain't really *Sean,* you dig? But don't tell nobody! My real name, it's *Johnny*—John. But I really *dig* Sean. I *Mean* it. Sounds kind of *special,* know what I mean? I figure, man, if I'm fixin' to play rock 'n' roll, I ought to have me a good Stage Name. You know? I *dig* Sean."

I allowed as how *I* thought Sean was a much better stage name than Johnny, and this made him happy. Michael growled gently.

Little Sean/Johnny was born and reared in Fort Worth, a town I remembered well enough from visiting it in the sixties that I could understand his wanting to escape.

He wasn't seventeen, as we'd imagined, at all, but eighteen, which made a difference, and, like almost everyone else in the Village that summer, he'd been to college for not quite a year. His family didn't understand him, which was neither unusual nor important, though he believed otherwise.

"They wanted I should sell insurance like my *dad,* man. What a drag!"

He was evolving a more detailed autobiography than I really wanted to hear, but I didn't interfere. After all, I'd *seen* this puppy making butterflies.

Between crises of poached egg, he explained how he'd become a rock 'n' rolly, and I threatened to introduce him to some of his heroes. Two eggs later he gave me the indelible details of his stark-by-our-standards love life: an Oklahoma girl called Mary-Bob with whom he'd once gone All the Way in the back of an abandoned pickup truck while his folks were out of town. I silently envied him the surprises Greenwich Village had for him.

Michael, all the while, seemed to be dozing lightly through this wash of random data, a trick he'd copped from Nero Wolfe. At least, that's what I hoped he was doing.

Another cup of maté, more toast, and my assurances that he'd done nothing unforgivable with Mary-Bob (though who can say?) brought Sean at last to his arrival in New York.

"I was kind of scared right off, on account of everything's so Big an' all, an' I don't—*didn't* hardly know anybody, know what I mean?

"First two, three days I was kinda lost, you know? When I got off the bus, I asked this taxicab driver take me out to Greenwich Village, an' it costed me two-fifty an' I didn't find out for two, three days I was really in some place called Bronnix."

"The Bronx."

"Right. What's a Bronk?"

"Forget it. What happened then?"

"Oh yeah. Well, I just set in some big ol' park out there an' played my geetar till some of these kids with the long hair got to talkin' to me, an' one of 'em was a pretty good geetar player hisself. So they said *they'd* take me on down to Greenwich Village, an' they did, too." He was going to have to learn to control that accent of his, but I didn't intend to muddle things by mentioning it just then.

He'd also hung around the Village two, three days, sitting in Washington Square or in some nameless basement coffeehouse, looking very brave. That's all interpretation, not what he actually said. It was a familiar scene. After a while he was befriended by a roaming tribe of teenyboppers, "an' they give me these ol' *pills* to stay awake, an' they taken me off to this *party* somewheres near some river.

"This was at some real *fancy*-lookin' pad, you dig? But they was all rollin' their own cigarettes, an' I thought that was kind of funny."

It must have lasted several days. Village parties often do. They take on a life of their own, if you're not careful. People kept rolling cigarettes for Sean and showing him how to smoke them.

"They tasted kinda *weird* at first, you know? But I sort of got *used* to 'em after a while. Besides, I was plumb outta smokes myself."

Then, two days ago, "This cat—I think his name was Lizard, somethin' like that—he shows up an' he's got this bottle of like little blue *pills.*"

Michael's eyes snapped open.

"Lizard?" I doubted.

"Like that. With an *L* an' a *L*. I dunno."

"Laszlo," Michael droned, closing his eyes again.

"Laszlo?" I verified.

"Somethin' like that."

"Anyhow, this *L*-and-*Z* person called his little goodies Reality Pills. Wasn't that sweet?"

"Yeah, man, Reality Pills. Well, everybody else taken one, so I figure what The Hell? an' I taken one, too. He was givin' 'em away for Free.

"Then I got to feelin' kind of *dizzy* like, so I went away, an' all of a sudden I had me them goddamn Butterflies."

That's where I stopped him. Reality Pills indeed. I felt a mystical need to sit down and think about it all.

We removed to the living room. Michael sipped glum maté and stared through the wall. I fumbled through some easy sonatinas on the harpsichord. Sean watched the harpsichord's mechanism as though paralyzed. None of us said a word for a long time.

Reality Pills?

6

Andrew Blake was less than happy with his halo. He realized the moment it hit him (his word) that it wasn't going to give him anything but trouble, or so he claimed. Personally, I think his attitude was decidedly un-Catholic, even though events *did* shortly bear it, and him, out.

When, freshly enhaloed, Andy fled The Garden of Eden, the little Black-Haired Chick we'd all three been so busily impressing followed him. But for once he didn't particularly *want* to have a little Black-Haired Chick, no matter how thoroughly impressed, following him.

"What I wanted was to be alone. I kept hoping I could maybe wash the damned thing off."

Her name was Karen. Almost every chick's name was Karen that summer, just as almost every boy was a David. Names run in tides below Fourteenth Street.

This particular Karen was a Greenbaum by trade, and during the winter she studied Creative Writing at Bard College, an unofficial Village training ground. She was nineteen, and she thought Andy's halo quite becoming.

Andrew broke free of The Garden of Eden and turned left toward Sixth Avenue. Karen was nine feet behind him. When he reached the avenue, three-quarters of a block later, she was still nine feet behind him.

"Go away," He felt neither gallant nor gracious.

"My name's Karen." She meant well. "I read your Book."

"No. God, no. Go away."

Andy was making a distinct impression on everyone who saw him, and, the weather being good and the afternoon being

Saturday, just about everyone saw him. Even in the violent sunlight his halo was clearly visible, flickering about him like an obstinate Saint Elmo's fire.

"I said," teeth clenched, "go away!—*Taxi!*"

Every cab he hailed came just close enough for the driver to make out Andy's halo, then squealed away, leaving only burnt rubber to show it'd been there.

"What could I do?" he told me. "I had this Halo. No cabby's gonna stop for me an' I'm not *about* to try the subway. So what can a man with a halo *do* in New York City?" Beat. "I walked."

Karen walked nine feet behind him. Why nine feet? No telling. Maybe she got it from the *Ananga Ranga*. Who knows?

Andy was aiming for the Brooklyn Bridge, the old one. Somewhere along Houston Street, a reporter collecting local off-color spotted him and tried to stage an interview. Andy blurted something incoherent about me, mentioned Michael's name, and started running.

"So there I am, running down Houston Street. The temperature is ninety-five, it's broad daylight, I'm wearing a heavy wool suit, and I'm running. Also I have this Halo."

Karen trotted along three yards behind. Sometimes she said, "Please wait," but mostly she just trotted silently. Her long black hair grew limp with sweat, came undone, dangled lankly on either side of her pale face like a frame. Her dress, cotton but black, also grew first damp and then wet, and hung from her thin shoulders like a clinging sack.

They must've looked like a saint being chased by a witch. When they crossed the Bowery, untold dozens of vagrants took the pledge, according to Andrew. They turned south off Houston and plunged through the pious depths of the Lowest East Side's most conservative ghetto, and their coming was proclaimed by slamming doors and windows, and their going was marked by heart attacks.

The reporter had long since given them up and phoned his ambiguous scoop in to the city desk, but Andrew continued to run, and Karen stayed nine feet behind him all the way.

"I don't know. Maybe I was afraid she'd catch me, or maybe I just wanted to get home in a hurry. Who knows? All *I* know is, I never once considered walking or stopping. You know how it is. I had this Halo: why should anything *else* make sense?"

Somehow, despite the spreading confusion and the complex problems of mental and physical health they left in their wake, they didn't attract official attention until they gained the Brooklyn end of the bridge. Then two cops in a prowl car noticed them.

One: "At first I think he's a purse snatcher, this guy. Then I see he ain't holdin' on to no pocketbook or nothing, and this lady can catch him anytime she wants to. *That* looks suspicious."

Two: "Yeah, an' then I sees somethin' *real* funny an' I says, 'Manny,' I says, 'Hey, Manny, get a load o' that guy,' I says. 'He's glowin'!'"

The brisk-witted fuzz instantly deduced that Andrew was an important government scientist glowing on account of some top secret experiment or something, and that Karen was a dangerous Commie spy, and that either she was chasing him or he was running away with her, one. Either way, the law felt called upon to lend a hand.

Andy's kid brother Jeff bailed them out instantly. "But why *both* of us, for Christ's sake? I'll never understand how my brother's mind works, never." Andrew was hard to please.

To forestall further hassle—the thought of a blue halo running loose in Brooklyn made twenty-year-men blench—the kindly fuzz drove Andy and Karen, in separate cars about three yards apart, to Andy's Brooklyn Heights pad. En route they warned Andrew not to leave the house until he Did Something about that goddamn Glowin'.

It was quite dark when they arrived, and Andy's gross candlepower was amazing. He attracted more attention than he could reasonably handle—even the local moths were a problem—so he had to endure the ultimate public indignity of being escorted to his own front door by an armed guard with all the neighbors watching.

"I'll never be able to show my face in the neighborhood again. I may have to take up a disguise. I may have to shave my beard!"

Karen trailed forgotten behind the guards and slipped between them into Andy's pad. Then she placidly refused to leave.

From then until he called me, Andy did original research on hell. Not only did he have a halo—an utterly undignified and embarrassing ornament, fatal to every aspect of his meticulously structured self-esteem—not only that, but he was additionally encumbered by an overtly adulatory, erotically interesting witness to his total humiliation, imposed on him with the implied blessings of the New York City Police Department solely to lacerate and sting his countless wounds. Andrew Blake was up tight.

I got all this unsponsored melodrama during Andy's second, more polished phone call—he was suppressing video for the duration—which broke in on our contemplation of the Reality Pill's probable significance like a flatulent apocalypse. But while Andy was extolling his own gentility in waiting so long before calling 'cause he didn't want to wake me up or anything and for Christ's sake, Chester, Do Something, I realized what must have happened and how to extract a few more data therefrom.

"Andy," I interrupted, "let me talk to Karen."

"Karen? Oh—oh. That Karen. Sure."

There were footsteps and phone-bumping noises, during which I grimaced expressively at Michael and Sean. Then came an incomprehensible dialogue, more bumping noises, and a high, slightly nasal voice that asked, "Hello?"

She was a multiple-greetings girl, and it took us awhile to establish that we could really hear each other. Then I said, "Karen? Listen, do you take drugs?"

"Do I . . . ?" She was coy. "Now *listen,* that's an awfully— personal question, isn't it?"

"Oh good Lord!" I wanted to go back to bed. "Look, do you know who I am?"

"Uh-uh, no. Andrew just said to . . ."

"Great. Good old Andy. I'm *Chester.* Remember Chester? You saw me with Andy yesterday when . . ."

"Oh! I Know You! I Read Your Book!"

Groovy. I was in. I might even be a halo candidate myself. So I carefully explained that I was only asking these personal questions for Andy's sake—didn't she want to help Andrew?—

and didn't give a damn personally whether she took dope or chewed terbaccy, but *did* she ever use drugs?

Pause. "Well . . ." Longer pause. Then, quite softly, shyly, "sometimes," in a maidenly whisper.

"Sure," very heartily. "Everybody does it Sometimes. It's nothing to be ashamed of." Sometimes I make myself sick. "But tell me, have you ever had, I think they call it, a *Reality Pill?*"

Pause. A whole bunch of silence. Maybe she hung up? "Hello? Still there? Karen?"

"Uh-huh." Still there.

Silence stretched between us fine as copper wires, hissing. At last Karen took a deep breath, held it, and whispered, "Yes."

She sounded oddly different, as though she were sorry she'd said anything. This in turn made me feel as though I should've worn black leather, which would've been just a little more silly than everything else that's happened so far.

"Yes," she whispered again.

I cupped the mouthpiece in my hand and stage-whispered, "Sean, how long were you high? Figure it out."

Then back to the phone: "Karen dear, this is very important. *When* did you take that Reality Pill?"

"Which one?"

Oi. "The last one, dear."

This was a tough one. She was teenyboppishly uninvolved with clocks and suchlike trivia, and we had to determine when she'd dropped that stupid pill the hard way. It was at a party, she recalled, and it was in the nighttime somewhere, and this poet called Lazarus gave it to her.

"Lazarus?" A clue. "Do you mean *Laszlo Scott?*"

Could be, but she wasn't sure, except he had a blond beard you could hardly see and—Oh, wait a minute! He gave her *two* pills, and she took the other one just before she found Andrew.

Sean said, "Must've been something like thirty hours."

Karen screamed then, and Andy either shouted or cried out in strong emotion. Damn vidiphones anyhow, and damn Andrew Blake for squelching his damned video. "What's happening? Karen? Hey!"

"It's Andrew! Oh! Oh dear! He's *fading!*"

While she paused to gulp air, I thought of Andy's red beard slowly turning morning-glory pink, bleaching away at last, looking first like smoke and then like dust until there was nothing left at . . .

Loud noises. New noise. "Chester?" View screen lighting up in pastel glory.

"Andy, what happened?"

"It's gone." Now he sounded like a French horn with adenoids. "It just Faded Away. Only a minute ago. Just faded away." *That* was more like the usual bassoon.

"Congratulations. Tell Karen not to take any more pills and everything will be all right. It wasn't your halo, baby, it was *hers.*"

I hung up as soon as I decently could, for the talk had lost its savor and I had some thinking to do. I felt just about to solve the butterfly problem, I knew not how.

Mike and Sean shared my silence for a few minutes, then Mike drawled, "Well?" and we did us some mind-picking.

This pill was obviously a brand-new drug, we decided, some kind of projective hallucinogen. You have the hallucinations and everyone gets to see them. This would've been harder to believe than to imagine if it hadn't been for Sean and his butterflies, which were clearly nothing but public hallucinations. Not mass hypnosis, either: these were as substantial as any other, more orthodox butterflies, and they caused extensive and quite objective damage, too. But when the drug wore off and Sean came down, the hallucinations ended and the butterflies vanished. Interesting.

"Consider," I said, prepared to mark points off on my fingers. "We've never heard of this stuff before. No newspaper has mentioned it. Nor rumors. Nothing. All highly unlikely."

We agreed. A revolutionary drug like this should've made headlines long ago. Quaint.

"Therefore," I continued, "this thing was *not* produced by one of the big drug houses. We'd've heard."

"Right." Mike was excited. "My God, you couldn't even *test* the damn thing secretly. The first pill that worked . . . Well, you saw what happened with the butterflies."

My turn. "Who could've developed this Reality Pill and really kept it a secret?"

"Nobody." This was Mike's field of special competence. "There's just no way to *keep* that kind of secret. Not even in China. No."

We stared at each other with matched expressions of unbridled surmise, and then, in chorus, said, "The Pill from Outer Space!"

I dropped to the floor, laughing, and rolled about a bit, now and then gasping, "No! Mother of God! Oh wow!" but mostly, "No!" Mike was doing much the same thing, and Sean looked unusually tentative.

"It's absurd," I yelped. "Also corny. It's impossible to take seriously. It's worse than third-class pulp science fiction. It's just unthinkable. Therefore," one of my favorite words, "once you've eliminated the unthinkable . . ."

Michael, still semihelpless on the floor, agreed. "It's a Communist Plot," he chuckled. "Elementary."

This bit of unreason was only a little easier to take, but eventually we calmed down and took it. I had a few reservations, but Mike—who was hooked on spies and such to begin with— was wholly smitten by the notion. His eyes hinted at incredible schemes.

"Well," he said at length, "what're we going to do about it?"

"Do?" I hadn't considered that angle.

"Yeah, do. We're not gonna let 'em get away with this, are we?"

"Of course not, I suppose."

"Right. Whatever this plot is, we've got to thwart it."

"*We* do?"

"It's our duty, baby. They're trying to overthrow society, Chet. And where would *we* be without society?"

It was an interesting question, but I didn't like any of the answers.

"Okay," I resigned. "What're we gonna do?"

We discussed it for almost an hour, confusing Sean beyond repair and swearing him to absolute secrecy. He was already a little afraid to open his mouth anyway, and when Mike casually mentioned *plastique,* you could almost see Sean shrivel up. But his eyes were just as excited as Mike's.

"We've got one solid handle," said Michael the Theodore Bear.

"Which is?"

"Laszlo Scott," he replied. "Sean and that chick got their pills from Laszlo. But where did *he* get them?"

Another interesting question. Laszlo Scott was an exceptionally slimy creature, capable, to my mind, of any enormity, but he was also imposingly stupid, and I couldn't imagine any really competent Communist Plotter making use of him.

"Where indeed?" I counterqueried.

"Right!" Mike snapped. "That's what you've got to find out."

"I?"

"Who else? You're the local Laszlo Scott expert. It wouldn't do much good if *I* tried to follow him, would it? Sean can help you."

"You want Me to follow *Laszlo?*"

"Only for a few days, until he gets more pills. That's when the fun begins."

"Following *Laszlo?*"

"C'mon, it won't hurt you. It'll be Fun, Chester. Really. You can take notes."

Groovy. So I resigned myself to tailing Loathsome Laszlo, but I was already sick of the whole routine. I had a whole anthology of arguments against this project, beginning with, "If this is really a Communist Plot, we ought to notify the FBI," and ending with, "I'm a musician, dammit, not a spy," but it was already evening, and we had to go west.

I didn't really want to follow Laszlo.

7

It turned out to be an exceptionally quiet Sunday, especially by Village standards. Aside from the horde of teenyboppers, none of whom represented enough money to matter, plus half a spate of bewildered-looking tourists who were most likely hunting for Chinatown, the streets were deserted.

"It's a turndown day, baby," Chaz said when I reached The Mess, something like eight thirty. He was right. There were more performers in the house than audience.

"Yesterday must've worn 'em out," I probably explained.

Anyhow, Charley closed The Mess a half hour later, and all of us—we Tripouts, Al Mamlet, and a banjoist from Chicago I'd never seen before who somehow knew what he thought was all about me—split for The Garden of Eden.

M. T. Bear and Sean were already there, of course, along with Gary the Frog, a few Davids, and the customary strangers. They were clustered around our family table, overflowing slightly into the aisle, interfering with the waitress, chattering like a tribe of typists, and generally carrying on as was their noisy wont.

Gary, his face even more of an acne farm than usual, was loudly endeavoring to master a twelve-string guitar he'd neglected to tune, while one of the Davids kept saying excitedly, "Hey, baby, let me try it? Huh? Huh, Gary? Kin I try it?" All very natural.

Mike was doing his standard best to catch everyone's ear, saying, "But it's a Plot, don't you understand?" but everyone's ear remained blithely uncaught. Mike'd hollered Plot too often. Everyone believed him, but nobody cared. Constant excitement is a drag.

The Garden of Eden, immune to Sunday doldrums, skirled about the table like a neurotic river, babbling, jostling, everyone sort of accidentally groping (sort of) everybody else, all of which made it hard for me to get through to Mike. "Pardon me," I said politely once or twice, *pro forma,* with no visible effect. Then "This is a Raid!" I yelled in a thick bass voice. "Don't nobody move!"

The noise was something awful—high-pitched shrieks, low thuds, lots of Oh Wow's, and other hip chaos—but when the dust cleared, I only had to shove and push a little bit to get through to the table.

"Why didn't you just yell Fire?" asked Mike.

"Howdy, baby," added Sean.

And, "Where's my Geetar?" croaked Gary the Frog, thank God.

I sat down gratefully. Some David surrendered his seat to Sativa, who whispered what I chose to think was thanks. Patrick, Stu, and Kevin pulled up chairs obtained from somewhere. A version of quiet descended on The Garden of Eden. Even the Kallikak box took five.

"What's happenin!" I smiled, pretending nothing was.

"They don't believe me," Michael grieved.

"Why," I shrugged, "should they?"

A slow voice, like a tawny port, breathed, "Who is *That?*" into my left ear. "He's *Pretty!*" Sativa always talked like that.

"Sean," I explained.

"Huh?" He hadn't heard the question.

Okay. "Sean," I said with flawed formality, "this is Sativa. Sativa love, meet Sean."

"Oh yeah!" Vast enthusiasm. "You sure sing Good."

"Pretty." She had a few-track mind, like most of us in those days, but more openly. She slithered from her chair to a position directly behind young Sean and started to stroke his hair ever so gently. At the first stroke he twitched slightly, being unaccustomed to such things, then leaned back and enjoyed it.

"Ai-yah," I told myself. "Well, I won't have to worry about those two for a while," not that I'd intended to.

"Hi!" That was Harriet, Gary the Frog's fan club et cetera, surging through the crowd like an amiable elephant. "Guess who I just saw outside?"

I knew better than to bother.

"Laszlo!" she lisped.

"Oh God," said the rest of us.

"Laszlo Scott," she went on. "He says he'll have more you-know-what tomorrow."

"Groovy." That, of course, was Gary.

"Laszlo." My evening was shattered. I'd forgotten about that. Laszlo Scott indeed, whom my best friend Mike said I had to dammit follow tomorrow. I thought about that for a while, missing out on the activity around me. When I got back, Sativa was on Sean's lap, and I couldn't quite tell whose arms were whose, which was splendid; Gary the Frog was sitting on Harriet's lap, which made more sense than chivalry; Michael and Patrick were trying to understand each other, a hopeless hobby they were fond of; the Kallikak box was playing one of Our songs, by God; and Laszlo Scott, alas, was flowing up the aisle toward me, and I didn't have a tourist's chance to get away.

Laszlo was easier to understand than to believe. He throve on ridicule, an amazingly complex perversion. Not just any old ridicule, mind you: Laszlo was a connoisseur. He was perfectly willing to endure the esteem of young female tourists, on which he made his living, as long as Mike and I and other such Village aristocrats, all of whom he hated in proportian to his need for them, put him beautifully down. (Once, in an excess of something I'd rather not think about, Laszlo got a coffeehouse gig that involved his being beaten up by the manager after closing every night. He held that job for six months, until the manager got busted in New Jersey for aggravated assault and the coffeehouse closed down.)

Laszlo stood some five plump nine in his fragrant stocking feet. His hair was so blond it was almost invisible, wherefore he sported a translucent pussycat beard that gave his (let us call it pasty) face a patently absurd ambiguity, an almost aggressive absence of form. In the middle of this face, which might be ugly if anybody cared, sat two little eyes, wet blue, beady red-rimmed, and porcine, surrounded by no visible lashes or brows.

"Laszlo," I once said in a fit of divine inspiration, "is a blue-eyed maggot in drag." No one ever disagreed.

(Laszlo was coming closer. His progress up the aisle was slow, because he stopped to manifest himself at every table on the way, but he was now only three and a half tables away and my stomach was beginning to turn.)

Laszlo was a poet, so to speak; a coffeehouse poet, of course, given to clambering up on stages and reciting his works at helpless audiences, hopefully for money. This was his claim to membership in coffeehouse society, and even though his poetry was generally incredibly bad or stolen or both, we honored his claim, without necessarily honoring Laszlo himself—a superhuman task not worth the effort.

(Now he was two tables off and clearly audible, alas. Mike'd noticed him and was trying to communicate with me by vague and frantic hand signals that I carefully ignored, preferring to sink into happy catatonia.)

The trouble with Laszlo, however, was none of this. The trouble was that Laszlo was a skunk, a nerd, a slimy loathsome thing whose major joy was to bring trouble and discomfort to everyone he encountered. For kicks he sold oregano to high-school kids from Queens. He stole from people poorer than himself as a matter of habit. He invented foul stories about innocent people and circulated them for a hobby. He once caught a social disease and spread it broadcast, especially among the naive and virginal, for upward of six weeks, until it got too uncomfortable even for him.

Laszlo was an incurable backstabber. In the Village society, where trust took the place of law, he could not be trusted. He was a wolf in black sheep's clothing, a one-man plague. Even worse, he was a notorious drag.

The thing is, if Laszlo had been at all intelligent, or even kind of clever, or if he'd just had something like a sense of humor, we'd've pretty much ignored his faults and weaknesses. I myself was moderately fond of one or two worse characters who had the saving grace of being interesting. With such people, you take their flaws into account, more or less automatically doing whatever you must to protect yourself, and then enjoy these people as you'd enjoy anyone else. After all, no one's perfect. But Laszlo, alas, was stupid, which simply could not be forgiven.

And now he was finishing off the table across the aisle ("Is it true your old lady's hustling?" he was asking a hyperjealous drummer), and we, especially I, were next. Oi. Laszlo had a special fondness, so to speak, for me, mainly because I was pretty successful in a number of arts he pretended to practice. I'd published two small books of pretty good verse, and a few novels, and I used to write for the *East Village Other* until it sold out to the Establishment and went slick, and I was a mildly famous rock 'n' rolly, and so on. In other words, I was popular in a world he wanted to rule. I was a number of things he'd've liked to've been, on his terms, which made me a natural target for him, and here he came.

"Good evening, *Mister* Anderson. How's your commercial little world tonight? Have you heard the news?" He was dressed, as he'd been for the past six weeks, in tattered cavalier poet garb—rusty purple patched tights, formerly black shabby high-heeled, knee-high boots a size or so too large, a lace-front shirt nearly as dark as his boots after six weeks' uninterrupted wear, a swallowtail coat that might've once been black but was mainly green by now, a battered three-cornered hat with a limp and dirty plastic feather sagging down from it, and an opera cape of indeterminate color badly patched in some other indeterminate color. Furthermore, he smelled.

"Ah yes," I less than sneered, "it's little George." When he arrived in the Village, two years ago, he changed his name from George Harper to Laszlo Scott, and I never let him forget it. "I suspected you were around. Something in the air, if you know what I mean." I never talked like this to anyone else.

"And there's little Mike," ignoring me. "Saw Maidy yesterday, baby, hangin' out at Times Square. Dig?" Maidy Clark was Mike's immediate ex-mistress, about whom he was going to be sensitive until the next one came along.

Mike stood up, clenched a fist, said, "Laszlo . . . !" and then remembered that we had designs on Master Scott and, shaking his head like a bear among bees, sat down again.

"What news, Georgie?" I was hoping to get it over with as quickly as could be.

"Well, baby, I just signed a contract. With Columbia, you dig? They want me to tape my own songs, baby, with a *band.*" He purred unwholesomely.

"Sure, man, sure. Just like Dylan, right? What happened to that contract you signed with Victor? Gonna do both? And how about that book you were doing for Viking?" Laszlo's greatest personal weakness was that he could never remember to whom he'd told which lie. "So what else is new?" I hated to hear myself talking like that. I wanted to go away and take a bath.

Laszlo promptly changed the subject. "I s'pose you've heard about my Pills," he sneered.

Mike's ears came to a visible point.

"Well, I heard about *some* pills," I confessed.

"Mine," he exulted. "Reality Pills, you dig? An' I'm the only connection, baby. Me. You want some?"

"What do you mean, you're the *only* connection? Bullshit. Where'd *you* get 'em?"

"That's *my* secret, baby."

"Not for long, Georgie, not for long."

"Long enough, baby. Want some?"

Mike was obviously memorizing all of this and ready to spend the rest of the night analyzing it. He took being a spy and/or detective seriously, the only way really to enjoy it. The rest of our group, for various reasons of their own, were listening almost as intently. Only Sean and Sativa were ignoring our discussion. They had other things to think about.

"You want some Reality Pills?" Laszlo repeated.

"I dunno," grudgingly. "Maybe."

"Sure, Captain Cool. Yeah, maybe. Tell you what I'll do: I'll have some more tomorrow, dig? If I see you, baby, I'll give you a special deal, just for you, Andy, 'cause you're sort of a poet, too."

"I thought you were *givin'* 'em away," croaked Gary the Frog.

"Just creating a demand, Froggy. You know." One very smug Laszlo.

"Yeah," I said, cynicism dripping from my words so strong I was half afraid my teeth'd rot. "The first one's always free, right? We know how it is, Georgie. But how do we know the next batch'll work? You've got a great name for oregano, baby."

It was next to impossible to predict what would offend Laszlo, but this seemed to. He drew his cloak around himself in a dramatic gesture that knocked two cups of coffee and a Coke off the table behind him, elevated his nose some fifteen degrees, and sniffed, "That's your problem, baby. See you then."

He huffed off aromatically to bug some other table. I took a deep breath. Sativa giggled. Gary the Frog started to say something, forgot what it was, and snapped his slack mouth shut with a liquid click. Mike was bursting to say something, but not till Laszlo was out of range.

"Michael," I whispered loudly, "can you really believe that biped fungus is a Communist Plotter? And besides," I'd been thinking about this for a while, "how could that damn thing be a Communist Plot if it couldn't be tested secretly?"

Mike looked around cautiously. "Siberia," he hushed.

"Siberia?"

"Right. They used monkeys or something. Obvious. Who'd notice a monkey's hallucinations anyway?"

"Well, *I* would," said Harriet from under Gary the Frog.

"Me, too," I agreed. "And what about Laszlo?"

"He's a tool." My density seemed to annoy Mike. Pity. "That doesn't change the plan, though."

"Oh." I'd been afraid of that.

"Tomorrow," Mike went ruthlessly on, "he's getting more, right? That's our chance. It's all so simple." Mike had a habit, at such times, of spreading out his hands as though he were trying on a crucifix for size. This meant he was practicing superhuman patience with such clods as myself, who were unable to understand such obvious schemes.

"Are you people, you know, like Talkin' 'bout *Somethin'*, man," Patrick stumbled, "or is it one of your rants?" We'd put him on by accident once with the plot of a spy story we never got around to writing, and he'd wondered about us ever since.

"Just a rant," said the security-conscious M. T. Bear.

"Groovy."

Whereupon the table talk turned to fairly general subjects, mainly yesterday's adventures, the Reality Pill, who was sleeping with or without whom, what bands were rumored to be breaking up and why, the Reality Pill, who might be selling what for how much, the apocryphal history of Andrew Blake and everybody we knew who wasn't there, modern techniques of counterespionage, wiretapping, housebreaking *et al,* and other quaint topics dear to our twisted hearts, but especially Reality Pills.

"I don't care," Stu insisted. "I want 'em." Mike had been expounding his Communist Plot theory.

"Sure," I said loyally, "it's probably a great high for people like us, but can you imagine the Whole World on that stuff?"

"Why not?"

"Sturgeon's Law," Mike explained, Sturgeon's Law being: 90 percent of everything is crap, mildly speaking.

"That's cool," Stu capitulated.

"What's it like?" Kevin asked. None of us had thought to ask that question, but Kevin was scientifically trained.

"Yeah, Sean," I agreed. "How does it feel?"

"Uhmm!" Sean was still involved with Sativa. They seemed to be developing a really intricate relationship.

"How does What feel?" That double reed voice again.

"Andy!" Several voices.

"Hello there." And not just Andrew, best Edwardian threads and all, but Karen Greenbaum as well, and hand in hand, too. Somebody's plot was thickening nicely, thanks.

Mike and Stu scurried about collecting chairs for them, but Andy said, "No, no. Don't bother, we can't stay. We're off to see *Fox and Hare,"* the in-est flick that summer. "We just dropped in to see what you were up to. Do you know Karen?"

All of us but Sean and Sativa (who were busy) rose to be introduced and shake hands or, in Mike's case, kiss hands, that being one of his favorite riffs. Karen blushed, giggled, tried to say hip, sophisticated things, and generally embarrassed everyone but Sean and Sativa (who were busy) and Andrew Blake, who was temporarily blind.

"What happened," Patrick said uncoolly, "to your Halo?"

"Halo?" Andy gestured casually. "Oh, that was just a misunderstanding."

I gasped, Mike choked slightly, and even Sean looked up from whatever tactile intricacy he was involved in at the time.

"Misunderstanding?" I amazed.

"You know."

I didn't, but what the hell. I was still rabidly curious, though, so I unkindly said, "And, ah, Karen?"

Give him credit, he hemmed and hawed a little first. Then he embarked on a rant involving such classic phrases as, "really quite intelligent," and, "very sensitive for her age, you know," and, "really Understands my work," et standard cetera, during which Mike and I, having heard it all before and before, shrugged eyebrows at each other.

Then, with a fanfare of literate billing and cooing, the new lovers split to *Fox and Hare* to dig the latest Technicolor version of the life the rest of us were living.

It was almost ten o'clock, technically early but I was beginning to feel a trifle eroded, as though this Sunday had been crawling on for days. A combination of Laszlo and Andy within the same hour, perhaps. Anyhow, as soon as I could catch Mike's eye, I yawned significantly, whereupon he ordered me another cup of coffee. Life with Mike has certain disadvantages.

From then on the evening disintegrated. At that point, doubtless much later than he ordinarily would have, Sean tenderly dislodged Sativa and staggered to the john.

"Oh," she whispered in my ear in a tone that'd certainly be sinful for any other two people, "he's *Pretty!*"

"Right," I said. Why not?

"Ah, what's his, ah, name?"

Oh my dear Sativa. "Sean," I sighed.

"Oh. *Sean.* Pretty!"

I couldn't tell whether I was weary or amused. Two cases of young love in one evening were a bit much. Still, I was sort of glad for Sean, who was about to recover from Mary-Bob, so I guess I was basically amused, or at least entertained. Mike, meanwhile, was trying to convince Kevin, of all people, of the basic truth of his Communist Plot hypothesis.

"I think," Sativa said in an amazingly unmystical tone, "I'd best go to the john and fix my diaphragm."

I goggled. She split. I suspected I knew where she meant to use that device. Sativa had four cats, a dog, three roommates, and two rooms—a standard Village hangup.

Sean came back, registering absolute dismay at the absence of Sativa.

"She'll be back," I comforted him.

He sat down. "You know," he said, "I think she kinda Likes me." He was announcing miracles.

"You may be right." Then Sativa returned and I lost track of them.

Somewhere later I hunted around for my current notebook and found it in front of Mike, being filled with left-handed illegibilities concerning the Reality Pill project.

"What the hell are you doing?" I foolishly inquired. I'd meant to do some scribbling in that notebook myself.

"It's really very simple," he beamed, waving a page at me that I couldn't've read with the aid of a computer.

"Oh yeah?" I'd heard him say those words before, and so far they'd never been quite accurate. One of Mike's famous simple plans'd involved installing ten illegal phones and three bookies in our living room, resulting in a noisy police raid that coincided with my finally taking to bed a chick I'd lusted after for more than a year. I never saw her again. "Simple, huh?"

"Right. Look, all you have to do . . ."

"Later." I didn't want to know all I had to do, but Mike happily misunderstood.

"You're right," staring quickly everywhere. "Somebody might hear us."

"Groovy."

Later Sean borrowed my keys and he and Sativa vanished.

Later yet, with no intervening events I could remember, Mike and I were walking east on Eighth Street, heading home, I became aware of this in the middle of a sentence: ". . . but the thing to remember is that the power behind Laszlo very strongly does not *want* to be discovered, and might even try to kill us if they notice us. Might even succeed, in fact." It was one of my sentences.

"Right, but as soon as we find Laszlo's connection, we call in the FBI. We're not doing anything really dangerous."

"No?"

"Nuh-uh. All we're gonna do is follow Laszlo. See?"

"Oh yeah? Who you callin' *we*, white man?"

"You know what I mean."

"I'm afraid I do."

The rest of the way home I worried about tomorrow. Following Laszlo was bad enough, following him into possible danger was just ridiculous, but tired as I was. I couldn't think up a dignified way to chicken out. Maybe it wouldn't be dangerous. And maybe the sun would rise in the south. Sure.

The guest-room door was closed when we got home, but the noises from behind it were sufficiently explicit. Sean was learning fast. He had a few Texas practices—yelling "Yippee," for instance—I hoped he'd get over in a hurry, but by and large he seemed to have a lot of (call it) talent going for him. Sativa sounded pretty happy too, which pleased me, for it meant she'd sing a lot better than usual for a while.

"Well, good night, Mike," I whispered, privily hoping my closed door would muffle the Sean and Sativa sinfonia.

"Set your clock for seven thirty, right?"

"Seven thirty!?"

"The early bird routine."

"Worms?"

"Good night."

Sean's noise ignored my door completely. I might as well've been in the same room. I halfway wished I were, but I set my alarm as instructed and went to bed like a good boy.

Noise and all, I fell instantly asleep, still half dressed, and dreamed all night of a million Laszlos trailing me on rancid butterflies.

8

onday started poorly enough. I staggered naked and disheveled out of my room at half-past heathen seven to find Sean and Sativa, mutually radiant, fully occupying the living room and wearing nothing but wide grins.

"Groovy," I complained. "Let's have an orgy." Instead I stumbled back into my room to find a bathrobe.

Sativa, I noticed, took this collective nudity in her cool stride, but Sean blushed all over—an impressive sight in so tall a kid—tried with a wholly inadequate hand to salvage his modesty, gulped "Oh wow," and fled awkwardly to the guest room: a complicated reaction I was quite unable to understand.

Decently robed and less than half awake, I fumbled into Michael's room and tried to rouse the master planner. This was far too much work to start a morning with, but if I had to get up, I'd be carefully damned if he was going to sleep.

Mike asleep is a fairly charming sight. His mouth is full of his right thumb, his face is round and innocent, and he isn't saying anything. Nevertheless, I pulled his thumb out of his mouth, shook his head and shoulders fairly roughly, and yelled, "Reveille! Reveille! Out of the sack, soldier!" much more loudly than I liked.

"Gargh!" His eyes flashed open, his jaw snapped shut (which is why I pulled his thumb out first), and he sat up like an overwound automaton.

"Good morning, Michael," I regretted, dialing his lights to full.

"Morning?"

"Right. Up and at'em, more or less. Busy day. Get up."

"Oh yeah. Sure. I'm awake."

This I rather doubted, but I let it pass. Leaving Mike's door aggravatingly open, I set my wobbly course back toward my own room, intending to get shaved and dressed or whatever seemed appropriate.

Sean was back in the living room, his native modesty staisfled by a pair of not quite transparent briefs that were little more than a token gesture. He was grinning a high-grade idiot grin and holding hands with Sativa, who was still wearing mainly Sativa.

"Morning, children," I begrudged as cheerfully as could be.

"Morning," they burbled, not looking at me.

A shower woke me, shaving reconciled me to being awake, and dressing—inconspicuous loud silks, a paisley scarf and high suede boots, bright green—pretty well sealed my fate for the day. The whole process carried me through to eight ten, and I finished by dousing myself in patchouli. Then, I went in search of Mike and breakfast.

Sean and Sativa seemed not to have moved, but he was apparently getting excited.

"Cool it," I told them. "Mike up yet?"

"Mike? said Sean as though he'd never heard the name, and, "Nuh, uh," Sativa added, which might easily mean anything.

"Right." So I returned to Michael's room and there he was, thumb firmly in mouth, at beautiful peace with the world. I was not pleased.

"Michael!" I yelled in the bosun's mate voice I picked up in the Navy in my puppy days. Windows rattled gratifyingly. Even Mike went so far as to pull his thumb our of his mouth and mutter something inarticulate and vaguely placating.

"Wake," I bellowed, "up!" I knew I wasn't going to be able to speak above a whisper for the rest of the day, but Michael, by God, was going to get up.

He stirred uncomfortably. Sean and Sativa, hand in hand, came in to see what might be happening. "Up! Up! Up!" I screamed frantically.

"Oh," Sativa said. *"I* can wake him up." She dropped Sean's paw, flowed over to the bed, sat down on it, and put a hand on Michael's shoulder. Sean began to turn a purplish red.

"Michael, poochie," she whispered in his ear. *Michael, poochie?* She stuck out her tongue and did something to Mike's ear with it. I grabbed Sean and held him back.

Mike sat up, opened his eyes slowly and wide, and reached out for Sativa. She, giggling, got off the bed and backed toward the door—truly an inspiring sight. Mike got out of bed and followed her. Sean, still fuming, and I stepped out of the way.

She waited until Mike was half an inch short of touching her, then turned, and, laughing, skipped out into the living room. Michael followed blindly. When he passed through the door, I slammed it shut, released Sean, and said, "Good morning, Michael," almost as maliciously as he deserved.

Sean and Sativa joined hands again, disillusioning Mike completely. He stood stock-still in the middle of the living room, looked around in marshmallow confusion, then realized with a start that he was both awake and up.

"Gnurph!" he said in horror. He headed back toward his room, but I fended him off and aimed him toward the john.

"Not today, old buddy," still rather maliciously. "Communist Plot, baby, remember?"

"Gnurph!" he repeated, but he waddled toward the john.

Midway through breakfast most of us were wide enough awake to lay plans of a sort. Michael, his mouth ringed quaintly with milk, immediately took charge.

"The first thing we should do," he said, *we* meaning myself and possibly Sean, "is search Laszlo's pad. Right?"

"Why?" To me the idea lacked appeal.

"He probably keeps some kind of record," very patiently, "of the source of those pills, or at least of how many he got and what he did with them. We'll need that sort of thing for evidence when we go to the FBI. Why do I always have to explain these simple things to you?"

This wasn't worth an answer, so I poured myself another cup of maté and thought about things for a while. Sean and Sativa—still holding hands and having a hell of a time trying to eat that way—weren't saying anything, and I doubted that they were hearing much either. She was still wearing mainly herself, which gave the breakfast table an unduly festive air.

"Hey," I realized, "just how're we planning to go about searching Laszlo's pad?" I suspected I already knew.

"Simple." Mike sniffed in well-bred disgust. "We wait around until he splits and then break in."

That's what I thought. "As I recall," I said sarcastically, "that's called breaking and entering, and there are laws against it in this town."

"Oh wow. Since when are you allergic to breaking laws?"

He had a point there, but, "I like to think I'm more or less selective about what laws I break. I mean, well, I like my felonies to be fun."

"Breaking into Laszlo's pad and searching it isn't fun?"

"Hmmm."

"Besides, it's your patriotic duty to society. Remember that."

"Um."

"And if you find those records, you won't have to follow Laszlo."

"How do we do it?"

At quarter of twelve we stationed ourselves in a grubby candy store across the filthy cobbled street from Laszlo's Avenue A pad. Mike phoned Laszlo, hanging up as soon as he answered.

"Still there," he told us.

We settled down for a moderately long siege, sipping the worst chocolate egg creams on the Lower East Side. While I tacitly counted my woes (I *like* chocolate egg creams, generally), Mike taught Sean how to operate the two-way wrist radios we were using on this lark.

"All you have to do," he said for the third unduly patient time, "is press the blue button and slide it to the right to send, and press the green button and slide it to the left to receive. The little gray button controls the volume: slide it to the right to get louder, to the left to get softer. It's very simple."

"Yeah," Sean whispered. "Man, how old *is* that chick?"

"What chick?" Mike derailed fairly easily and didn't like it a bit.

"You know." Long Texas smile. "Sa-TI-va," very slowly.

"Oh wow. *I* don't know. Twenty-five?"

"Yeah?" Sean's face looked as dreamy as a custard pie in August.

"Now," calmly, "about this Radio . . ."

On and on they went, while Laszlo stayed perversely home and I swallowed endless lousy egg creams. The plan was for Michael to follow Laszlo, when and if he left, keeping in touch with us by radio, thus leaving Sean and me free to ransack Laszlo's pad with little chance of getting caught, an arrangement of which I basically approved. Sean, however, didn't seem to have much of a gift for wrist radios.

"Blue button," he said ruefully after a prolonged while; "green button" in bewilderment; *"gray* button! Hey, man, which is which?"

"What?" Mike looked grievously stricken. "What do you mean?"

"I mean which is which, man? I can't tell them goddamn buttons apart."

"What do you mean, you can't tell them apart?" I'd seldom heard Mike sound so utterly offended.

"I think," I drawled, interrupting my catalog of sorrows, "I think," again, "Sean's trying to tell you something."

"So *tell* me, dammit."

"It strikes me," prolonging Michael's agony, "that our young friend's a trifle color blind. Right, Sean?"

"Yeah," he confessed, embarrassed. "I got these goofy contact things I'm s'posed to wear, but I don't like 'em."

So I ended up wearing the radio, though Mike's generally reluctant to entrust me with electronic gear, being of the odd opinion that every communications gadget I touch falls apart instantly, which has only happened a few times and was never quite my fault.

And still we waited, sipping flat egg creams, telling Sean imaginative tales about Sativa, drawing progressively unfriendly looks from the Puerto Rican counterman and his fat wife or whatever, and cursing Laszlo fluently. None of us was particularly happy, and the day showed signs of becoming interminable and drab.

Laszlo finally left home at half-past two. Mike gave him the traditional half block lead and then slipped out after him, first making sure my radio was on. He doubted I could safely turn it on myself. Fine roommate.

Half a tepid egg cream later my left wrist said, "KRD 429B, mobile unit one, to KRD 429B, mobile unit two. Come in mobile unit two."

"That's Michael," I explained to Sean and the suddenly downright hostile counterman.

"KRD 429B, mobile unit two," I told my left wrist as Sean and I scuttled out just before the counterman could scuttle us, "to KRD 429B, mobile unit one. Hello there. Do we really need this KRD garbage?"

"You have to," Mike's voice said tinnily. "The UNCC may be monitoring."

"Groovy. Considering what we're up to, I don't want to be that easy to identify. Are you there?"

My radio crackled thoughtfully for a bit, then, "Right."

"Great. What's happening?"

"He's trying to flag a cab. No, he's got one. It's cool to begin the exercise, understand?"

"Robert."

"Robert?"

"You know, Yes."

"Roger!"

"I thought that was some kind of British vice."

"I've got a cab. I'll follow him. You get to work."

"Roger?"

"Right. Keep in touch."

Sean and I played truck dodge from one curb to the other, leaping about inconspicuously, and ended up in the aromatic downstairs hall of the hyper-substandard brick antiquity that Laszlo Scott infested. Sean wanted to read the archaic obscenities on the walls, but I hustled him along upstairs. My main ambition was to get this whole thing over with as quickly as possible.

Laszlo's den, third grimy floor front, sported a shiny metal door with five count them five locks of elaborately different kinds. The homemade universal key Mike'd issued me opened all of them but one, which turned out to be neither locked nor working. I began to feel a treacherous sense of confidence rising within me.

I slowly pushed the door open. It didn't creak. This bothered me. Laszlo's door by rights *should* creak. I stood there wondering about that, and Sean pushed past me into the pad.

Nothing happened to Sean, so I shrugged and followed him in. "Hello there," I told my wrist before I even bothered to look around. "Are you there?"

"What's happening?"

"Contact, smooth and easy. Where are you?"

"Third and 28th Street headed north."

"Groovy. Keep in touch."

Then I looked around. It wasn't exactly the kind of pad I'd expected Laszlo to have, but it was obviously Laszlo's kind of pad. The internal walls had all been torn down, not quite neatly, making the pad one huge and thickly littered room, in the midst of which stood Sean looking shocked. I got the impression he wasn't used to dirt.

The walls were whitewashed, mostly, and decorated with Laszloish slogans in gaudy colors, like: Art is Fredom; The Cretor is The Onley True God; the Futur Belongs too the Poet—the rest being unprintable, just as poorly spelled, and pretty dull.

The windows were covered over with colored tissue paper pasted directly on the panes—the standard poor man's stained-glass effect—which was covered over in turn by a few year's geological accumulation of good old city filth. The light that found its way through these barriers was dim and resigned, unable to give a damn, precisely what Laszlo's litter needed. Complete darkness would've been even better, aesthetically, but might've had some practical drawbacks.

"Well, Sean, this is a New York poet's pad. How do you like it?"

"You mean he *lives* here?"

"That's what he calls it. There's his bed."

It was over in the farthest, darkest corner of the mess, a bare and superannuated mattress on the floor, torn and filthy with historic dirt, surrounded by discarded bottles, beer cans, chocolate milk cartons, creme-filled cupcake wrappers, sandwich bags, used tissues, mummified corned beef sandwiches, obsolete stockings, assorted dingy female undergarments, badly used torn comic books—the enduring moldy record of Laszlo's Village life. The place smelled of mature cat box, too, though there seemed to be no cat.

Sean clearly didn't believe a word of this. "You say this cat's a Poet, man?"

"That's the general idea, baby. A genuine twentieth-century bard."

"Oh *yeah*?" Sean was learning fast.

"Hey!" my left wrist suddenly demanded. "What's happening?"

"We're inside," I assured him, while Sean, tiptoeing fastidiously, touching whatever he thought he had to as little as possible and wiping his fingers nervously on his Levi's afterwards, more or less began to search the pad. The litter was six inches thick on the average, deeper in drifts, and the task before us had a lean and hopeless look.

"What the hell are you doing?" Mike insisted.

"Talking to you," I said reasonably enough. "What's happening?"

"We're in Grand Central. Subject's waiting for someone under the clock. Looks worried."

"Great. Keep up the good work, fellah." Sean had found a chartreuse desk minus a drawer or two, and was cheerfully ransacking it, emptying it onto the floor, creating an additional mess Laszlo was unlikely to notice.

"Are you, ah, proceeding with the exercise?" Poor Mike.

"With great viguh, sir, in spite of all but insurmountable obstacles."

"Results?"

"Ambiguous."

"Oh? Well, ah, keep in touch."

"Later," That done, I joined the hunt.

Sean and I in record time formulated a neat set of ground rules for the search. Nothing on the floor, we agreed, was worth considering; anything carefully stashed anywhere was. That made our job 90 percent easier. Another rule prohibited putting things back where we found them, which would just be wasted time and needless charity. Working thus, we went through Laszlo's midden with a gap-toothed rake.

It took an hour or so, during which Mike called frequently to report that Laszlo hadn't done anything yet and ask us what we'd found.

I was getting dragged by the mess, my tiny respect for Laszlo was clear gone, when Sean yelled from the bathroom, "Hey, what's this?"

And Mike tinned, "Chester, are you there?"

"Aye, aye, sir," to Mike and, "Hold it," to Sean.

"He's gone!" Mike shrilled, buzzing the speaker.

"Where'd he go?"

"Dunno." The fidelity was poor, but good enough to carry the embarrassed tone of Michael's voice.

"You *lost* him?" Considering Mike, this was hard to believe.

"There was this ChicK, you understand?"

"Chick?"

"Yeah. She asked me for a light, and when I turned around again, he was gone."

"Oh. A ChicK." I thought it over, then, "Pretty?"

"Wow!"

"Figures. Well, we'll cut out like now, okay?"

"You better." Pause. "Oh, find anything?"

"Not particularly. Agent 002's got something in the john, but I haven't seen it yet."

"Hmm. Right. Anyhow, get out as fast as you can. He may be heading back, you know. See you at the pad."

"Roger! Keep in touch."

Well. That was interesting. I supposed. "What've you got?" I yelled at Sean.

"C'mere an' see. I cain't tell"

Laszlo's john couldn't surprise me anymore, not after the rest of the pad, but it certainly was unusual. Yeah, unusual. It looked like a cross between an explosion in a pharmacy and a condemned abattoir, just what I expected but more than I could take. Nevertheless, I took it. I'm a dedicated man now and then.

Sean was standing in the middle of all this, skitterishly shying away from anything. He was holding a medium-sized brown paper sack, well-filled, over his head.

"What seems to be the matter here?"

"Dig." He handed me the bag. It was full of crushed, dry green leaves. For a moment I felt a thrill course through me, but then I remembered Laszlo's slimy practices.

"It's probably oregano," I regretted.

"Don't smell like it," he offered.

He was right. "Step into my office," I suggested, and we moved back into the big room.

"I happen to have with me," I said, pulling my trusty little pipe from my pocket, "an extremely sensitive testing device."

"Groovy," my faithful assistant exclaimed.

I dipped up a pipeful of Laszlo's unknown green stuff, lit it, and inhaled deeply. "Nope," I said after a while, "it's not oregano."

"What is it?"

I dropped my voice to a solemn whisper and said, "Marijuana, baby. Loathsome Laszlo's private stash."

"Hey, man, what a gas! Let's cop it."

"You want to steal Laszlo's grass?" The idea had an appalling charm.

"Why not, man?"

"Well—he'd notice. Mike doesn't want him to know we've been here."

"Oh, man, like *you* know bards can't count."

Years ago, before we knew what Laszlo was, I'd innocently paid him twenty bucks for prime spaghetti seasoning, so, "Okay, but leave some for Laszlo," there being a kind of honor in every minority group.

"Right."

And so we split, Sean carrying our share of Laszlo's treasure. I closed the metal door silently, carefully relocking all five locks, and we started to tiptoe down the stairs.

Halfway down we stopped dead. There was a strange noise below us, a familiar strange noise, an absolutely Laszlo kind of noise.

"Trapped!" I cursed.

We turned and tiptoed double time back up the stairs, past Laszlo's pad and two flights farther, all the way up to the door to the roof, which was locked from the other side.

"Yeah," Sean whispered while I swore inventively, "trapped." Meanwhile Laszlo loudly climbed the stairs below us. He seemed to consider each step a personal offense, and kept it no secret. He wasn't a happy Laszlo, not at all.

He reached his landing and the Laszlo noise abated. Then there were crisp metallic noises, four sets of them: the Bard of MacDougal Street unlocking his door. This developed into a furious muffled rattling, punctuated by spurts of amateurish profanity. The rattling grew louder, and there were vigorous percussive sounds most likely made by kicking.

Under cover of this racket Sean whispered, "Hey, man, did you do something to that other lock?"

Clatter bang.

"Other lock?"

"You know, man. They was five locks, only one of 'em didn't work. Remember?"

Thunderbash clamorbang cuss!

"Oh Christ," I admitted. "You're right"

"You locked it?"

"I locked it."

Sean and I huddled at the top of the stairs, waiting. It didn't seem likely that Laszlo'd come upstairs and find us, but considering Laszlo, that wasn't much security. I became acutely conscious of the rustling paper bag in Sean's hand. That could take some explanation. It might be easier just to slug him, but Mike wouldn't approve. Too inelegant, he'd say. Too crude.

Suddenly Laszlo fell silent, except for a thin low mutter that was probably his detailed opinion of the situation. Sean and I held our breaths. Laszlo's muttering grew louder, and there were footsteps approaching. Complications threatened to set in.

Laszlo climbed up two flights, to the landing half a flight below where we were huddled in the insufficient darkness. He stopped before a door in plain sight of us, stood fuming for a moment, then rapped abstract invectives on the door.

Sean and I were paralyzed. This was clearly a situation out of which no good could come. All Laszlo had to do was turn around and we'd be had. He was bound to wonder why we were lurking around his pad, and we could count on him to think the worst—especially since he'd be right.

He rapped again. No answer.

"Why me?" he wondered bitterly. "What have I done? Why do these things have to happen to me?"

I could've told him, but it didn't seem wise.

"It's a plot, that's what it is. They're out to get me, that damn Anderson and all his stinkin' crew. *I* know what's going on here. Oh yeah, *I* know where it's at, baby." Louder rapping. "I'll show them bastards." Further rapping.

I felt better already, but, "Hello there," said the wrist radio into one of Laszlo's silences: transistorized instant traitor. I squelched the gadget before it could say any more, but too late.

"Who's there?" Laszlo panicked in anger, revolving like a paranoid top. "Who said that?"

Sweating foolishly, I pretended to be invisible. Doubtless Sean played some such desperate game as well.

Laszlo stopped twirling, his silly-putty nose aimed straight at us. "All right," he snapped in a scared falsetto, "I see you. Come down here. Come on."

"Okay," whispered something in me that was half stubbornness and half humiliation, "I've been caught by Laszlo Scott, fair and square, but I'll be damned if I'll cooperate. If he wants me, let him come and get me." So I sat rock-still and didn't make a sound. Being pretty much stuck behind me, Sean had no choice but to do the same.

"Quit stalling," Laszlo said with less conviction than before. "Come on down here."

We didn't move. Presently Laszlo said something common-place and foul and stomped ungracefully away. We heard his cloddish feet descend two flights; we heard him rattling his door again; we heard him clomp the rest of the way downstairs to the ground floor, and we heard him slam the front door, hopefully behind him.

Still we did not move. Very gradually we realized that somehow Laszlo hadn't really seen us after all. This was very strange, for Sean was wearing a white shirt and the stairwell wasn't really all that dark.

But we didn't hang around to work it out. As soon as we understood that Laszlo'd actually split for someplace, we tiptoed cautiously but swiftly down the stairs. (I was getting sick of all this tiptoeing. My green suede boots weren't made for it, and my feet were starting to hurt.)

At the street door, Sean—whom Laszlo conveniently didn't know—poked his head outside to reconnoiter, keeping his left hand and Laszlo's verdant treasure safely out of sight.

"It's cool," he announced, and out we went, looking so exactly nonchalant and casual we were almost invisible to ourselves.

We got home five minutes after Mike, and Sean instantly abandoned himself to Sativa again while I tried to explain to the irate M. T. Bear why I hadn't responded to his last radio signal, why it took us so long to get home, and why we found nothing more significant than the bulging paper bag. Mike liked his plots to work the way he meant them to.

"Apparently," he said when he'd digested my report, "Laszlo missed his connection at Grand Central."

"He wasn't very happy," I agreed.

"So you'll have to start tailing him tomorrow."

"Oh." That again.

But the time had become five o'clock, and we felt justified in calling it a day. This left us gloriously free until the morning, because it was Monday night, the Village sabbath, and all the entertainment coffeehouses were closed, and nothing, praise God, was happening. We could all use a little nothing happening. So we settled down to sample Laszlo's grass.

An hour or something later we all nobly admitted that just this once we had to admire Laszlo's taste. We were all absurdly pacified.

"Man," I drawled for all of us, "I'm stoned. All I want to do now is move as little as possible. Wow."

"Oh yeah," Sativa languidly remembered, "I forgot."

"That's cool," Mike said. "What'd you forget?"

"She can't recall," Sean answered, but:

"Oh no," she corrected. "Somebody called. While you were away. I'll remember in a . . . oh yeah, Harriet called."

The rest of us groaned. We dearly loved Harriet, but only in conservative doses and never on the phone. She could burn up an hour saying good morning.

"What," I queried bravely, "did she want?"

"It's her anniversary. She and Gary the Frog have been living together for seventeen and a half weeks Tonight. Isn't that sweet?"

"Better him than me," said Mike. "Better *her* than me, too, come to think of it."

"Well, *I* think it's sweet. And they're having a party tonight to celebrate." "Forewarned," I uttered, "is forestalled."

"Right," Sativa gleamed. "And we're all going."

That produced the finest stunned silence our pad had heard since Mike's third-last mistress announced that she was pregnant. (It turned out that she wasn't pregnant at all, and that Mike didn't do it anyway, but for a while there our atmosphere was very oddly charged.)

I recovered first. "A," I insisted, "I do not go to parties. Ever."

"But . . ."

"B. If I *did* go to parties, I still wouldn't go to parties where Gary the Frog and Harriet were likely to appear."

"But, Chester . . ."

"C. I didn't accept the invitation, wouldn't've accepted the invitation, and didn't authorize you—sweet little songbird though you may be—to accept it for me."

"But I promised!"

"D. I've had a hard day and I want to rest."

"You and Michael are the guests of honor."

"E. What with one thing and another, I can barely move at best and have no eyes for that crosstown hike to Harriet's seventh-story loft."

"We can take a taxi."

"And F, I do not go to parties. Ever."

"You said that before."

"It's still true, and it goes for Mike and Sean, too. Right?"

"Right!"

"But I gave Harriet my word . . ."

"Sorry about that, love. You're free to join the gruesome orgy if you wish, but the rest of us aren't leaving this house, and that, my sweet, is where it's at."

It's kind of refreshing, now and then, to exercise authority in your own home.

9

From the very beginning, the party was as horrid as I knew beforehand it would have to be. The guests, more than a hundred, were just about evenly divided between people I didn't want to see and people I didn't want to see me. The loft was too hot, too narrow, too crowded, too dark, too smoky, and stank to high someplace of elderly cat box. There were, furthermore, two low-fi sets, one at each end of the loft, each blasting a different record I'd never have listened to otherwise, plus an atrocious and overstuffed rock-n-roll gang abusing megawatt amplifiers at about midway through the loft, plus everybody shouting to be heard above it all. Untold numbers of guests were extravagantly overdue for baths. Other hordes of guests were shakily holding foul-colored drinks ready to spill on the nearest available me. A few guests, most definitely the wrong ones, had already reached the disrobing stage, and some weren't limiting their efforts to themselves.

And just in case we were somehow able to withstand all this, the creature that opened the door and let us in was Laszlo Scott.

"Well, well, well," he ad-libbed, "Chester the Great and Michael the Cross-Eyed Bear. You might as well come in; it can't make any difference now."

We wedged our way in, escaping Laszlo in the crowd, and moved by a process much like osmosis through the steamy loft, hunting for Harriet so we could pay our counterfeit respects and split. Perfect and preferably strangers, most likely female, shrieked, "Darling!" brutally through my tender ears. Anybody stepped on my feet all the time. Something tried to remove my clothes, I hope. My well-known *joie de vivre* signaled TILT.

(Sativa—that unprintable lady Machiavelli—wasn't with us, nor was Sean. They stayed home to take advantage of our absence, and I still don't know how she engineered it. Under my breath, and sometimes above it, I invented gorgeous ancient curses for her head.)

We reached the back of the loft without encountering Harriet, which was odd, she being a lot too large to miss. We'd not found Gary either, but in that environment this single lonely blessing went unnoticed. We had, however, mysteriously acquired tall glasses full of a swampy bluish liquid that, remarkably, didn't taste at all bad, considering. We emptied our glasses, tossed them out the nearest window, and started back toward the front of the loft.

Just as we were sneaking past that felonious rock pile again, it blew an untuned fanfare that plastered us against the wall. When this was over, silence or studio deafness fell upon the gladly smitten horde.

"Cats and chicks," a regrettable voice boomed from the rock group's biggest amplifier. That explained where Gary the Frog was lurking. "Cats," it regibbered, "and chicks: welcome to our little party."

"Yes," came Harriet's equally amplified baritone, "we're *so* glad you could make it tonight," which might mean a number of things but probably didn't.

We were trapped, Mike and I, trapped and doomed. Even when no one was talking, the air pressure from that six-foot amplifier's humming kept us pinned against the wall. We couldn't get away, and the wall had splinters.

"Farewell, Michael," I sighed at the top of my lungs. "I will sleep now."

"Courage, *mon brave*," he bellowed nobly. "We are not yet dead."

"That's half the problem," I explained.

Then, "Cats and chicks," the talking frog attacked again, "on account of this is our anniversary, me and Harriet've fixed up something superspecial for all our buddies here tonight. Right, Harry?"

"Right, Gary!"

"You bet. An' here to tell you all about it is a local Village celebrity who needs no introduction, a cat who we all know an' dig the most, a great artiste that his accomplishments are all the talk of MacDougal Street and envirions, none other than your old buddy, Mis-ter Lasz-lo Scott!"

"Michael," I said in what currently passed for a whisper.

"Yes?"

"I think I'll start worrying now."

"I'll help you."

Amid sporadic cheers and weak applause, Laszlo climbed over the bass drum and grabbed the microphone.

"Friends!" he lied. "Nah, let me call you colleagues."

I was too weak to resist.

"Doubtless you have all heard about my Reality Pills, no doubt. Some of you have dropped 'em for yourself already, and even if you haven't, you seen what they can do, right?"

Once more, "Michael," I whispered, so to speak.

"Speak."

"I think it's too late to worry now."

"Check."

The only bright spot of the evening so far was that Laszlo kept making full stops for applause, but no one was applauding. Guessing this might be the only bright spot, I treasured it carefully.

"Now, everybody knows," Laszlo hinted, "that I'm the only connection for my famous Reality Pills. Nobody can't score 'em offa nobody else, you dig: just me, Laszlo Scott. An' everybody knows how I been a Good Guy an' just *give* 'em all away, mostly: just layin' my famous Reality Pills on everyone I see, right? 'Cause that's the kind of cat I am. I just can't help it. If ol' Laszlo's got it, baby, it's yours. Just ask me."

I was growing ill, for any one or more of a number of reasons, take your pick. Two from Column A and one from Column B, but no one was applauding. Pass the mop.

Laszlo fumbled on. "An' that's just what I'm gonna do for each and every one of you people here tonight. In fact, dig it, I already *done* it. There's been a great big dose of Laszlo Scott's famous Reality Pill in Liquid Form in everything you people drank tonight. So all you people just go have yourselves a ball, an' remember good ol' Laszlo Scott's the cat who turned you on.

"An' now I want to close up with a brand-new poem I have wrote for this occasion."

"Michael!" I was fighting like a netted panther, but Laszlo, the bastard, the inhuman friend et cetera, turned the volume up for his epic and I couldn't even move my arms.

Laszlo made a great show of searching his pockets for the manuscript (though a rumor, made up by myself, that he could neither read nor write was generally accepted). Finally he gave up.

"Shucks," he promised. "I must've left it home." Tantalizing pause. "But I think I can remember how it goes."

I doubted I'd be lucky enough to die.

Laszlo threw his cape back in a silent movie gesture that knocked Gary the Frog and the bass drum to the floor, struck a plaster of Paris pose, and began: "Love Song in a Summer Loft, by Laszlo Allen Scott the Fourth.

> "Your grandfather hates me be-cause I
> Am twict as good as any other guy.
> He don't like me. He don't even try,
> But someday your grandfather's gonna die, baby,
> An' this is what I'm gonna do to you—
> I'm gonna f.".. ZAP!!

All the lights went out. The amplifiers quit. Mike and I fell to the floor in bruised and splinter-ridden heaps. Laszlo became blessedly inaudible.

"There *is* a God!" I yelled.

"Where are the fuses?" some idiot asked.

"Don't tell him," ordered Mike.

Lots of people screamed, but after what we'd just been through, the peace, though merely relative, was wonderful.

"Let's get out of here," I suggested.

"Great. How?"

"Crawl."

"Which direction, pray?"

"Any direction. If we can't find the door, I'm willing to make do with the windows by now."

"Seven stories?"

"You'd rather stay here?"

"Lead on."

I did, keeping my right shoulder against the wall for a guide and crawling staunchly toward what I was almost certain was the door.

"Keep in touch," I whispered back to Mike.

"Roger."

"That word again."

"Right." He grabbed my left heel and held on.

"Toot! Toot!" I stated in my best steam locomotive accent. This was fun! In fact, the whole party had been fun, come to think of it, but this was clearly the best part. I felt great.

Part of me worried about that. Why should I feel so good? After ("Pardon me, ma'am") what I'd just been through, at the very least I ought to ache all over. ("Excuse me, sir or madam.") Instead I was feeling downright euphoric, which wasn't natural. Something ("Toot-toot, toot-too . . . Oops! Sorry 'bout that.") was wrong. ("Toot-toot.")

Then my prancing fingers found the doorjamb. Aha. Anderson was right again, as usual. When would these fools ever learn not to doubt me?

"This way," to Mike as I pulled myself erect. He joined me and we slipped quietly out of the loft and into the hall. It was much darker there, but the air was clearer and there was no crowd, so I could find my way around by ear nearly as well as I could've with my eyes if the lights had been on, but I stuck close to the wall to keep from worrying Michael.

We found the stairs with no trouble at all and started carefully down. I was feeling better by the second. To think, a few moments earlier I'd been worrying because I felt good. How absurd! Why should anyone worry about feeling good? What sort of old-maid Protestant thinking was that? Probably thought didn't deserve feel good, right? Bull. Felt great. Greater. Greatest. Yeah!

In fact, I felt so unprecedentedly good I could almost hear Handel's *Water Music* playing behind me, my favorite happy music;

Halfway down I said, "Are you okay, Mike?"

"Of course." Hmm. He sounded lots more vibrant and virile than usual. Echoes from the stairwell, doubtless. "Why shouldn't we be okay?"

"Groovy." *We?* Really? Poor old Michael. All that noise upstairs must've finlly unhinged him. I'd seen it coming years ago, but what can you do?

I could still hear the *Water Music*. It was an amazingly lifelike illusion: the sound seemed to reverberate through the all but deserted old building, and the interpretation, which was brilliant, was completely unknown to me. I realized I'd have to have something done about that tomorrow, but for now it was a gas.

"Chester?" My God! Michael sounded ten feet tall.

"Yeah?"

"Must they play so loudly? We can hardly hear ourself think."

"They?"

"That orchestra."

I stopped. Mike bumped into me. He wasn't ten feet tall.

"You," I said, "you can hear them, too?"

"I could hardly fail to. They're probably audible in Brooklyn. Do they have to play so loudly?"

"Hmm. I refuse to believe any of this."

"Believe what you like, but *please* ask them to cool it. They're hurting our head."

And then the lights came on.

Mike says it was five minutes before I could move again, but he's probably tinting the facts a bit. I distinctly remember that the gaudily liveried baroque orchestra that filled the stairs behind us played a little less than half a minuet before I screamed.

The music stopped. "Your pleasure, sire?" said the fiddler in the fore, bowing deeply, fiddle straight out at a forty-five-degree angle behind him and bow held horizontally across his chest in what was clearly a salute, though I'd never seen it done before.

"What," maintaining my cool, "is all of this in aid of?"

"Doctor Handel's *Water Music,* sire. I was given to understand that you were fond . . ."

"No. I mean *you.* The orchestra."

"Ah. Your privy band, sire. Did you not, upon many a time yet fresh in memory, express a fond desire that such as we might . . ."

"Cancel."

"Sire?"

"Tilt."

"Your pardon, sire."

"Forget it. Please play on, maestro, *ma un poco mezzo forte,* if you please."

"Your most humble servant, sire." He bowed again, then nodded his white-wigged head, and the minuet I'd screamed to pieces began anew, but softer now. We all continued down the stairs.

I was quiet for another flight—not thinking, just reacting—and then said, "Yes. It's obvious enough, once the shock wears off, and even rather flattering, in a mildly introspective way. But, Michael, why have you taken to calling yourself *we?"*

"No room," Michael gestured crossly. "None at all. Your walking jukebox takes up more room than a teenyboppers' fan club on parade. Humph. Inconsiderate, we calls it, but we'll wait."

"Oh. You've become a convention?"

"No, more like an invocation."

"Invocation?"

"Possibly."

We walked the final flight in silence, not counting my personal band. That, by the way, seemed to leave a little something to be desired. Every now and then a false note rang out through the otherwise exceptional ensemble. Not a wrong note, mind you, just a slightly out of tune one. Bassoon, from the sound of it. This bugged me mainly because, the orchestra being merely an external figment of my own imagination, the false notes were my fault The implication was humiliating.

Meanwhile I took time out to admire how well I was taking it all. Very calm. Very cool. Very natural.

"Wow!" Mike said as we approached the door. "That's a relief."

"Oh? Are you alone now?"

"More or less. Wow. Now I know how a tenement building feels."

A crowd of not-much-stranger-looking-than-usual people across the street beckoned, whistled, and waved to Mike. A rowdy bunch, not really our kind of people, but he sauntered over to see what they wanted.

I was more interested in the orchestra. Oh, it was a doozy! Authentic livery of purple watered silk and plum plush with lots of lace; authentic instruments like serpents, recorders, krumhorns, sackbutts, oboi d'amore, cornets, brasses without valves and woodwinds without keys, two almost Turkish kettledrums carried by two husky 'prentices each, all absolutely authentic and brand-new and being played by virtuosi—with the exception of that bassoon; authentic interpretations such as no man had heard since the early eighteenth century; authentic musicians, running roughly six inches shorter than modern average and ruddier complexioned than we're used to: it was perfect—except for that bassoon.

While the leader arranged the orchestra in street formation—four abreast and God help anyone else using the same sidewalk—I searched for that bassoon. There were fourteen bassoons, but I found the culprit at first glance by instinct. Except for being shorter, he was Andrew Blake's double, stiff red beard and all. My imagination has a better sense of humor than I do and I'm jealous.

"My good man," I addressed him, falling into character, "you seem to be a little out of tune."

"Aye, sire," tugging his rusty forelock, "so I seem," and he sounded exactly like Andy's famous Irish impersonation, the one he uses to con free drinks on St. Patrick's Day.

"I trust you will correct the defect."

"An it please you, sire," the forelock bit again, "I'm not allowed."

"No?"

"'Throw 'im a clinker now and again for authenticity,' they tells me, beggin' your pardon, sire."

"Oh." How was I supposed to handle this? I decided to try ignoring it. But, "Pardon me, do you have any relatives named Blake?"

"Relatives?" He laughed. "God love ye, sire, you know the likes o' me ain't got no relatives. We're all too poor, beggin' your pardon. You want relatives, sire, you go talk to the leader there. 'E's got himself a Nephew, he does, playin' second fiddle. Or them four drum boys, now. They're all each other's Brothers, so they say. But I ain't got no relatives, sire. Not me."

"This is turning into one hell of a night." Michael was back, with company: those oddly dressed rowdies from across the street. I wasn't at all sure about those people. They looked like the kind of Saturday types I generally avoid, but Mike was my best friend so I held my peace.

"What are we going to do with all this?" I wondered, waving florid circles in the air.

"Who am I to question the dictates of the gods? Onward to The Garden of Eden. Why not?"

Why indeed. "That's boss."

It took awhile to start moving. The orchestra was already in order, but Mike's associates couldn't agree on who ought to walk where. They exhausted the possibilities of discussion and negotiation in less than five minutes and asked Mike's permission to retire to the nearest alley for a conference. I found myself wondering about Mike.

The rowdies' conference took some fifteen minutes. Then they returned, none the visible worse for wear, and took up stations flanking the orchestra, four on each side. They stood there glowering and making highly improper and hostile gestures at each other while Mike and I, both a bit puzzled, walked to the head of the column.

"At your pleasure, sire," the leader bowed.

"You may begin," I nodded.

And we did.

There are problems associated with marching an orchestra in full throat through lower Manhattan after midnight that the average man can't possibly imagine, and I envy him. The police were no problem—not after the leader produced, on irate demand, an appallingly official city permit to hold a parade through those streets at that hour playing music—but the people who lived in the buildings we passed were difficult to cope with. They threw some of the strangest things, and I couldn't see just how they *were* being coped with. I was starting to develop some faith in the Reality Pill, though. It seemed to give good service.

Mike's acquaintances continued to worry me. "Michael," I inquired as we columned right onto Broadway, "your—friends—look very interesting."

"Yes." he beamed. "Aren't they great? I'm really very proud of them."

"I can see where you might be. Ah, what are they?"

"Gods, of course. A whole pantheon. It's a *little* pantheon, I'll grant you, but it has a certain fey charm of its own."

"Gods, eh?" They were still tossing graphic threats at each other and their fey charm was moderately difficult to see. Acquired taste, perhaps. "Gods of what?"

"Oh, this and that. You know. I'll introduce you." He turned and yelled, "Hey, Mick, front and center!" then turned back and said, "You'll like Mick. He's quite well done."

Mick, it seemed, was the god of teenyboppers, and quite well done. A little under seven feet tall and glowing, with shoulder-length gold hair, deep blue vacant eyes, and a pretty face that managed to look healthy, sensitive, pouting, and cheerful all at once, he was slimly dressed in white-net T-shirts and tights over gold and brown paisley briefs, and shod in supple fawn suede boots that tapered three inches higher aft than fore. He exuded, furthermore, an almost irresistible electric adolescent sexuality. Once more I wondered about Michael.

In the prettiest boy-man voice I'd ever heard, Mick spoke a few choice words so flawlessly fatuous I forgot them before he'd finished speaking, then returned to his place beside the orchestra and set to snarling at his collegues once again.

"That's unfair criticism, Mike," I pointed out. "Most rock and roll musicians are . . ."

"Cool it. I'm not criticizing them."

He wasn't, I realized, not at all, and God help MacDougal Street.

Then we had the incident of the parade permit, after which I met Tok, the god of pot, just as tall as everyone but skinnier than most, no particular age, quaintly dressed in nickel bags and cigarette papers, with a hempen wreath in his shaggy hair (the very same color as yours) and reeking of patchouli so strong I could almost walk on it: another threat to MacDougal Street's stability.

We took a left from Broadway onto Bleecker. By then we'd started gathering satellites—a minor crowd of young girls trying to touch Mick—and my orchestra was playing something that sounded suspiciously like "Hard Day's Night," with more false notes than usual from the unrelated bassoon. A six-foot-tall blue lobster—another little something of Mike's, I gathered slightingly—watched us make the turn.

That reminded me. "Shouldn't we be taking notes?"

"Do you think we can forget?"

"Anything's possible."

"You've got a point there."

The Village proper, if there is such a thing, was still some four blocks ahead, a sudden bright island in Manhattan's after-midnight dimness. Already we could see that even though the entertainment houses were closed, Bleecker Street was as crowded as usual, hopefully with nobody we knew. Michael, therefore, stepped up the tempo of introductions, calling the rest of his pantheon front and center double time and dismissing them before they had a chance even to say hello, which was all to the good. They were:

* Fellatia, the goddess of something she and Mike coyly refused to name. She was a bulbous chick of moderate ugliness, aged anywhere between eighteen and thirty, and dressed all in pretty-colored Kleenex. Despite Mike's brusque dismissal, she tried to assault me for nameless reasons of her own, but we beat her off. I began to think MacDougal Street might not survive the evening.

* Phlipout and Phlippina, twin deities of disorder, were muscular male and female teenyboppers—very healthy and confused—in whose presence, Mike claimed, all things tended to dissolve into the most spectacular chaos imaginable. The

blithe madness lurking in their eyes made this seem all too likely, and I noticed that their place in the marching order was right beside my friend the out-of-tune bassoonist.

* Moe, the god of tourists, was forty-five, fat, crew-cut, drunk, bellicose, and gifted, so Mike said, with superhuman powers of abuse.

* Buldge, the goddess of minor disasters, was a kind of accidental fertility figure, very pregnant, incredibly naked, alarmingly busty and genital, with unkempt brownish hair hanging down to where her waist used to be, whose merest glance could delay a chick's period two weeks.

* Chuck, the god of miscellany, was a super-Mike of sorts, taller and leaner but with the same look of bland malevolence and random fanaticism that so endeared Mike to everyone who could put up with him. I suspected Chuck was basically road manager for the rest of Mike's crew.

"And this," Mike boasted less than half a block from West Broadway and the frontier of the Village, "is Zap, titular deity of changes, in whose presence nothing is ever the same." Zap was pretty formless and it hurt my eyes to look at him.

"Are you sure you're doing the right thing?" I worried. Michael only smiled.

Then we entered the Village. Suddenly Mike blew three loud blasts on a police whistle. The orchestra—*my* orchestra, mind you! —struck up a march:

heavy on the piccolos and very loud. Michael's gods and goddesses scattered to the five winds, and the action instantly became too confused to follow.

Mick ran up Bleecker Street, and every teen-aged girl he passed screamed and followed him. He zigzagged back and forth across the street, ignoring traffic, and the girls, screaming, followed him, making traffic impossible. Weeping girls performed incomplete flying tackles at his legs as he passed. Overwrought female tides brutally washed over anything, especially people, that stood between themselves and Mick. The clamor of auto horns, shrill screams, and breaking glass threatened to drown out my orchestra, and I rather wished it would.

Mick was built for running and stayed easily ahead of his following. Every now and then he paused to kiss some unsuspecting chick, who promptly fainted. The sidewalks on both sides of the street were littered with broken glass, abandoned escorts, and the limp bodies of kiss victims.

Close behind Mike came Fellatia, vigorously propositioning the abandoned escorts, who fled in yelping droves before her.

Phlipout, Phlippina, and Toke ambled into every coffeehouse, restaurant, street food dive and bar on the street, all the patrons of which instantly ran outside in noisy panic, there to encounter Moe, who yelled, "All you people'sh jush a bunch a' flippin' faggots! C'mon, lesh fight!" and struck out indiscriminately at everyone in reach.

Meanwhile Buldge, smiling vacantly, strolled up to every female, conscious or not, who remained after Mick's army had passed, saying, "Oooo, are *you* gonna have a little baby, too? I bet you *are*," causing every girl who hadn't fainted yet to faint.

Behind Buldge came Zap, now nine feet tall and formless, shooting purple rays from his (perhaps) fingertips at every overt hippy in sight. "Oh WoW!" or the equivalent the smitten hippies yelled. "Oh WoW!" and took off like stampeding hippies, running in tight circles and pleading, "Get out of my head! Oh WoW!"

Through this confusion, Chuck, the super-Mike, strode calmly, giving orders ("Come back, Buldgie love, you missed this one!") and tending to such minor details as cops, mounted cops, and cops in prowl cars. Cops he passed developed uncontrollable urges to disrobe, horses tried to climb light poles, and prowl cars suddenly issued vast clouds of black, evil-smelling smoke.

The carnage swept forward faster than we could walk, and soon turned north at MacDougal Street and passed out of sight, though not out of earshot (whatever that might be). Bleecker Street looked like something out of World War II: broken windows, overturned cars, and fallen bodies as far as we could see. Only Mike, the orchestra, and I were still erect and functioning. The orchestra played the dead march from *Saul* and we picked our way delicately through the rubble.

Despite the devastation all around me—my own, my native land, in ruins—I still felt great. The Reality Pill, I thought, had much to recommend it, if you didn't mind a little chaos on the side. But, "Is this what you really wanted?" I asked Mike.

"Well," he said, looking slowly around him, "I am a little disappointed."

"Oh?"

"I was expecting something a little more colorful," he sighed.

"Oh."

The sound of screams *et cetera* grew faint as Mick and Company tore up MacDougal toward West Eighth, where they were sure to do such things as I shuddered to imagine. In the distance an approaching chorus of sirens could be heard. A few photographers had already appeared—that was a big summer for photographers—and flashbulbs popped around us like exclamation points.

MacDougal Street, when we reached it, proved to be utterly impassable. Cars and trucks, not all overturned, sprawled every which way like mechanized spaghetti, blocking street and sidewalks equally. Dazed survivors of all types and genders wandered aimlessly through the ruins, mouthing strange, poetic expressions of dismay. Every window above street level was crowded with frightened people gibbering in nameless tongues. An acrid blue haze hung over everything, pierced by sporadic flashbulbs. A very blonde girl, naked except for an arcane blue and red tattoo above her navel, sat cross-legged atop an overturned chrome trailer truck playing aimless squiggles on what seemed to be a soprano recorder.

"Busy," I observed.

"Indeed," said Mike.

"Detour?"

"Detour."

So Mike and orchestra and I went on to Sixth Avenue, which was still untouched by the gods.

Rescue vehicles started arriving as we walked up the avenue— dozens of police cars, lots of ambulances, three or four full fire companies, and some odd National Guard equipment left over from Saturday.

"That's what I call prompt action," I said.

"Right. Sort of gives you confidence, doesn't it?" Mike answered.

Despite the orchestra—which I, for one, would've noticed right away—we attracted no attention as we made our melodious way toward Third Street. This was mainly because the rescue vehicles, arriving from every possible direction, created an instant chaos of their own, a modern consort of horns, sirens, screeching brakes, tearing metal, and obscure, thickly accented obscenities.

"I don't know," I worried. "It doesn't give me all that much confidence, really. I mean," waving expansively, "look. I've seen better organized games of pick-up-sticks."

"Nobody's perfect," Mike forgave them.

The orchestra played Telemann. That bassoonist played Vivaldi.

The Garden of Eden was packed with jabbering refugees, but its windows were intact.

"Jesus Christ!" Joe yelled from behind the cash register as we entered. "Wha's happenin'!?"

We shrugged eloquently and groped our way to the table. Only strangers were there, none of our people. We unseated two of them, ordered coffee, and relaxed.

"Are you satisfied?" I asked.

Mike looked doubtful. "I'm not sure," he said. "There's got to be more to it than this."

"Excuse me," said another tall blue lobster, making its way to the john.

"One of yours?" I wondered. "I thought it was one of yours."

"I don't *like* blue lobsters."

"Oh. I guess the party's broken up."

That gave us something to think about, so we did. We weren't the only people roaming through the city high on Laszlo Scott's famous Reality Pills in liquid form. Not a bit of it. And what were those other few hundred maniacs doing? Our minds mutually boggled.

There was a disturbance at the door, but we carefully ignored it. We'd had enough disturbance for a while. The disturbance got louder, harder to ignore, but still we managed. Then a new note was added to the disturbance, a flat note, obviously uttered by a skitterish bassoon. "Uh-oh," I commented.

"Hey, Andy!" Joe barged through the crowd toward us. "There's these People outside that they say they're like friends of yours, and . . ."

Something tripped him and he fell. The orchestra marched sedately over him, playing somebody's Trumpet Tune full blast. The Garden of Eden became unwholesomely crowded.

The orchestra grouped itself in a cramped semicircle around my chair and finished the trumpet tune with flourishes. "We missed you," the leader said. Then the orchestra plunged into Bach's first *Brandenburg Concerto.*

Joe, disheveled and flamboyantly annoyed, shoved past the trumpets, yelling, "Get these people outta here!"

"Something wrong?" in Michael's blandest tones.

"I ain't got no license for no band," Joe yelled. He was verging on hysteria. "An' I can't have all them people in here. It's illegal." His swarthy face was turning an unappealing purple. "An' they all gotta order. Jesus Christ!" He turned and drove back through the orchestra, rending his garments melodramatically as he drove.

"Excitable type, that Joseph," I murmured.

"Lousy insurance risk," said Mike. Then Joe screamed magnificently treble in the near distance.

"Yoo-hoo!" somebody yelled. "Michael!"

"Oh?" we said.

"Michael!" someone yelled again. We could feel lines of panic form in the mob like lines of force around a magnet, and when Michael's gods tore through my orchestra (putting that bassoonist out of business for a while), we weren't at all surprised.

"Hey, boss," Chuck said, "we finished Eighth Street."

"I don't doubt it."

"Eek," said a number of people tritely as Mick deftly dealt with them.

"What next?" asked Chuck.

"Hey! Help!" from Joe, who was completely surrounded by Fellatia.

"Zap!" from Zap.

"WoW," from everybody else. All males present clutched their groins convulsively. Mike and I seemed to be immune.

"Yoo-hoo!" That was phlipout and his sister. Behind them untold crockery broke noisily.

"Have you tried Washington Square?" Mike was being businesslike.

"Got it on the way back."

The confusion was spreading to the orchestra. This dragged me. I like the first Brandenburg.

"Yow Yow Yow Yow YOW!" Joe yelped all the way back to the cash register.

Mick was surrounded by a squirming pile of shameless female teenyboppers, plus a few shameless males I'd never suspected before. There seemed to be enough of Mick to go around.

"What about Sheridan Square?" Mike asked.

"Where's that?"

"West of here,"

The noise was impressive and growing. It was almost too loud to hear, and the walls were shaking like drumheads. All the gods were working overtime, the orchestra was doing its high baroque best, and Mike and Chuck were planning strategy. No good, I decided, could possibly come of this.

I was right.

"All right, all right," said a bullish voice. "Move along." The law had arrived, lots of it. At least a dozen irate fuzz in riot helmets beat a path through the melee, past our table, to the rear of the room. Hippies and other innocents, forgetting gods and chaos, ran shrieking to the front and out, overpanicked by the presence of police. I was getting sick of all that noise.

"Shall I?" Chuck suggested.

"Forget it," Mike explained.

"This is all your fault," I told Mike.

"Eh." He shrugged.

"All right, all right," said the cops. They had portable loudspeakers. "Everybody out. Come on, now. Move."

Everybody turned out by then to be the gods, the orchestra, Mike and, irritated, I; not quite seventy-five people, so to speak. We moved.

Outside we were herded into green buses with barred windows.

"Are we under arrest?" Mike blandly asked a cop.

"Move on there," he explained. We moved.

Thanks to the pill, I was simultaneously euphoric and enraged. Arrested, by God! And it was all Michael's fault.

Despite Mike's efforts to engage me in light banter, I preserved a fairly stony silence all the way to the Charles Street precinct house. There we were herded out of the buses and into the station like so many oddly dressed cattle, the orchestra going fairly quietly, the gods giving everyone their usual hard time, Mike and I pretending to be meek and somewhat invisible. Inside, the orchestra began the Bach again, the gods flew madly about spreading disorder, and we took up inconspicuous positions at the rear of it all.

We were in a large, high-ceilinged, dingy room, poorly lighted, with fly- and spit-specked dirty marble floor and grimy plaster walls, drab green, that echoed without mercy. At the far end of the room, at the foot of a rusty flight of wrought-iron stairs, half a dozen plainclothesmen tried to look unalarmed, with indifferent success.

A uniformed elderly cop with lots of gold braid, sitting at a brightly lighted, battered oak desk at the east side of the room, looked threatened. Fellatia was crawling gracelessly over the desk toward him, despite the efforts of two burly patrolmen to restrain her.

"What's goin' on here?" the man at the desk wanted to know.

"It's like this, Sarge," said a cop, launching into a highly colored report of the events at the Garden of Eden. Words like *riot, indecent exposure, disorderly conduct, vagrancy, resisting arrest, attempted bribery, felonious assault,* and *disturbing the peace* ran through his monologue like a wearisome refrain.

Michael looked elaborately unconcerned. I worried.

"Oh yeah?" the sergeant said when the cop had finished his gory report.

"Yeah," the cop insisted.

"Lemme go, you great big handsome brutes," Fellatia told the two cops who were holding her.

"I better call Centre Steet," the sergeant said. He did so.

Meanwhile, Mick, Toke, Chuck, and the twins were sneaking up the stairs, apparently unnoticed by the huddled plainclothesmen.

"Chuck's clever," Mike said admiringly.

"Hmph," I said.

The sergeant hung up. "They're sending over a Special Investigator," he said, visibly impressed. "Now," collecting himself, "who's in charge here?"

"I am," said the leader of my orchestra. I softly groaned.

"Oh, *you* are, eh?" the sergeant sneered. He opened a large notebook and uncapped a fountain pen. "An' what's *your* name, buddy?"

"Begging your pardon, sir," the leader said in calm, reasonable tones, "but, a name being clearly unessential to my function, I wasn't given one."

"No name?" The sergeant was upset. "What're you tryin' ta pull?"

"Pull? Nothing, sir. I don't pull anything at all. I merely play the violin. "The sackbutt players, now . . .""

"Ahr, a wise guy, huh?'

Just then there was a loud disturbance upstairs. Mike chuckled. We heard loud, metallic hangings, drunken yowls, and the sound of many heavy feet. Then an extra motley crowd poured, shuffled, stumbled, and staggered down the wrought-iron stairs, ridden herd upon by Mick, Chuck, Toke, and the twins, who were followed in turn by a brace of cops yelling, "Come back here," and, "You can't get away with this."

The gods had been freeing prisoners.

"What the hell is all *this!*" The sergeant was becoming hoarse.

Half the prisoners were women of one sort or another. As soon as they reached the main floor, they forgot about escape and started reacting to Mick. Mick encouraged them. While the sergeant stared in speechless horror, a medium-sized orgy took shape in front of his desk.

"Whoopee!" yelped Fellatia. She broke free of her guards and started toward the sergeant, clearly bent on some unwholesome and unnatural variety of rape.

The sergeant yelled and stumbled backward. Fellatia charged. He picked up a chair and held her at bay, almost, but she had longer arms than he'd counted on.

Several cops tried to rescue the sergeant, only to be trapped in the growing orgy around Mick.

Mike fell laughing to the floor. I tried to kick him and missed. Somebody started shooting in the air, and chips of plaster from the ceiling floated down like pregnant snowflakes.

Every alarm in the building went off at once. A cop, minus trousers, ran screaming up the stairs, pursued by several naked lady drunks.

The uproar was decidedly oppressive.

"If there's anything I dislike," I yelled at Michael, "it's . . ." I couldn't think of a word for it, so I made a wide gesture intended to take in the whole scene. Unfortunately, the gesture caught an approaching plain-clothesman right in the Adam's apple, and he fell to the floor, not quite saying anything.

Mike got to his feet, saying, "Bad company down there," and giggling disgracefully.

"Hurrah!" Fellatia bellowed in a window-breaking tone. Several windows promptly broke.

"Our Father," the sergeant yelled, "who art in Halp!"

Then, "What's going on here?" said a voice so deep and authoritative that everyone stopped whatever he or she or it was doing and fell silent for a minute.

A tall, grizzled man in conservative red business clothes, full of dignity and power and the majesty of the law, strode through the middle of Mick's temporarily frozen orgy. He stopped in front of the desk and looked around disgustedly.

"You," he told the sergeant firmly. "Get dressed."

"I can't!" the sergeant wailed. "This broad, she . . ."

"Quiet. I'm Special Investigator Blake." I wondered about that.

Fellatia subtly advanced on him.

"Back," he ordered. She moved back. I was impressed.

Then, "You," clearly meaning us. "I want to talk to you." He looked around at the still frozen orgy with incredible disdain. "Come with me." He started toward the door, and we followed. "No use trying to talk in this madhouse."

We reached the door together and passed out into the cool, still darkness. "Come with me," he said again, heading toward Sheridan Square. We went.

We hadn't gone half a block when the noise broke out anew in the precinct house behind us. The special investigator sniffed disapprovingly. We said nothing. The noise was louder than before.

We turned a corner and passed out of sight of the station, but the noise remained impressive.

"Where are you taking us, sir?" asked Michael with unusual respect.

The special investigator stopped, regarding us both with grim intensity. Then he grinned, tipped his hat, and vanished.

"Wow," I said after a while. "How did you do that?"

"Me? I thought you did it."

The noise followed us halfway home.

10

So there I was at half-past ten on Tuesday morning, feeling a good bit less than myself and not at all happy about it, sitting in that same old two-bit candy store across the street from Laszlo's pad, waiting for the Bard of MacDougal Street to appear. That same suspicious counterman was being suspicious again, and surly to boot. The coffee tasted foul. The street looked foul. The thought of having to follow Laszlo, that notorious author of cacography, was insufferably foul, and I could think without straining of forty-seven places I'd rather be, none of which I even liked.

The counterman and an absurdly ancient crone in clothes her mother must've given her were conducting in some nameless tongue an acrimonious debate of which I was probably the subject.

Once again I tried to contact Michael on the wrist radio. No soap. I was not pleased.

All through breakfast I'd tried, with my best talmudic logic, to prove that Laszlo had obviously scored on Monday and that it was therefore foolish to follow him today. But Mike is always unreasonable in the morning, and there I was.

There I was alone, furthermore. Sean, who was supposed to be helping me, was at the doctor's instead, recovering from some excess of Sativa's. Great. And I couldn't raise Mike on the radio.

I was inconspicuously dressed, as is my wont; this time in early-eighteenth-century French costume: swallowtail red satin coat with gold brocade, white on white linen shirt with lace front and cuffs, knee-length gold satin breeches, anachronistic black patent leather high boots with silver buckles and high heels—a fairly popular outfit that summer, but, I was learning, much too hot for the day and the job before me. Thanks to my early-morning inner smog, I was also carrying my trusty briefcase, empty.

And then it was eleven, and there were four count 'em four old crones huddled with the counterman in highly foreign languages. Now and then one of them would point a crooked finger at me. I was becoming somewhat uncomfortable.

It kept getting later—eleven ten, eleven thirty, you know how it does. No Laszlo. No Michael on the radio. The coffee got no better. The old crones multiplied. I spilled coffee on my shirt front. It was being a middling bad day.

"Hey, you," the counterman said after a while. "Whaddaya doon here, hey, whaddaya doon? Gedoudda here, ya flippin' beatnik freak. Whassa mattah, ya Crazy'r sumpin'? Gedoudda here. I youghtta calla cop ya flippin' freak."

I decided to leave. The coffee was pretty bad, anyhow.

The counterman followed me to the door, saying impolite things. The assembled crones egged him on in Etruscan or whatever it was they spoke, if that's what they did. One of them aimed arcane gestures at me.

Still no Laszlo. Still no Mike. I pretended to be interested in a hardware window for a while, until the proprietor came out and offered to help me. Then I feigned interest in a window full of dusty lingerie.

I was being fascinated by an altogether empty store window when Laszlo finally appeared, somewhere on the other side of noon. By then I was so far gone that I'd've missed him altogether, but he passed right by me and his aroma—a complex mixture of funk and other essences distinctively his own—jarred me into moderate awareness. I let him get a half block lead, as Mike'd suggested, and then doggedly set out after him.

Aesthetic considerations aside, Laszlo wasn't hard to follow. He was wearing a battery-powered electric green tuxedo, some four years out of style, that would've stood out like an electric green tuxedo in a London fog at midnight, and he walked so slowly that my only problem (aesthetic considerations aside) was to keep far enough behind him.

"The lame duck has flown the coop," I hopefully told the radio, using the code Mike and I'd agreed upon at breakfast. "I am following. Do you read me?" No response. Perhaps, I wished, my radio just wasn't receiving.

Laszlo ranged the East Side like a slug in a rose garden, making numerous stops at this, that, and the other disreputable dive, but no stops long enough for me to grab some lunch or get rid of the coffee I'd taken on whilst waiting for him. You can always count on Laszlo, yes indeed.

I kept my mute wrist radio fully informed of Laszlo's movements, on the off chance that Michael could hear me, but the longer we walked the less hopeful I was. Laszlo was clearly embarked on an endless chain of trivial errands, and I was doomed for my psychedelic sins to follow him forever. The temperature, furthermore, chose to linger in the nineties, and the smog became alarming, and I'd left my smog mask home.

We roamed through the East Side, always tending down-town, never stopping long enough for me to satisfy any of my needs, until just past five. We were on Canal Street then, Laszlo on the south side, I on the north. He stopped in front of a grotesquely ruinous loft building, one of those hundred-year-old, seven-story horrors, blackened brick and rusty fire escape, that leaned a nervous five degrees foward over the street. I hid myself in a urine-scented doorway and watched.

All at once Laszlo was being furtive. He looked suspiciously in all directions, peering myopically into infinity. He checked a watch I'd not have guessed he owned. He looked around again, then ducked into the building.

"April Fool," I told the radio. "April . . . no, I mean Mayday. This is It." I ran recklessly across the street, buffeted by the backwash from a million turbo-trucks. "Mayday," I repeated. "Two three nine Canal Street. Mayday." Then I was at the door and didn't dare say anything more.

I pulled the door open with an unfortunate shriek of unwilling old metal, at which I cursed ingeniously. I stepped into the hall and stood there silently, listening. Somebody, hopefully Laszlo, was several flights above and climbing, oblivious to the music of the door.

"I'm going in," I whispered to the radio and started up the stairs. They were marble stairs, blackened with time and deeply rutted, and next to impossible to climb silently in the boots I was wearing, but I managed, more or less.

The stairwell and halls were unlighted, darker than Laszlo's heart, and malodorous and dank. I imagined Laszlo and a horde of Communist thugs waiting for me on every landing. My nerves went through a whole year's wear and tear in less than seven minutes. I couldn't imagine this job's being worth what it was costing, but this was no time to be arguing about that.

I skulked up four dim flights—each step threatening to squeal—until I saw light of a sort oozing out an open door. I paused on the stairs.

Then, "We got it made, Chief," I heard Laszlo whine.

Contact. Now I had two choices open to me, according to the one-sided discussion Mike and I had had at breakfast. I could either cut out homeward, calling for help, or I could stick around and gather data. Without exactly saying so, Mike'd made it more than clear which choice he preferred.

I disagreed, but, "What the hell?" I admitted, "I'm already here." So I tiptoed the rest of the way up to the fourth floor, found the landing and hall to be conveniently full of packing cases, picked a good-sized case to hide behind, and hid.

There were two voices: Laszlo's overly familiar mush and an odd, somehow pedantic voice, low baritone, that spoke in a strange accent involving clicks on every consonant that allowed them, like a professor of philosophy accompanying himself on castanets.

"Most good, youthful Laszlo," said that voice. "It performs to satisfaction then, our little chemical?"

"Dig it," Laszlo pushed.

"This indicates accord?"

"Groovy."

"Groovy? Yes. It is so quaint, your language. here, so poetical, with such a richness of analogy. Yes, groovy."

"Dig it, man," Laszlo pressed on regardless. "Them pills are where it's at, baby. I mean, like, I could sell 'em for . . ."

"Now," interrupting, "we commence to—what is it, your clever word? Yes, escalate. Now we escalate to phase two. You agree?"

"Phase two?"

"Of course."

I couldn't place the other voice's accent. (I couldn't place Laszlo's, either, but that was mainly because he'd made it up himself.) It didn't seem particularly Russian, but who knows? Commies weren't necessarily Russian, in those days. There was still China, for instance. "Red China," we called it. But the accent didn't seem particularly Chinese, either. Oh well.

"No more small tests, youthful Laszlo, no. No further pills."

"Hey!"

"Now must we begin to operate upon a grander scale. Mass testing now is called for. Phase two. Then comes phase three and finishes. Soon now, youthful Laszlo, very soon, and you shall come into your own, as we agreed."

"No more pills?" Laszlo sounded gratifyingly pained. "Hey, baby, wait up. We gotta try it out some more, you dig?" He was nearly articulate in his despair. "I mean, like, dig it: we ain't tried it out, you know, on teachers an' like that, you dig? I mean . . ."

"Maintain a lowered temperature, youthful Laszlo. The pills are grown unnecessary now. Obsolete? Yes, obsolete. Now we must all think of larger things, and soon . . ."

Laszlo groveled fluently, never quite saying what he had in mind. I knew what he was after, of course. No more pills meant no more Laszlo Scott monopoly. But the strange accent kept explaining dispassionately that the pills were no longer necessary. I imagined Laszlo could've had as many pills as he wanted for the asking, but I couldn't imagine him doing anything so honest and overt as asking for them. Neither, it seemed, could he.

For once, though, I was on Laszlo's side. Now that I'd had some experience with the pills myself, the thought of phase two—whatever it might be—was frightening.

The discussion grew heated, at least on Laszlo's side. The air grew thick with phrases like *you dig?, like man,* and *dig it.* I decided, hardly noticing how brave of me it was, to sneak up to that door under cover of Laszlo's broken rhetoric and try for a peek inside. First, though, I whispered my plans into the radio. "Keep in touch," Mike'd told me.

"But you must comprehend, youthful Laszlo, that the pills are inefficient on such a scale," the voice was saying as I silently removed my boots—an engineering feat of which I was briefly proud. "Tomorrow night this city, then this world," the voice continued. This sounded ominous, and Laszlo sounded unimpressed.

More stealthily than the cats of Queen Berúthiel I made my way to the door and peered in ever so cautiously. I was lucky: they had their backs to me, and I got a good, long look.

My mind very carefully boggled.

"Well," I told myself, sneaking back to my packing case, "so much for Mike and his Communist plot."

The other voice belonged to a six-foot-tall, deep blue lobster. This was getting more interesting than I really liked.

Half an hour later, nothing worth mentioning had changed. Laszlo and his lobster-friend were still inside, I was still behind my packing case in the dark hall, all that coffee I'd absorbed while waiting for Laszlo was still where it had been for altogether too long now, my lunch (I kept thinking of lobster thermidor) was still in the indeterminate future, Mike was wherever the hell Mike was, alas, and things showed little sign of getting better.

I'd spent the half hour whispering to my left wrist and trying to get my boots back on, with little luck in either project. My feet seemed to have swollen.

Some days it's hard to maintain one's native dignity. If I could've gotten my boots on I'd've split, having lost my taste for heroism, but I couldn't bring myself to walk home in my stocking feet. "Anything," says an old Anderson proverb, "is better than embarrassment."

What I'd been saying to the radio all this time, disregarding random words on which the UNCC would frown loudly if I was being (hopefully) monitored, was mostly along the lines of, "Help! Get me out of here! Call out the Marines! Like, help!" plus everything the lobster was telling Laszlo.

Laszlo being Laszlo, this was plenty. The lobster, with amazing patience for a lobster, explained everything at least five times before I stopped counting, everything in this case being an elaborate extraterrestrial plot to conquer the Earth.

Honestly. It offended my sense of propriety something fierce, this hackneyed invasion-from-outer-space routine, but the lobster sounded quite sincere, and who was I to doubt the word of a six-foot-tall blue lobster?

Who indeed?

So all this while I crouched behind the packing case, elaborately not sneezing, ignoring even more pressing other needs, becoming acutely uncomfortable and frustrated, listening to an absurd blue crawdad telling Loathsome Laszlo how the Reality Pill was going to conquer Terra without endangering precious lobsters or involving them in anything so crude as physical violence.

Lobster: "We, of course, cannot inflict pain or," rattling shudder, "death upon another rational being, dissimilarly to you so vicious aborigines that do such things for—what is your word?—kicks. Impossible. Not since we left our oceans, now some ten to the seventh years ago, have we been able to commit such things except as final acts of defense, and few of us could long survive such acts. You must comprehend that we are a mature culture, we Kkkkk," a sound like a flam paradiddle, doubtless what the lobsters called themselves.

Laszlo: "But dig it, man, you're pushin' it too fast, you dig? We gotta—you know—test them pills like Uptown, unnerstan'? I mean, like . . ."

Anderson, uncomfortably: "Michael? *Oh,* Michael. Do you, what'd you call it, *read* me? Oh hell. Michael?"

Lobster: "But, youthful Laszlo, we need room, new shorelines and new seas. We Kkkk are a growing race and long-lived. We must grow or die, and to grow we must conquer. Do you comprehend?"

Laszlo: "Look, man, give it another week, you dig? I mean, like, in a week I can prob'ly . . ."

Lobster: "However this is not the paradox it might seem to your unsophisticated intellect. Your science, biochemistry, is to us an art form. Likewise your psychology. We need but study any race some while in order to produce such clever drugs as will induce said race to be its own conquistadores. Yes? Nor is our skill in forming psychological devices any less."

Laszlo: "At least gimme another day or two, huh? Whaddaya say?"

Lobster: "Whereupon we show ourselves when the native violence subsides, reestablish order, and become as gods or heroes to our newly subject peoples. All so simple. Many hundred times has this been done, nor have we ever failed. We cannot fail."

Laszlo: "You don't unner *Stan'!*"

Lobster: "We are kindly masters. Have no fear."

Anyhow, after thirty minutes of this double monologue, something finally happened. I was standing, boots in my right hand, briefcase in my left, peering over the top of my friendly packing case at the shadows Laszlo and the conquering lobster cast on the hall floor, trying simultaneously to figure out what to do and how to get away, when something hard and cold, but not metallic, suddenly grabbed me under both armpits, hoisted me a good four feet off the floor, and carried me off toward the lighted room.

I screamed, spectacularly gave up on the coffee problem, dropped my boots and briefcase, and kicked vigorously, all to no avail at all. What had grabbed me was another blue lobster, somewhat taller than Laszlo's buddy, who took great care not to hurt me or let me go, and paid absolutely no attention to my attempts to hurt him.

Moving more smoothly than I'd though a lobster could, my chitinous captor hauled me to the lighted doorway and stopped there. "Ckckckckck," he said, or words to that effect.

Laszlo's eyes bulged. His friend's eyestalks fully extended themselves and examined me from wildly unlikely combinations of angles. My captor continued to rattle like a baritone snare drum. I continued to kick, my heels hitting my captor's cephalothorax with a dull booming sound, until he grabbed my ankles with two lesser pincers and held me motionless.

My hands remained free, however. I raised the wrist radio to my mouth, turned the volume up to full, and yelled, "I'm caught! I've been captured! Send help!" I intended to say much more, but a prehensile segmented feeler curled down from behind me, removed the radio, and crushed it like a grape before my eyes. Okay, I'm easily convinced. I went limp and waited to see what would happen.

Both lobsters were rat-a-tatting on at a great rate now, and Laszlo's expression was slowly changing to something I knew in advance I wasn't going to like. I was right.

"Well, if it ain't Mister Wiseass Anderson hisself," Laszlo drooled. "Fawncy meeting you here." Then he laughed, an uninspiring sound.

"Aha, youthful Laszlo," said the first lobster, while the second continued to clatter. "This person is known to you?"

"Dig it," Laszlo admitted. "This here's ol' Wiseass Anderson."

"Oh. What is it, this *wiseass?*"

"He's jus' another MacDougal Street bum, man. That's all *he* is."

"Indeed. And did you bring him here, Laszlo Scott?"

"Me? Hell no. He brung hisself, man. Like, he's jus' tryin' to Spy on me, that's all. He's always, you know, tryin' to Spy on me an' like that."

"A spy?"

"Dig it."

"Indeed." The lobster advanced toward me menacingly, its huge blue claws snapping fiercely bare inches from my face. "Well now, we know exactly what to do with spies. Indeed we do. Exactly. Oh my, yes."

I missed Michael very much. Indeed I did. Oh my, yes.

11

nd where *was* Michael all this time?

As soon as I was safely on my way to Laszlo's, Mike went back to bed, of course. After all, he explained, it was only eight thirty, and he was still tired from last night's adventures with the pill, an he knew Laszlo wasn't likely to be up and moving much before noon, and he knew I'd want him to be at his best—alert and well-rested—in case following Laszlo led to complications. Right?

"It wasn't as if I were deserting you or anyting, Chester. Really, I don't see how you can discuss it in those terms, not even in jest. Look, I even had the radio on the nightstand by my bed, turned up to full volume, to make sure I'd wake up if you called. Christ, Anderson, when you get into these unreasonable moods . . ."

But sleep is Michael's finest art. I've seen him sleep through a fire in the same room (complete with firemen et cetera, some of whom thought he was dead until I pulled his thumb out of his mouth and they heard him groan), the big Los Angeles quake of '69 (or was it '70?), countless deadlines, appointments without number, three exceptionally loud recording sessions, one very raucous birthday party (his)—in short, through just about everything that might wake up any normal person. If Mike ever gets famous enough to rate a biography, I mean to write it myself and call it *The Magnificent Sleeper,* or maybe *The Man Who Slept Through Everything.*

Anyhow, Mike had no trouble sleeping through my early-morning efforts to call him. No, what finally woke him—at half-past one, when I'd already shadowed Laszlo back and forth across Tompkins Square three times—was the vidiphone, to which he is psychically attuned.

The call was from a chick named Yvonne on whom Mike'd once had improper but futile designs, whom he hadn't seen in eighteen months. She was just in from some far place and was entertaining improper designs on Michael for a change. Would he care to have lunch with her?

This call took an hour—Mike's phone calls often do—during which several lesser calls of mine went quite unheard. Meanwhile Sativa got up and, with much banging about of pots and pans, made Mike a second breakfast. Furthermore, Sean came home from the doctor's with an awkwardly placed dressing, a large jar of ointment, and a shamefaced expression.

Mike arranged a luncheon date with Yvonne for three o'clock at her hotel room and hung up. Sean immediately turned on my harpsichord and set out loudly to discover how it worked. Mike showered. Sativa, who grooves behind parties and/or noise, confusing the two, dialed a fairly loud detergent drama on our seldom used 3V.

The dentist who occupied the floor below my place tried to complain about the noise by banging on his ceiling with a broom handle, something he'd never done before in all the three years Mike and I had lived there. No one heard him, nor did anyone hear my sporadic attempts to communicate with Michael.

By somewhat more coincidence than I'm used to, Mike never happened to be in his bedroom when I called. He dressed, as is his wont, in motion and everywhere, ducking into his own room only to pick up garments to be put on elsewhere, wherever in the house the action was.

Mike, dreamy-eyed, horny, and glittering, left for his date with Yvonne at two thirty. Sean and Sativa left with him, bound on little missions of their own. At last the place was quiet, and my voice could doubtless be heard in every room, coming at full tinny volume from the wrist radio Mike'd left, forgotten, on the nightstand by his bed. I haven't asked, but I hope Yvonne was worth it.

At just past five, when Laszlo'd led me to lobster headquarters on Canal Street, Michael was still engaged in an air-conditioned hotel room with Yvonne, possibly discussing politics. (He was very anti-Kennedy that year, for reasons unknown to me.) Ten minutes later, when I was discovering that Laszlos Reality Pill connection was a deep blue shellfish, Michael and Yvonne were just leaving her room en route to The Garden of Eden.

"You see, she was very eager to meet *you*, Chester. I mean, she'd heard so much about you and all, the usual thing. But I knew you wouldn't want her at the pad—she being just a little bit stupid, among other things—so I took her to The Garden. Where else?"

And at something like six o'clock, when I was in the claws of one lobster and being threatened by the other whilst Laszlo gloated moistly, Mike and Yvonne were well established at The Garden, talking with Andrew Blake and Karen about me—or so Mike claims.

"The thing about Chester," Andy's supposed to have said, "is that his genius works in so many different directions at once."

"Right," from Mike, theoretically. "Music, poetry, novels— the only things he can't do well are things he hasn't tried yet."

And so improbably on and on, Mike still insists, for several hours in a choral recitation of my varied virtues that, if I could only believe it really happened, might almost have made my captivity worthwhile.

And if I work hard enough, I may believe it yet

12

Anyhow, there I was, tied hand and foot to a pillar in the middle of the loft, being surveyed with varying kinds and degrees of avid interest by two blue lobsters and Laszlo Scott.

One of the lobsters—they all looked alike to me—said something that sounded like popcorn popping, and the other lobster went away. I could hear them, out in the hall, pushing heavy packing cases around like so much air. I worried.

"Yes indeed," the remaining loster said. "We know how to deal with spies. Oh my, yes."

"Kill the wiseass mother," Laszlo hinted. "C'mon, Chief, tear 'im up. Yeah, man, yeah! Kill the bastard."

Being basically unprepared to believe in a pacifist lobster, I expected it to act on Laszlo's suggestions, but, "Oh my, Laszlo Scott!" the lobster quaked, turning light azure in distress. "Kill? You know . . ." It couldn't go on.

This was encouraging. Getting killed would've spoiled my chances to foil the lobsters' plot, among other things, and getting killed with Laszlo in the audience would've been distressing. Instead, I allowed myself to hope. Hope is good for you.

Still shaken by the thought of killing, the lobster said, "Excuse me, please," and went out to the hall to consult, like a snare drumming contest, with its colleague. This left me alone and helpless with Laszlo.

"Nyah! Nyah! Nyah!" he chanted, war-dancing around me in clumsy circles. "Now you're gonna Get It, an' I'm Glad! Nyah!"

"Cool it," I said.

"Nyah!"

The lobsters were wheeling large electronic devices into the loft, most likely for *my* entertainment. I gave them all my worried attention, leaving Laszlo to his own damp devices.

He went on nyahing furiously for a while, until he saw that I wasn't watching. "Nyah?" he said.

He looked furtively about and saw that the lobsters weren't watching him, either. (By then, knowing Laszlo, I was.) He clenched his pudgy fist, shouted Nyah! lunged for my solar plexus—and was gone! Of this, at least, I heartily approved.

But, "Hey?" came a frightened Laszlo noise from overhead. I looked up, grinned, and said a nyah or two of my own. Laszlo was spread-eagled on the ceiling, face down, and his terror and discomfort were a pleasure to behold.

"Now there, youthful Laszlo," said the English-speaking lobster solemnly, "you *know* you ought not do such things. Feel shame, Laszlo Scott, transgressor: feel regret."

After the briefest little resistance, he obviously felt just that.

I, on the other hand, suddenly felt a good deal more respect for these blue crawdads than I'd meant to. That levitation stunt was even more impressive than Sean's butterflies. How, I wondered, had such highly gifted lobsters taken up with Loathsome Laszlo? And why?

"Violence," the lobster went on sternly, "is intrinsically bad. Say that."

He didn't want to and he tried not to, but, "Violence is intrinsically bad," he choked out just the same.

"Very good. Now believe it," the lobster ordered.

Saying to myself, "Oh *Yeah?*" I watched Laszlo's putty face go through uncommon changes for almost a minute, until, against his own will and most likely without knowing what *intrinsically* meant, he obviously believed, without the slightest reservation, that violence is intrinsically bad.

"That's better," said the lobster. Laszlo sank slowly, feet first, to the floor.

I was impressed. Anyone who could do a thing like that to a thing like Laszlo was clearly someone to reckon with.

Furthermore, I recalled with a start, I myself was about to have to reckon with that someone. This did not comfort me.

Still, I wasn't as worried as I had been. I couldn't believe that so firm, deep-rooted, and irrational a prejudice against violence was likely to prove healthy on this planet. And nothing, I hoped, is intrinsically anything.

"Nyah?" I asked Laszlo when he reached the floor, but he didn't answer me. He just looked at me wide-eyed and scared, and then skittered off to someplace out of sight. I nearly laughed.

Then it was my turn.

"What is your name, Spy?" the lobster asked. I didn't answer. I wasn't going to give him anything for nothing. Then I felt a pressure in my head, discomfitting rather than uncomfortable, a very gentle pressure, and I heard my mouth say, "Chester Anderson." The pressure went away. Oh?

"Indeed. And I am Ktch. I am in charge here." I didn't doubt it for an instant. "You shall answer my questions." I certainly hoped not, but the odds were on his side. "What," he said ill-advisedly, "do you do?" After a moment of pressure, my mouth started telling him, in alarming detail, what I did. It began on the metabolic level describing with some oversimplification the process whereby I changed food into feces with myself as an inconsequential by-product. The lobster—Ktch—listened to all this drivel with rapt attention.

I stopped listening whilst my mouth was still describing the process of salivation, and discovered, to my delight, that I didn't have to listen at all. My mind, that is to say, was not engaged in this activity. Aha. A possible weakness in the lobster's plans.

I carefully imagined a hundred-piece rock 'n' roll orchestra—fifty guitars, twenty basses, fifteen harpsichords and organs, five harmonicas, ten drummers drumming: all, including the drums, highly amplified—with a two-hundred voice chorus: an impressive ensemble. I set these three hundred imaginary noisemakers to work on "Love Sold in Doses," one of Wild Bill Mosley's better tunes, in a gloriously impractical endless arrangement I'd been toying with since 1966.

> "I offered you riches an' all of them things;
> For all of your fingers I offered you rings;
> To cover your body, silk fabric that clings:
> And you gave me Love Sold in Doses."

The noise inside my skull was something awesome, but my fool mouth was still chattering away. It had gotten to the treatment of fatty acids in the upper intestine, a basically uninspiring topic.

I turned my imaginary amplifiers up a notch. My idiot mouth rattled on. Maybe, I resigned myself, this wouldn't work.

I turned the volume up another notch. Nothing happened. Up another two notches: nothing. With a subliminal shrug I turned the volume all the way up, so loud it should've been audible outside, thinking that if I couldn't keep myself from talking, maybe I could kill myself with noise.

My mouth faltered, stumbled, hesitated, groped for a master volume control set at one on a scale of one hundred.

Ktch's feelers stood at attention. "You have stopped talking," he complained in frictive tones akin to wonder. "Why have you stopped talking? Do not stop!"

The pressure in my head—hardly noticeable in all that din—increased sharply. My mouth began to say something. I turned the master volume control ever so slightly.

"What are you doing?" The lobster seemed upset. "Stop that, Spy. At once. Stop. You shall answer my questions, Spy, you *shall*!"

The pressure increased. So did the volume. I could play this game all night.

Ktch began to pale, a charming sight. His feelers wilted slightly and his eyestalks twisted themselves into a true lover's knot. His claws clicked nervously.

I noticed he was clicking his claws in time to "Love Sold in Doses." Groovy! So I wrote in a lobster-claw obbligato.

Halfway through his big solo Ktch realized what he was doing. "Stop that, Spy!" he commanded, clicking brilliantly. He doubled the pressure and I turned the volume up to five.

Then, aside from his claws, Ktch went as limp as a lobster can and turned as pale as New York City milk. "There are twelve of us here," he said flatly.

"We have always worked in teams of twelve. It is our tradition. Four chemists, three zenologists, three technicians, one communicator, and one coordinator. I am the coordinator. I am called Ktch."

And then, so help me Dylan, while "Love Sold in Doses" thundered in my skull and Ktch's claws clicked time, he told me Everything. It took awhile.

"After four months of group study, we developed the proper weapon, which you call, I believe, Reality Pills. Then we cultivated a vector, Laszlo Scott, a typical member of your species." I let that pass.

He explained how the weapon was made—a process I didn't understand but carefully memorized—and how it worked.

"It does no harm, of course. We cannot do harm. It merely generates confusion, disorder, anarchy—you might call it chaos. Whereupon we intervene to restore order. Always. We are often hailed as heroes."

The explanation was long-winded, and I was getting sick of "Love Sold in Doses," which, for all its hip innuendos, is, after all, just another tune. So I turned the volume up to ten.

"This project is organized in three phases," he went on hurriedly. "Individual testing, mass testing, and diffusion. We have finished phase one, the individual testing, with completely satisfactory results, as usual. We always have completely satisfactory results."

At this point, "Hey, Chief, wha's happenin'?" Little Laszlo chose to manifest himself again. "Why you tellin' him all that stuff, huh?"

"Love Sold in Doses" collapsed. So did Ktch. Pity. "How did you do that?" For a lobster, he sounded downright respectful.

I shrugged my shoulders eloquently. A wisp of pressure began to make itself felt in my head, then turned tail and ran away. Groovy.

"Laszlo Scott, why did you not tell me about this?"

"'Bout what, man? Why didn' I tell you . . ."

"Yes. I must think about you, Laszlo Scott. Also about you, Spy. I—no, We have been misinformed. Something must be done. Yes. Come with me."

He led Laszlo out of the room. I whistled "Love Sold in Doses" hopefullishly.

"Stop that!" the lobster yelled. I did. Why not?

Laszlo and the lobster were away some fifteen minutes, during which I wondered where the hell my beloved roommate, manager, and master planner was. I also noticed, for the first time in awhile, that I was disgracefully wet and beginning to smell, and that I still hadn't had lunch. I wove these three themes into a disgruntled fugue and waited for further developments.

Somewhere in the near distance a voice, probably Laszlo's, made odd sounds expressive of distress. This was little comfort.

Then Ktch came back. Alone. He'd got his deep blue color back and his eyestalks untangled, but he looked, to say the least, a bit offended.

"What you did," he said hurtly, "why can Laszlo Scott not do the same? Were you taught to do this? Where did you learn it?"

I whistled another half-bar of "Love Sold in Doses."

"No," he surrendered.

Out of unabashed nastiness and the absence of lunch, I whistled through the whole tune once, with flourishes. He kept time with his claws.

"I'm afraid," he said when I was quite through, "that I shall have to resort to methods I myself deplore. But you are too strong for our usual procedures. Quite unexpectedly strong. Nothing had prepared us for . . . Ah, well. You yourself have forced us to this point. We shall have to use torture, alas."

Torture?

"Of course, I wouldn't hurt you for the world," Ktch explained, while setting up the electronic devices I'd worried about earlier. "In fact, I don't believe I could, really. Just thinking about it makes my eyestalks twitch. Conditioning, you know. There."

He flipped a switch. The devices—there were four of them that I could see, all very bulky, gray, and ominous, with lots of knobs and dials and, on the biggest one, silvery thin tentacular extrusions that were probably going to be attached to me somehow—the devices hummed rather threateningly, lights lit up and flashed or not as they saw fit, a psychedelic op-art disk on the tentacle device rotated with obvious hypnotic intent, and the air around me suddenly grew heavy. Ktch looked as pleased as an azure lobster can.

"These won't actually hurt," he said. "That is, there's no physical pain involved." He started attaching tentacles to me. "Of course, if you choose to interpret the sensations they produce as pain—and you probably will—well, that's your doing, not ours."

There were lots of tentacles, and he fastened them to me in all sorts of unlikely places, many of them personal. I kept a stiff upper lip and wondered where Mike was.

"This is the first time we've used these instruments here," he apologized at last. "With Laszlo Scott they were not needed— or so we were led to believe. In fact, the last creatures we used these on were amphibious, if that's the word for it, and had four sexes. A charming arrangement but quite impractical. One is best, or at the most three, but Four . . ." He waved a fluent feeler in mock despair, while I silently vetoed his opinions.

"Anyway," he went on, "the calibration is perhaps a trifle rough. I'm sorry about that. We'll watch your reactions and refine our settings, but that will take some time. Here goes."

He flipped another switch, I braced myself, and the torture commenced. Like everything else so far, it was impressive, if that's the word for it. Yeah, impressive.

13

By then it was eight o'clock, and my disappearance was beginning to attract some belated attention.

Sean and Charley Wainright noticed it first, which was to be expected. "Where's Chester?" Chaz bellowed when Sean wandered into The Mess. "He's late."

"He ain't here? I'm lookin' for him; figured he'd be here. Where's he at?"

"He's late. Do you know where he is?"

"No, man. I thought he was Here." And so on for a few minutes. Communication tends to be a bit problematical in the Village.

Sean checked the back room, where he found the rest of The Tripouts pleasantly stoned but no trace of me at all. "Where's Chester?" everyone asked everyone else. Sean split to seek me in The Garden.

Where I was was being fiendishly tortured by the inhuman devices of a dozen large blue lobsters bent on conquering the Earth, but that was neither here nor there. At The Garden of Eden, Sean found Mike and Andrew Blake. Help, so to speak, was on the way.

"Hey, Michael the Theodore Bear, you know where Chester's at?"

Mike said, "At The Mess, no?" and Andrew said, "That's an interesting question. Do you mean it? I mean, *all* of it?"

"No, man, he ain't there," Sean said. "I figured he was Here."

"In a manner of speaking, he is," Andrew Blake explained, but Mike said, "Oh shit," very softly, and I was as good as saved, in a manner of speaking.

"Pardon me," said Mike, rising abruptly to his feet. "I seem to have forgotten something. Pardon me."

He rushed out of The Garden, closely followed by Sean, while Andy said, "It's hard to tell about Chester. Sometimes he's . . ." then noticed that he'd lost his audience and quit.

Mike and Sean took a taxi home—$1.37 plus tip, cash, Mike having forgotten his General Credit Card. They had to pool their resources to make it, and the driver was eloquently displeased with his tip.

"What's happening?" Sean begged as they ran up the stairs.

"I may have goofed," Mike explained.

They reached the pad, dashed to Mike's room, and, after a bit of confused scrabbling, found the radio on the floor where it'd somehow fallen when Yvonne called.

"Chester?" Michael asked the radio. "Chester? Do you read me? Come in, Chester."

"You don't gotta yell like that," Sean winced.

"Sorry," yelling. "Chester? Can you hear me?"

It took him awhile to admit that I probably couldn't hear him. Then, "Oh shit," he dropped the radio and ran out of the pad, closely followed by Sean.

"What's happening, man? You gotta *tell* me what's *happening!*" Sean was getting excited.

"I did goof." Mike seldom made such damaging admissions, but Sean didn't know him well enough yet to appreciate this.

Ever since the St. Mark's Place disturbances of a few years back, cabs had carefully avoided our neighborhood, so Mike and Sean rushed back to The Garden on foot, more healthy exercise than Mike'd had in years. En route, gasping, Mike explained the situation.

"We better call the cops," was Sean's suggestion.

"You kidding? You don't know much about New York cops, my lad. They wouldn't do a thing, not in a case like this. Missing rock 'n' roll musician. Right. They'd only laugh. That I can do for myself. Listen. Hah. Hah-hah. See? Nothing to it." Michael was upset.

Rescue Operation, Step One: they stopped off at The Mess, roused my fellow Tripouts, explained the situation, and sent the group out scouring the Village for me in a random manner that would have worked, ordinarily.

Chaz demanded wergild for the scattering Tripouts, so Sean remained to play guest sets at The Mess, his Village and professional premiere. Mike returned to The Garden.

Step two: "Chester's missing!" he announced.

"Define your terms," said Andrew.

"Where?" asked Gary the Frog and Harriet.

"We've got to find him, don't we?" Karen Greenbaum wondered.

"What," it dawned on Andrew, "do you mean, *missing?*"

Mike explained at length. Then Andy said, "In other words . . ." and counteracted Michael's explanation. Gary the fatuous Frog asked foolish questions. Mike explained it all again, loudly with dramatic gestures.

"Oh," said Andrew Blake. "We've got to find him, then. At once. He may be in some trouble."

"That's what I said," said Mike. "Now look, I've got this all planned out. Everybody . . . Hey, wait! Come back!"

Too late. Everybody was dashing off to find me—Andrew Blake, Gary and Harriet, little Karen, even a few strangers (probably named David) swept up by the excitement—leaving Mike and his plan all alone in The Garden of Eden.

"And it was such a lovely plan," he grieved much later. "It wouldn't've worked, of course, but it was very pretty. Very professional, you might say."

That was just past nine, and I'd been suffering roughly calibrated agonies for something like ninety minutes. As tortures go, these were very, let us call it, Subtle, and I wondered a lot about Ktch's last victims.

To begin the program, I experienced a deep, perverted yearning to refrain from sexual intercourse with three of the most improbable creatures I've ever been forced to imagine. As a torment, this was fairly easy to take.

Then Ktch wandered in, read a few dials, said, "Tch tch," quite convincingly, turned a knob or three and wandered out again, leaving me to suffer through act two in solitude.

Act two, which they must have picked up from Laszlo somehow, was an extraordinarily vivid hallucination of myself reciting my own poetry. I took note of a few stagecraft errors to be avoided next time I read, but was otherwise fairly unagonized. My admiration for the subtlety of these blue lobster deepened.

Then Ktch returned, Laszlo in tow and looking most uneasy, to check the readings again. It's hard to tell with lobsters, but he seemed a bit surprised. One stalked eye examined the dials intently, the other, extended full length—four feet—examined me. Laszlo shuffled his feet and tried to be inconspicuous.

"Tch tch," Ktch repeated. "Your fortitude is most impressive, Spy. Indeed, quite admirable. Not at all what I'd been led to expect."

Laszlo cleared his throat and tried, without moving, to hide.

Ktch flipped a switch and the torture stopped right in the middle of one of my favorite poems.

"You must realize by now that we cannot be defeated," he said. "There is no resistance you can offer, no strategy by which you may hope even to delay our victory. You, after all— or rather, your people—will do our fighting for us, and you cannot think to defeat yourselves. We will merely restore order. You can't fight that. In fact, there's nothing to fight. Surely you understand this?"

I kept mum. Laszlo, for reasons of his own, looked enraged, embarrassed, and humiliated—an intriguing combination.

"You simply can't win," Ktch continued. "Why then, Spy, do you not cast your lot with us? Your people have a folk saying: 'If you can't run your tongue across them, merge with them.' I ask you to give this quaint wisdom your serious consideration. If you join us . . ."

Oh, that's what he wanted. I whistled him another chorus of "Love Sold in Doses."

"Admirable," he said, "and wholly unexpected. Such a waste." He devoted himself for a few minutes to the torture devices— refining the settings, I supposed—while Laszlo stared at me with the most illegible expression I've ever seen.

"That should do it," Ktch finally said. "Now I must leave you to our own devices for a few hours, while Laszlo Scott and I are fed and otherwise refreshed. But remember, surrender under torture is no disgrace. Farewell."

He flipped a switch and floods of odd sensation burst upon me before I had a chance to mention that I was overdue for feeding myself. But I hadn't been going to mention that anyway, I guess.

"Farewell, Mister Spy," the lobster said, and he and Laszlo split, leaving me to act three of my torment: the complete adventures of Donald Duck, 3V, wide screen, with full sensory participation. Fine. I've always enjoyed the classics.

A tiny corner of my mind wondered what it was these lobsters imagined they were doing to me. Another corner wondered where Mike was. Donald Duck defied the universe.

There being nothing better he could do, Mike stayed in The Garden. "If you were going to show up at all, that's where you'd go," he explained later. He drank lots of coffee and worried a bit, mostly about what I was likely to say about all this.

Laszlo arrived at half-past ten with his last consignment of Reality Pills and, being Laszlo, made a warped beeline for Michael, sneering, "Hallo, Michael the Bareassed Theodore. How's about a little taste of ol' Reality on Laszlo, huh, baby? Wanna get High?"

So Mike grabbed him by one padded shoulder, yelling, "What've you done to Chester!? C'mon, talk, you goddamn freak! Where is he!?"—sweet music for the Laszlo ears.

"Anderson?" a nasty purr. "How do I know where your buddy's at, man? He's *your* buddy, ain't he? Hey, man, turn me loose!" It was his moment of glory, and I hope he made the most of it.

But Mike was too worried to be cool. He shook Laszlo briskly, ripping his jacket, and said, "I'm going to beat the living Shit out of you, man," loudly enough to be clearly heard on the sidewalk outside.

"Lemme go!" screamed Laszlo, grinning. "Halp! Call the fuzz, somebody. Halp!" enjoying every second of it.

Nobody rallied to Laszlo's defense, but Joe came over and said, "Take 'im outside, will ya, Mike? I don' wan' no trouble inna Club, y'unnerstan'?"

"Forget it." Mike released the Bard. "It couldn't possibly be worth it."

Laszlo backed a prudent four feet off and extended an unkempt hand, saying, "No hard feelings, Mike, okay?"—a line he must've copped from The Hardy Boys a hundred years ago and never found a use for until then.

Mike winced nobly and turned away. "Oh, go paint yourself purple and moo," he ordered. "Go away."

Laszlo didn't get it, but he went—with Michael hot and hidden on his trail. The game was afoot, or vice versa.

I, meanwhile, had troubles of my own. The Magnificent Duck had abandoned his biography to play endless Brahms sonatas on a do-it-yourself-kit homemade harpsichord, which came closer to what I'd call torture than I really liked and prompted intermittent second thoughts about what the lobsters could possibly do to me with all those alien gadgets of theirs. I *like* Brahms, you understand—but played by a paranoid duck?

Ktch himself remained offstage for a while yet, and Laszlo— had I but known—was already getting his arcane jollies on MacDougal Street.

I was hungry. Highly entertained, after a fashion, but mainly hungry. Hunger is a notorious drag.

And everybody else was having good times, too.

Acting on the principle that that's where *he* usually went when he was lost, Andy took the E train to Forty-second Street and sought me out in every semidirty-book emporium between Forty-first and Forty-seventh Streets, where he was well-known and respected as the pseudonymous author of classics beyond counting. It hardly mattered that I wasn't there.

"I wasn't really worried," he explained. "I knew you could take care of yourself, and I supposed that if nobody knew where you were, it was mainly because you didn't want them to. I mean, Every man has a Need to get away from People Who Know Him once in a while. It's perfectly natural. You see, I under*Stand* these things, and that's what I thought *you* were doing. Right? Now, if Michael had only bothered to *explain . . .*"

And Sean, taking my place at The Mess on MacDougal Street, was discovering, to his lasting surprise, just how well he played and how much fun an audience could be.

"He was Great!" Chaz reported. "Fabulous! I mean, he really *grabbed* them. Understand? They wouldn't let him off the stage. Really. Encores for hours, honest to God, and a standing ovation and all that. I've never seen anything like it before. Never. I mean to tell *you*, son," slower and more serious, "I was sorely tempted to hire him on the spot, get it?"

And, "Yeah, the kid's pretty good," Al Mamlet seconded. Al's a very funny man whose taste I trust implicitly.

"Shucks. All I done was play a few old songs I learned in *Fort* Worth," was all Sean had to say about it, but he was hooked, all right. Utterly hooked and instantly addicted, and it showed. He was sporadically insufferable for weeks afterward.

Gary the Frog and Harriet combed the Village streets and parks, saying alternately, "Hey! Have you seen *Chester?*" and, "Hey, mister, got an extra dime you can spare?" more or less depending on whether they were bracing friends or strangers.

They made $1.37 in coins plus a Boston subway token in this manner, and gradually evolved their line on me through, "Hey, have you heard about Chester? He's been kidnapped!" to, finally, "Hey, what happened to Chester? I mean, somebody told me he was Dead or something"—all the market would bear—which took a lot of explaining to clear up afterward.

Sativa and the boys, with impeccable logic, hunted for me in every high-class teapad in the Village and still don't know whether they found me or not; and Karen, for a wonder, spent the whole night in the front pew of Our Lady of Pompeii Catholic Church praying for my safety.

All told, it was quite a night, and I'm still kind of sorry I missed it.

Ktch came back at twelve or so, read the dials, looked very grave, made further adjustments, and said, "You are very brave, Spy. Very brave."

No comment but a tight-lipped grin of indomitable courage.

"Please," haltingly, "believe me when I tell you how sorry I am about having to do this to you. I assure you, sir, I have no personal motive in doing this to you, none whatsoever. It is the Rules, you understand. The Rules say I must put you to the torture if you will not talk. The Rules Must Be Obeyed. But if I had my way . . ." He made a percussive noise roughly equal to a sob. I was touched.

"You are very brave," he repeated after a solemn brief pause. "But now I must leave you alone here for some time. It is my shift to sleep—The Rules. I have programmed you for eight hours of increasing intensity, as prescribed, but I trust, Sir, that your courage will not fail you. Spy, adieu!" He extended his upper three left limbs and feeler in a crustacean salute, then stiffly marched away.

And that's when all the fun began.

14

had to think! Ktch and his cohorts were snugly tucked away in their slumber tanks or whatever—it was difficult to imagine them using anything I'd recognize as a bed—and Laszlo was safely gone about his usual business of soiling the Village. This was my big chance—maybe my last chance—to dream up some way to foil the lobsters and save the world, or at least to escape from that loft and find Mike and let *him* save the world. I had to *think!*

However, I was still being tortured. All around me I could see tiny noises intertwining like spaghetti in the air. My body was covered with acute perceptions of color in flux—solemn reds, introspective blues, pulsating greens and browns—all intimate and not to be ignored. My ears were full of the flavor of hot buttered corn with salt and lemon juice. (And oh, yes, I was still hungry, which felt a bit like being underwater.) I could taste smoothness and abrasiveness and sharpness alternating in intricate patterns of what was not quite motion, and the temperature of the air— night-cool, growing cooler—smelled . . . I don't have a word for how it smelled. Like calculus, perhaps?

This was not at all unpleasant. In fact, I'd spent lots of money in my day for exotic pharmaceuticals I'd hoped would produce some such effects. No, it wasn't unpleasant (though the taste is probably an acquired one), but it interfered with thinking something fierce.

"I've got to ignore all this," I told myself in a moment of fleeting clarity. But the only sensation I'd ever practiced ignoring was pain, the one sensation I wasn't currently experiencing.

It was impossible to keep anything in mind. I'd start a train of thought going, and before it got past the verb it would dissolve in a welter of meaningless sensations. And the most frustrating thing about it was that I couldn't hold my mind still long enough to be frustrated.

I have no idea how long this went on.

Mike, meanwhile, was tailing Laszlo, an inherently thankless task.

"It wasn't as easy as it should've been. The freak seemed to be nervous about something. He kept looking back over his shoulder as though he were being followed or something, which kept me busy ducking in and out of doorways, hiding behind lampposts, crouching behind tourists, making an ass of myself in general.

"You know, it's kind of embarrassing when you're hiding behind some tourist and he turns around and asks you what you're doing and you say you're following somebody and he wants to know why. What do you say in a case like that?

"So he was hard to follow, and I didn't think that was at all fair. I mean, hadn't expected it to be much fun, but *work* . . . ?"

Nursing this comfortable sense of instant injustice, Michael followed Laszlo from The Garden of Eden half a block east to the corner drugstore, first stop. Laszlo slithered up to the prescription counter, and Mike ducked into a phone booth.

"What do You want?" said Dr. Lee, the pharmacist, who was a Villager and knew Laszlo.

"Can you, like, take somethin' an', you know, find out what it is? Huh, Doc? Can you?"

Laszlo was doing his best to be polite, which made Dr. Lee be wary. "Generally," he said, "I know what it is *before* I take it. Yes, Ma'am, can I help you?"

Laszlo tapped his feet and snapped his fingers anxiously for ten minutes while Dr. Lee listened with near-infinite patience to the overwhelming troubles of a fat Italian lady and sold her a box of aspirin for them. Then, "Are you still here?"

"Look, Doc . . ."

"What're you looking for, Georgie? I'm busy."

"Oh wow! Listen, Doc, s'pose I was to give you this Pill, see? Can you, like, ah, find out what's In it? Can you, Doc? Huh? Can you?"

"Yes, sir, can I help you?" Another customer.

Laszlo by now was almost dancing in frustration, which pleased Michael no end, but the customer only wanted a pack of cigarettes.

"Let me get this straight," said Dr. Lee resignedly. "You want me to analyze some pill for you. Is that it?"

"Yeah, yeah! Analyze. That's it, yeah. Can you, Doc?" He pulled a transparent plastic bag full of little blue pills out of his right coat pocket. Bits of lint and dirt and God knows what clung to the outside of the bag.

"Well," slowly and thoughtfully, "I *can,* I suppose. I've got a little lab at home that . . . Why should I?"

"Huh?"

"Why should I go to all the trouble of analyzing anything for you? Tell me that? What've you ever done for me, besides give me a hard time? You don't even buy your Cigarettes here."

"Oh wow!" waving the pill bag about in agitation. "Look, Doc, I'll Pay you!"

"Oh?" No one had ever heard Laszlo say those words before. Doc Lee thought it over for a moment. "Okey-doke," he said. "I'll try, anyhow. Those the pills?"

"Yeah. Here, Doc." Laszlo handed him one pill.

"I'll need more than one," said the kindly pharmacist, peering at the little blue pill in his palm.

"More than one?" Laszlo didn't like this.

"Right. Ten at least, maybe more."

"Ten?" He clutched the pill bag tightly to his chest. *"Ten?"*

Dr. Lee ignored this method acting. "Where'd you get this stuff?" he asked. "What's it for?"

"I, ah, somebody *gave* it to me. Yeah."

"Somebody gave it to you. Did he tell you what it's for? Diet? Headache? Cramps? Leukemia? It looks like a . . . Hmm!"

"What's wrong?" Laszlo backed a few inches away from the counter. "Somethin' wrong?"

"I just remembered. You're the maniac who's been handing out those whatchamacallim—Reality Pills. Right?"

"Who, me?"

"Is that what this thing is? Hmm."

"Look, Doc, ah. let's," backing away, "let's just forget it, okay?"

"Sure, I'll analyze the things, if I can. I've been wondering about them myself. But I'll need more'n one."

"Oh wow! Like, ForGet It!" Laszlo turned and ran for the door.

"Hey, what's wrong with you? Come back here. Laszlo! Take your pill . . ."

Too late. Laszlo was gone.

"How do you like that?" Doc Lee wondered aloud. "The wicked flee where none pursueth."

"Not this time, Doc," said Michael, laughing, as he left.

The trail led down MacDougal Street—Laszlo, looking apprehensively in all directions, on one side; Michael, taking advantage of every bit of cover, on the other—to Bleecker Street and then turned left, heading toward the East Side.

"I'd never seen Laszlo move so fast before," Mike said later. "He passed five whole coffeehouses without going in, and he passed dozens of chicks without coming on to any of them, and he walked right by Pat Gerstein without even slowing down to trade insults. Extraordinary, I told myself. Very odd.

"I was tempted to catch up with him and ask him what was bothering him, but I didn't think he'd understand, so I didn't. Laszlo has a flair for not understanding."

They crossed West Broadway almost at a run and faded into the anonymous night.

My long green fur could've used a brushing and my left fore-ear itched a little, but otherwise I was doing nicely, thanks. Of course, I wasn't really used to the sky's being orange, but I wasn't used to having six legs, either, or to being surrounded by hundred-foot-tall red ferns with stems ten feet thick at the base. No matter. I'd get along.

I took a bite out of the nearest fern tree. Good. It tasted just like hundred-foot-tall red fern, with lots of crunch and juice. I liked it.

There were some predators in the neighborhood—mostly those slimy brown and yellow snakish things with all the legs and teeth: the worst kind—but I didn't care. I could handle *them* all right.

My only problem was that I still couldn't manage to organize my thoughts, with, for some not quite remembered reason, I absolutely *had* to do.

Aw, to hell with it. I took another swipe at the fern tree.

Laszlo was being clever. Well, tricky. Backtracking, hiding in doorways to wait for whomever to pass, going in one door of such buildings as had more than one and coming out another, turning corners and running like mad, striking up conversations with policemen (a most unusual stratagem for him), and otherwise boring Michael with his puerile games.

"I'd like to know who the hell he thought was chasing him. I'd also like to know what made him think he could lose a tail with stunts like that. Too many movies, that's Laszlo's problem."

Except that one of Laszlo's stunts worked. Michael turned the corner of Third Street and Second Avenue two and a half seconds after Laszlo did and found no visible Laszlo, none at all. Oh, the shame of it.

He checked the halls of all the nearby tenements and heard no Laszlo on the stairs. He checked the two bodegas and one bar that were open nearby and found no Laszlo lurking. He couldn't remember having seen a taxi on the avenue, so he checked the halls again, with no results. Finally, after maybe half an hour, he gave it up.

"Christ," he told himself in something close to shock, "the little bastard shook me. He actually Shook me. And I can't figure out how the hell he did it."

So the evening shouldn't be a total loss, Michael went to visit Sandi Heller and Leo Pratt, who were roughing it in an old law tenement a few blocks farther east. All the way there, he berated himself for letting Laszlo get away, wondering how he could ever bring himself to tell anyone about it.

"I was afraid I was either going to have to bear the shameful secret to my grave or take to haunting low taverns and unburdening myself to heedless strangers, as it were. Maybe I could hire an analyst? And how did the little freak do it, anyway? He couldn't've sprouted wings. Maybe he just vanished, like Judge Crater. Nah, that's too good to be real. Laszlos never vanish, no such luck."

And then he was across the street from the Heller-Pratt pad, waiting for the traffic light to change.

"Jesus H. Christ!" he whispered, crouching quickly behind a parked car.

Laszlo the Lost was cautiously emerging from the Heller-Pratt hallway. He opened the door, poked his little round head out, looked four or five times in every direction, scurried out into the nearest shadow, and slunk furtively toward the east.

Mike, considerably shaken, followed.

"Oh yeah, Laszlo," Leo explained some fifteen hours later. "Wasn't that something? Sandi was checking something out with the *I Ching* and I was trying to work out some new changes for 'Dark Girl' on this banjo somebody left in the john a few months back, and then there was this Scritching on the door. Chi-ki-chi-ki-chi-ki, you know, like mice—or a very Sensitive pussycat.

"So I said, 'Who's that scritching on my door?' and this real strange haunted kind of voice whispers, "Leo?"

"'Who's there?' I say, and this same voice whispers, 'Leo? Are you home?'

"'So what the hell? Friend or foe, I had to find out what that voice was coming from, so I opened the door and Wow, there stood Laszlo Scott in all his queasy glory, not the sort of thing I'm accustomed to finding on my doorstep, not at all.

"So I said . . ."

"Oh good Lord, Leo!" Sandi has a sense of style. "They just want to find out what he wanted. You don't have to make a novel out of Everything!"

"Oh yeah. Right. Well, once upon a time I told little Laszlo that I've got a friend who's an analytic chemist, spade cat name of Chauncy Mitchell. So Laszlo wanted Mitch to analyze something for him, that's all."

"Pills?"

"Yeah, I think so. Sure, little blue pills. Looked like some kind of laxative or something. He gave me a little aspirin bottle full of 'em and told me to ask Mitch to hurry, which was funny on account of Mitch's in Switzerland. But what the hell? I told him Mitch'd hurry and he split. That's all there was to it. He wasn't here five minutes. Was he, hon?"

"Groovy. What happened to the pills?"

"Nothing. I gave them to the chick across the hall. She'll take Anything. Thinks it's hip or something."

From the Heller-Pratt pad Laszlo went straight home, though it wasn't even two o'clock yet.

Mike stationed himself in the candy store doorway across the street and watched Laszlo's windows. Oddly dressed persons of unknown age and gender tried to proposition him in foreign languages, but he ignored them. Scrawny kids trying to look mean in skin-tight leather slouched by muttering obscure insults, and he ignored them. A rather pretty long-haired chick in standard artist's garb walked by, slowed down, smiled at him and walked on, and he even managed to ignore Her. Michael meant business.

After fifteen minutes of this, the lights went off in Laszlo's pad. Mike didn't believe a word of it. He stood firm in the candy store doorway, waiting for Laszlo to try some funny business, for upward of an hour, or until two wary fuzz approached and one of them, hand poised above his pistol, snarled. "All right, buddy, what's *your* problem?"

"Nothing, officer, nothing at all. Just catching my breath. Long walk, you know."

"What does it take you, an hour to catch your breath? C'mon, buddy, move along before I run ya in."

So Michael went home, feeling deeply unfulfilled.

I was motion in the boundless universe. I was the square root of minus one. I was covered with thick beige fuzz that moved of its own accord. I was ten feet tall.

I was a pastrami ice-cream cone. I was the key of G minor. I was full of tiny gears and printed circuits and my batteries needed charging.

I was pregnant and I knew the people responsible. I was law west of the Klamath River. I was without form, and void. I was a long-playing microgroove record.

I saw the best minds of my generation and I was appalled. I was a platinum gas tank. I was an army advancing toward I was as army.

I was the ghost of Christmas past. I was the rabbit in the moon. I was as corny as Kansas in orbit.

I wasn't thinking very well at all.

15

Click!
Zap!
"Good morning, Mister Spy. Do you wish to talk now?"

It was over. Finished. Dead. Ktch'd turned my torture off, plunging me with a morbid Click! from breathless peaks of subjective ecstasy to Wednesday morning. Wow, what a bringdown.

"Mister Spy?"

The lobsters were at it again, all twelve of them—a ghastly sight—scuttling here and there about the loft with fifty-gallon steel drums in their claws; all but Ktch, who was standing still with one pincer resting on the largest torture device and both eyestalks pointed at me. These were the kind of lobsters that liked to gossip while they worked, too—the worst kind of lobster—and the loft sounded like a firing range at rush hour. I *hate* loud noises in the morning.

"Can you hear me, Mister Spy? Are you all right?"

And *this* morning I was ready to hate almost everything. I was still drenched with metabolized coffee, for one thing, clammy and reeking. And I still hadn't had yesterday's lunch yet, not to mention supper, snack, and breakfast. The inside of my mouth felt like it was digesting itself, and tasted like it, too.

"You're not—oh my—you're not Dead, are you? Tell me you're not dead!"

And I hadn't slept, either. That was another thing. All-night torture sessions are fine and groovy if you dig that sort of thing, but I'm a cat who needs his sleep.

Furthermore, Michael hadn't rescued me—first time he'd failed me in three and a half years. The world was still unsaved.

These filthy lobsters' evil plans were still intact, unfoiled. Everything had gone wrong. Everything.

Oh, but I was in a foul mood that morning.

"Oh dear! Speak to me, Spy. Dear Spy, *please* say something!"

Ktch was turning pale again. That seemed to be a habit of his, and I was sick of it. His feelers were flailing weakly about in the air, his eyestalks were wilting, and he was rubbing his claws together in brittle, nervous polyrhythms: crustacean symptoms of acute distress. I was pretty sick of that, too.

"Oh, Spy," he wailed, "please, Please do not be dead!"

"Oh, for Christ's sake!" I comforted him. "Will you shut *up*!"

"Oh my!" He sank to the floor and trembled noisily.

"Stop that!" I yelled. "Cut it out!" I hate to yell in the morning. "Stop that flipping noise, God damn you! Quit it!"

Which attracted the rest of the lobsters. They lay down their burdens and gathered in a clackety cobalt-blue cluster around me. This was a little quieter, but Ktch was still trembling briskly, and the sight of twenty-two extended eyestalks waving in my direction made me nervous.

"Stop that!" And I was developing a sore throat, too. "Stop!"

They didn't seem to understand English, but the idea got across. They muffled their noise to a spring-rain patter that was merely aggravating, and retracted their eyes. Ktch, however, continued to clatter on the floor. It was shameful to see a grown lobster carry on so.

"You," I said quite softly, blending laryngitis with intense menace.

Ktch froze in midclatter.

"You," I repeated. "Stand up. Quietly."

He stood up. Shakily. Every time his shell clicked, he winced, producing another click. His feelers dangled limply down on either side of him, his eyestalks drooped, and his claws just missed dragging on the floor. For a six-foot lobster, he was a sorry spectacle.

"Spy?" he begged.

"Shut up. I want to think."

Now that I had them quiet, my temper wasn't half as foul as it had been, but I was still uncomfortable enough to generate a decent rage if I needed one. To prove it, I glowered fiercely at my dozen lobsters. It isn't easy for a face as bland as mine to glower convincingly, but I managed. Twenty-four limp feelers drooped like a grove of segmented willows.

"That's better." Still menacing. Not a carapace creaked.

It was clear that Micahel was not going to rescue me. I had some things to say about that, but they could wait till I saw him again, if ever. Right now the problem was to rescue myself, a task for which I was eminently unsuited.

But maybe I had a chance. Look how I'd managed to cow these twelve strapping lobsters with naught but a yell and a glower. Consider yesterday's interrogation scene with Ktch. Right. These bugs had chinks in their armor big enough to drive a seafood truck through: several helpful weaknesses I already knew about, doubtless many more to be discovered.

Their biggest weakness was this nonviolent nonsense. They'd sure as hell picked the wrong planet for *that* game. Human beings are just naturally violent animals, even the nonviolent ones. Hell, even the limp protesters who lie down in front of ammunition trucks and have to be hauled off the street like sacks of flour, all they're doing is imposing their will on others, compelling other people to behave contrary to their own desires, which is the crystalline essence of violence. And the rest of us tend to be downright brutal: we spank our kids, we step on bugs, we fish and hunt for pleasure, we enjoy 3V bloodshed, we play football and other battle games—we're a rough bunch, we are.

I didn't think the lobsters really understood this yet.

And old Ktch here couldn't even *think* about violence without turning pale. Groovy. If I didn't get anything else accomplished, I intended to see just how pale he could get. I was fairly confident I could persuade him that he was personally and directly responsible for every act of violence caused by the Reality Pill, I was looking forward to that.

"Click."

"Who did that?" Twelve lobsters faded. "Don't do it again."

I'd also like, I decided, to see friend Ktch's reaction to a seafood restaurant. A lobster house, for instance.

Another massive weakness: the bugs were basing their ideas about the human race on Laszlo Scott, for Christ's sake. You might as well believe you can handle wolves because you've had a dog. A yellow dog. If these blue plate specials thought they were dealing with a planetful of Laszlos, they were in trouble.

Anything I could do that Laszlo couldn't, I figured—like overpowering Ktch's mind control goody—almost anybody else could also do, Laszlo being pretty much at the bottom of the racial totem pole, wherein might lurk some nasty shocks should the lobsters ever come to grips with the human race at large.

Just to be mean, I filled my head with "Love Sold in Doses" again. Ktch winced. The others twitched rhythmically. Nice.

"All right," I said, still keeping it harsh. "I'm done thinking for a while. You can move again. But keep it quiet, you hear?"

Hesitantly, the eleven working lobsters went back to work, muffling clicks as best they could. Some of the starch returned to Ktch's feelers.

"Spy?" humbly.

"Yes?"

"The torture. Did you break under the torture? Ah, are you ready to talk now?"

"Not a chance."

"Oh my. I didn't really think so."

"Right. What are you doing?"

"Conducting the morning interview, as prescribed by The Rules. Ah, um, may *I* ask *you* some questions, please, Mister Spy?"

"Not a chance. What are the rest of them doing?"

"I'm not allowed to answer questions. The Rules . . ."

"Remember what happened yesterday?" I whistled a phrase in case he'd forgotten.

He hadn't. "They are making ready for phase two, which begins tonight, Mister Spy."

"Indeed. Just what is phase two?"

"Oh my. Large-scale testing of the chemical weapon, sir. We have already studied its effect on individuals and small groups. Now, Phase Two, we must observe its effects on large population masses before we can initiate Phase Three. The effect, you see, is—I shouldn't be telling you this—is both qualitatively and quantitatively different in large groups. There is a resonance factor, and . . ."

"That's nice. What are you going to *do* to get Phase Two started?"

"Please! The Rules specifically forbid . . ."

> "I offered you riches an' all of them things,"
> *fortissimo,*
> "For all of your fingers I offered you rings . . ."

"Ai! Stop! Oh, Stop!"

> "To cover your body, silk fabric that clings:
> And you gave me Love Sold in Doses."

"Please, no more." There's something in the sight of a cringing lobster. "I beg of you, sir . . ."

"It's an awfully long song, but I'll sing it all if you insist."

"Oh dear."

I rather liked the way Ktch kept changing colors. It lent variety to what would otherwise've been a fairly monotonous exoskeleton.

"Our plan," he whispered, "is to pour six hundred gallons of the liquefied chemical into the reservoir called Croton under cover of darkness. Laszlo Scott will lead us there."

"Oh yeah? Six hundred gallons, you say?"

"Shh! The others will hear you."

"That's nice. How many doses in six hundred gallons?"

"Doses? Oh, roughly ten billions, I believe."

That stopped me. But, "Isn't that a bit much for only ten million people?"

"We expect some waste, you understand. Besides, it's really quite harmless. There is no lethal dose. We couldn't do a thing like that."

"Um. You shellfish have some pretty twisty ethics."

That bothered him. He embarked on an elaborate defense of lobsterian ethics, full of feeler-flippings, claw-clickings, and similar rhetorical devices. Very dull. And I thought about Phase

Two: the whole city high on Reality Pills. My imagination was too good.

I could see it all. Birchites launching millions of missiles against Russia, starting at last the war we'd avoided so long. Racists suddenly become omnipotent. The persecuted manufacturing impossible revenge. Cops really stamping out crime. Kids getting even with grown-ups. Mental patients striking back at the world. Sadists getting infinite kicks. The weak grown powerful beyond endurance. Lovers crushing all things under love. . . .

And not just the city, no. The lobsters underestimated us. The whole world in flames at the very least. And back of it all the blond Abaddon, Laszlo Scott, leading twelve blue lobsters to the Croton Reservoir.

And only I could stop it. I felt ill.

Why me? *I* never volunteered to save the world. I wasn't even very good at saving myself.

But there it was, my job, whether I liked it or not, and time was running short. I reinstated yesterday's rock 'n' roll festival chorus and orchestra. "Untie the spy," they played and sang, "Untie the spy," over and over again, "Untie the spy," in B flat, a domineering key.

Ktch weakened. His argument began to run down, to falter, and his gestures grew sloppy. He took one tentative step forward, then another. The argument petered out and stopped. He moved around behind me. I could feel the small pincers he used for delicate manipulation working at my ankles.

The other lobsters had stopped what they'd been doing and were standing frozen in their tracks like polyethylene-extruded monster models, paralyzed by my music, I presumed. Just to be on the safe side, I changed my text to, "Let the spy go home." It had a catchy Latin beat.

There! My left foot was free. I wiggled it gratefully. Ktch was working on my right.

Then, "What're you *doin'*?" a shriek, and the whole thing fell apart. Laszlo had arrived.

Ktch backed away, gibbering percussively. The other lobsters took up defensive positions around me. One of them, ignoring my most vigorous kicks, retied my left foot. Phooey!

All the lobsters were clattering like up-tight teletype machines, and, "You was lettin' 'im Go!" Laszlo complained. "You was gonna let 'im Go!" It was all very noisy.

"Shut up!" I yelled.

It didn't work this time. That is, the lobsters shut up, but Laszlo didn't. He stomped over to me like an angry gob of mayonnaise, screaming, "He was gonna let you Go!" while Ktch scurried out the door.

That blew it. When Ktch returned, his carapace was covered with a silvery blanket-like affair that evidently shielded him from my musical assaults. Ignoring me altogether, he concentrated on directing the other lobsters' work.

That left me to Laszlo. "You know what I'm gonna Do to you?" he said, among other things, taking care no lobster overheard. "What I'm gonna do, soon's all these Blue cats split, man, I'm gonna Take Care of You, baby. Real dirty an' slow-like, you dig?"

He went into it in whispered detail, drooling over every indignity and pain he had in store for me. I'd never realized that Laszlo had such a fertile imagination. He must've been working on this for years. I was worried.

Then the loft fell silent. Laszlo shut up. The lobsters were gone, all but Ktch, who stood, glimmering in his silver safety suit, by the door.

"We are ready now," he said.

"That's boss," said Laszlo, his little eyes twinkling.

"Come along, Laszlo Scott. Your services will be required. Come. Now."

"Me? But, *man*," distress, "don't you want, like, someone oughtta Look Out for this guy? I mean . . ."

"No. He will be all right here. Come."

Laszlo slowly wilted and went. "Downstairs now," the lobster told him. "Hurry."

Then, as Laszlo thudded down the stairs, "Farewell, Spy," Ktch said. "I hope you will not be harmed in the disturbances tonight. You have been a brave and worthy opponent. Now farewell," and he was gone, leaving the door slightly ajar behind him.

I had failed. I was still a prisoner, still attached to the torture machines (they were lit and humming, but I didn't feel anything, so they were probably on standby), still absolutely helpless. So much for saving the world.

Aside from the hum in front of me and a clocklike ticking behind me somewhere, the place was deathly still. Not even traffic noises could be heard.

Time passed.

Bang! from downstairs suddenly, the street door opening. Heavy feet started up the stairs.

Laszlo! I thought. I began to tremble. I tried to brace myself against the trembling, but it wouldn't stop.

The feet came closer, moving slowly and deliberately, and still closer. They were on the landing one floor down. They came slowly up the stairs. They were on this floor. The door flew open.

I screamed!

16

This is how Mike told me it happened, but I suppose it's close enough for jazz:

Michael awoke at half-past seven, after less than four hours' sleep, in the grumpiest mood imaginable. Swearing muddily, he turned off the three alarm clocks that'd been trying to rouse him since seven and clumped out to the living room to answer the vidiphone.

He stabbed fiercely at the Accept button, cutting the poor phone's whistle off in midtweet. Colors swirled briefly on the screen, and then a pretty face appeared.

"Seven thirty, Mister Cowland," she said sweetly, "rise and shine."

"Rise and *Shine*?" Mike was offended.

"This is the Midtown Wake-up Service," she said primly, "and you placed a call for seven thirty."

"*I* did?"

"Yes, sir."

"I must've been crazy."

"I'm sorry, sir, I can't tell you about that. Here's your card." She held it up to the screen.

Mike read the card in total disbelief until he came to the space marked Special Instructions, where the words, "Find Anderson," were printed in big block letters.

"Oh," he said. "Why didn't you say that?"

"You mean, 'Find Anderson'?"

"Yes."

"Well, it seemed rather silly . . ."

"Rise and Shine isn't silly?"

"Please, sir, I have other calls to make." She hung up.

Michael was now awake. Not particularly happy about it, but awake.

He burst into Sean's room, interrupting something, yelled "Find Anderson!" and dashed off to the kitchen to brew a pot of maté.

Sean stumbled into the living room, looking bewildered. Behind him, still in bed, Sativa yelled, "What's happening?"

"Hey, *man*," Sean complained, "find Anderson?"

"Right." Michael scurried off to shave.

By eight twenty they were strolling down Avenue A toward Laszlo's midden. "Man, this is Stupid," Sean was saying for the severalth time. "Laszlo, he ain't even Up yet."

"Cool it! Duck."

They ducked into a doorway. Sean started to say something, but Mike pressed his hand over Sean's mouth. Sean bit Michael's hand (there'd been no time for breakfast). Then Laszlo walked by, looking as displeased with the time of day as everybody else, and Sean let go.

"Oh," he whispered.

"We'll discuss this later," Mike snarled, rubbing his abused paw. "C'mon."

Laszlo was ridiculously easy to follow that morning. In fact, Mike told me, he and Sean could probably've walked right beside him without being noticed. He seemed to be two-thirds asleep, which made Mike feel considerably better.

The chase paused for fifteen minutes at a dingy diner where Laszlo presumably took on some breakfast, then went on in a relatively straight line to a century-old loft building at 239 Canal Street. Laszlo went inside, Sean and Michael waited outside. It was nine o'clock.

At nine fifteen Sean became impatient. "C'mon," he urged, "let's go in."

"Cool it. They may have a whole army in there."

"So what? We gotta help Chester, man. C'mon."

"We won't be much help if the Commies catch us, too. Listen to me, Sean. We wait another fifteen minutes, see? Watch who goes in or comes out. Right? Right. And if nothing happens before then, okay, we'll go over and take a look. But we've got to be Careful, you understand? These Reds are tough."

So at nine thirty they ducked and dodged across the street and, very cautiously, into the building. They stood in the lobby for a moment, catching their breath and listening. From above somewhere they could hear, faint but unmistakable, the sound of small arms fire.

"Oh wow!" said Mike.

"Too late?" Sean asked.

Then they heard the elevator painfully descending. They dashed to the door and out, just in time to see a large green turbo-truck pull up to the curb and park.

Sean said, "Wow!" and Mike agreed. There was nobody driving the truck.

Then the elevator reached the ground floor.

"C'mon! We've got to hide." Mike grabbed Sean by the arm and dragged him away.

In front of the building next door there were half a dozen empty plywood barrels, about five feet tall, all dirty and battered, one or two with small holes punched through them. Mike scrambled into one of these, Sean into another.

They regretted it at once. Somewhere along the line, the barrels had harbored fish, and the memory was still fresh and vigorous. But it was too late to find a less fragrant hiding place.

The front door of the loft building creaked open. Mike, holding his nose, crouched down and watched through a conveniently placed hole.

First a long, segmented stalk, cobalt blue, with a bulbous swelling at the end that Mike thought might be some kind of camera, snaked out and turned slowly to the left and right as though surveying the sidewalk. Then another stalk joined it and did the same. Then the side door of the truck slid open and a ramp extended itself to the sidewalk. The two stalks retracted themselves.

Then Michael gasped, inhaling an unhealthy lungful of essence of fish, as six huge lobsters emerged from the building. Two of them stood guard while the others formed a bucket brigade from the door to the truck. Fifty-gallon oil drums passed from claw to claw while Michael goggled.

After the oil drums came four large crates. Then the lobsters themselves, plus five more from inside the building, went into the truck.

The ramp stayed down and the door remained open, otherwise Mike would've run for the nearest phone booth to get help. Instead, he remained in his fishy hideaway until ten o'clock. The hot July sun beat down on him, the stench of ancient fish conspired to turn his stomach inside out, and the cramped position he was forced to maintain began to hurt his legs. He was an increasingly unhappy Theodore Bear.

At ten o'clock, Laszlo came out of the building, looked around nervously, and went back inside. Michael forgot his discomfort.

A few minutes later, Laszlo reappeared, scouted the sidewalk again, and said, "It's cool, man."

Out came yet another lobster, this one wearing a fetching little silver jacket.

"Youthful Laszlo," it said, "you shall ride in the driver's seat." It started up the ramp.

"But, man, like, I can't drive!"

"No matter. Get in."

Walking as though he were hypnotized, Laszlo got into the cab. He didn't look at all pleased, which comforted Michael slightly.

The ramp slid back into the truck and the door slid shut. The turbos started with a loud whine. Laszlo looked scared. Then the truck pulled smoothly away from the curb and drove off.

Mike and Sean exploded from the barrels, saying "Phew!" and, "Did you see That?" interchangeably.

"Lobsters," Mike said, unbelieving.

"That's good. I was scared it was *me*."

They dashed for the door, trailing clouds of glory as they went.

17

roovy!" I screamed when they burst in, and then went on more quietly: "You sure as hell took your own sweet bloody time about it, mister. What kept you?"

"Later," Michael Superspy was casing the joint, standing in the doorway looking very hot and paranoid.

Sean didn't bother. He plunged in like the puppy he was, yelping, "You okay, baby?" without waiting for an answer. "I did a Thing at The Mess last night an' they really Dug it, man. What're *these* things?"

He'd reached the torture machines. Michael was beginning to enter the room.

"Torture machines," I explained. "Leave them alone." I had plans for those gadgets. If they could just be stolen, I could make narcotics obsolete in Greenwich Village.

"Hmm. They're turned on." Michael had arrived. "How do you turn 'em off?"

I said, "God knows. Just leave 'em be, will you? I want to save them if I can. How about untying me?"

"Torture machines, you say?" Michael eyes them with a hungry look I didn't like at all.

"Come on, Michael, turn me loose."

"Maybe this red button here . . ."

"No! Cool it! Don't touch any . . ."

ZAP!

". . . thing."

Sparks—green, blue, scarlet, quite electrifying—flew from machine to machine, a depressingly gaudy display. The room suddenly stank of ozone. Sharp popping noises and loud bubbling hisses issued from the depths of the machines. Wisps of plaintive blue smoke rose into the air.

"No," Mike said, backing off, "I guess not."

I had nothing to say.

It was Sean who finally untied me. Mike was too engrossed in watching the machines destroy themselves to move.

I'll admit it was quite a show. As the rainbow sparks continued to fly and the smoke grew thicker, the machines began to glow dully, then to sag, and then to melt. Liquid metal gathered in small pools under the machines, and then ran slowly across the room, setting the ancient wooden floor afire.

My boots and briefcase were up against the rear wall, beside an open barrel half full of those well-known little blue pills. Impulsively, I filled the briefcase with pills, "Evidence," I explained to myself. Then I grabbed my boots and cut for the door.

Sean was there before me, looking just about as puzzled as usual, but Mike was still involved with the machines. "C'mon," I yelled. "Let's split, man."

The smoke was getting thicker, the ozone was stinging my nose and eyes, and the fires were beginning to crackle a lot. I didn't really want to stick around much longer. "Kurland!" I yelled again, but still Mike didn't move. Dropping my boots, I ran over and shook him. Hard.

"Oh," dazedly. "Sorry 'bout that."

He came peacefully.

Halfway down the stairs I remembered my boots. Too late. The fire was already roaring, and the fourth floor didn't seem to be a healthy place to visit anymore. Those boots'd always been too tight anyhow.

When we reached the street, Mike said, "Torture machines?" He was still pretty dazed.

"When I tell you about it, you'll cry," I promised. "Sean, why don't you hail us a cab?"

Once he'd caught a whiff of us, the cabby didn't want our business, but it was too late. We were already aboard and in motion. He turned his air conditioner up as high as it'd go and drove on, muttering Brooklynoid curses.

"Hey, you stink," I told Mike. He was coming out of his trance.

"That's cool. So do you. What happened?"

"When I tell you," I repeated, "you will weep." Then I told him.

I was still telling him when we pulled up in front of the pad. I gave the cabby a five without interrupting my report and didn't linger for the change. All the way up the stairs I talked and into the living room. Still talking, I tore off my stained and fragrant clothes and ran for the shower.

"Yeee!" Sativa screamed.

"Sorry." I jumped in. She yelped and jumped out. "My need is greater than thine," I explained. Then I went on with the report.

Mike took a shower next, and then Sean, so I remained in the bathroom, talking a blue and lobster-ridden streak.

When, mod-ishly garbed in paisley towels, we returned to the living room, I was still talking.

"Hmph!" Sativa snorted. "Men!" She stomped off to finish her bath. We sat down and I continued to talk. It was a long story.

I wound it up over my second plate of poached eggs and kelp. "And that's it. They're on their way to the reservoir now. What are we going to do?"

"Is it okay if I just, you know, go back to Fort Worth?"

Mike sniffed. Then, "We've got to stop them. Obviously."

"Groovy," I observed. "With what army?"

Sean said, "I'm gonna call the cops. Right now!"

"Cool it," Mike cooled him. "They'll never believe us. And all the evidence is going up in smoke, too. We just have to do it ourselves, that's all."

I repeated my question.

"Easy," he said. "There are how many—*twelve* of them, right?"

"Plus Laszlo."

"Twelve and a half then. So we'll get all our friends to help." He sounded perfectly rational—but *our* friends? "We'll outnumber them, for one thing. And we shouldn't have any trouble anyway, not if these lobster critters are as nonviolent as you claim they are."

"Oh, they're nonviolent, all right. But I don't know, Michael: *our* friends?"

"Who else?"

"You mean Andrew Blake? Gary the Frog? Our friends? Are you sure?"

"Well, some of our friends. I'll start calling them now."

18

ave you ever tried to talk a bunch of hippies into helping you save the world? Forget it. Next time I save the world, by Starky, I'm gonna do it solo. Easier that way, less work.

To begin with, it was a little after three on a warm summer's Wednesday afternoon, which meant that almost everyone was hanging out in Washington Square and almost no one was home to answer vidiphone calls. When you're trying to collect an army in a hurry, it slows you down something fierce if Andrew Blake's the only person you can reach by vidiphone.

"I don't believe it," Andrew told us several times. "You've all been taking chemicals. You're on a trip. It's pretty, but I don't believe a word of it."

That's the sort of thing that discourages people who'd otherwise be more than glad to save the whole world daily, twice on Sundays.

I tried to explain. I knew better, but I tried. "We're not *on* anything, Andy. We're not even high. This is really Happening, cross my heart. It's real. It's just like your halo, only worse."

"Halo?" His voice changed from bassoon to oboe. "What halo?"

So I gave up. When Andrew doesn't believe in something, he's thorough. I *did* persuade him to meet us at The Garden of Eden at five, though, which would've been an accomplishment if it weren't that he was planning to be there at five anyhow.

So we hit the street, the four of us. Sativa was now a member of the Army of Deliverance. While we were phoning, she'd had her daily mystical experience and decided it was her karma to save the world single-handed, but she was willing to let us come along and watch. Sativa always appreciates an audience.

Except for a half million strangers, St. Mark's Place was empty. We'd expected that. But we wasted half an hour in Tompkins Square discovering that *it* was empty too, which we hadn't expected. Tompkins Square was home turf for the Psychedelic Conspiracy that year, full of almost everyone we knew.

"Dere aw oba dere inna Village," the Good Humor Man growled. "Dere aw oba dere watchin'a bal*Lett*, y'unnastan? All dem dencers."

So Sativa, little Sean, and I trotted west on St. Mark's Place, moving much too quickly for the temperature and trying not to notice, and Mike cut out for the garage, two blocks away in the other direction, to pick up The Tripouts' bus.

That was our most treasured possession, that bus. It was an old Army surplus ground-effect troop carrier, made in 1969 or so and obsolete before delivery, that we'd converted into a mobile rock 'n' roll dream pad. It could seat sixteen and sleep dozens, depending on how friendly they were, and was equipped with hot and cool running everything. The roof was a sun deck, planted with grass and dandelions. The back third was a fully stocked practice studio, complete with battery-powered duplicates of our regular instruments that couldn't play as loudly as the real things but were otherwise quite satisfactory. We'd toured the Midwest in it last summer, getting citations for maintaining a nuisance (the blowers weren't too well shielded, and produced authentic hurricane effects uninterruptedly as long as the motors were on), disturbing the peace (the battery-powered instruments weren't all *that quiet*), and general suspicion (the bus was painted in the highest psychedelic style, even to glowing in the dark) in every town we passed through. It was a great old bus. Well, it'd do to get our army to the reservoir at least.

Washington Square contained one *avant-garde* ballet company—free-form antigrav dancing to memorized but unplayed music—one dissociated light show that couldn't quite cope with the afternoon sun, and the entire population of the Greater New York region. The piquant tang of caprylic acid hung over everything like a panning review.

We stopped in the uncrowded east side of the park and planned. "Separate," I told my trusty aides. "We'll work through the crowd individually, Otherwise we won't get through at all. Look for The People." That's what we called our expanded peer group in those days, when we were still a minority. "Tell them— it's four ten now—tell them to meet us in The Garden at five. Got that?"

They had it.

"Groovy. And be sure *you're* there at five, too. Don't forget."

They promised to be there.

"Then there's nothing left to tell you but Good Luck," I told them. Then I yelled, "Charge!" and we charged.

The Square was as jammed as a subway at rush hour. Everyone was pushed into the most intimate and compromising physical contact with everyone else whilst nervously pretending there was nothing going on—a kind of casually erotic situation of which I'm generally quite fond, but hell to hunt for people in. You can't push through such a press, you either have to climb over it (which will rapidly impair your popularity) or get down on your hands and knees and crawl through a forest of anonymous legs (not the best way to find specific people, unless you've made a fairly close study of legs.)

Naturally, I crawled. Sean, I later learned, tried the other approach, but was soon converted to mine. Anyhow, I crawled, and no one even tried to kick me. America is losing its spirit of fun.

By a winning blend of luck and intuition, I located Stewart Fiske and Pat Gerstein standing together near Holley's bust, just beyond the stage where all that unheard music was going on. Stu's boots didn't match—same color, nothing else the same—and Pat was barefooted.

I popped up in front of them, told them what was happening, explained as little as possible; and got them to promise to meet at The Garden. Then, after a quick look at the dancers—they were awful—I submerged again and went on with my search.

Sativa and Sean were going through much the same routine, with only minor variations. Sean, for instance, had his hand stepped on by a moderately ugly girl. "I think she done it on purpose, man. You know, like tryin' to strike up a conversation. Didn't hurt me none."

Sativa discovered three male teenyboppers squatting in a circle in the middle of the leg-forest, unconcernedly smoking what they firmly believed was marijuana, which was still illegal then. "They were nice. Pretty! They wanted to turn me on, but I told them I only smoke pot."

Michael, too, had his share of quaint adventures, wrestling the Tripsmobile—our bus—from the far east crosstown to MacDougal Street and fighting against impressive odds to park it within walking distance of The Garden.

"She's still got a tendency to try to go *over* traffic instead of through it. In fact, she got halfway up a police car before I caught on. I thought she was just being friendly."

Nevertheless, we were all safely established in The Garden of Eden's supercooled darkness by quarter to five, and almost everyone we wanted was either there or coming. It was really quite a feat, considering.

19

S eriously, Chester," droned the double reed of Andrew Blake, "What's this really all about? You can tell Me."

"Wait a bit." I was tired of repeating my long, involved story, and even more tired of trying to condense it for popular consumption. "Mike'll tell you all about it Just wait till five, okay?"

The Kallikak box was playing our old arrangement of "Love Sold in Doses," and I was trying to remember the arrangement I'd pulled on Ktch and his fellow crustaceans last night, but I couldn't. In fact, I couldn't even remember the tune, not even while I was listening to it. This was a very odd sensation.

"Chester? Mr. Anderson?" That sweet and worried voice belonged to Karen Greenbaum, who was still going around in not quite circles with Saint Andrew, though by now you'd think she'd know better. "Is something wrong?"

"Wrong?"

"You look so—funny. You know."

"Oh. I'm just trying to remember something that I know too well to recall."

That seemed to satisfy her.

The Garden was full of our people, a professionally motley crew, with more coming in all the time. It was rather flattering to see how large a crowd our people were. I mused idly that it would pay some Village businessman to open a coffeehouse catering pretty exclusively to our crowd, then I remembered that that's what The Garden of Eden was and gave up musing for Lent. It was three minutes to five.

I turned to Michael the Theodore Bear and said, "Do you have some kind of speech worked out?" He looked worried. If it were anyone else, I'd say he looked nervous.

"That's the trouble," he fretted. "I've got *three* of 'em, and I don't know which one to use."

"Don't sweat it. You'll probably have a chance to use 'em all."

Sean and Sativa were holding hands and things, oblivious to the crowd and The Garden and Sativa's current karma—unless maybe Sean was part of that—an island of horny serenity in a lake of curious hipsters. Stu, Pat, and Kevin were huddled off in a nearby corner singing four-part harmony.

Four-part harmony? That brought me up. Oh: they had Little Micky with them. It's fairly hard to see Little Micky when there's anybody else in the room, unless you're looking for him. He's quite small. (He was also singing flat, which made him even harder to see.)

Sandi Heller and her old man Leo were sifting with a bunch of people named David several tables away from mine. Leo was grinning like a dentist's testimonial. Sandi, assisted by years of drama study and dance experience, was totally failing to communicate with me by means of beautifully expressive gestures and neat pantomimes. Nicely picturesque.

"What's happening?" I yelled to her when it became obvious that she really *did* want to tell me something.

"Mutter jumble mutter garble Baby," she explained.

"Oh."

And then it was five o'clock. Joe pulled the plug on the kallikak box, which had next to no effect on the noise level of the room. Michael, having previously obtained permission to do so, climbed up on the table. He spread his hands wide like an old-time revivalist and said, "Ladies and gentlemen!" in stentorian toones I'd never before suspected he possessed.

Nothing happened.

He said it again, even more loudly, and nothing continued to happen. Somehow he wasn't communicating. He tried it again, to be fair, and when it didn't work that time either, he puffed out his chest, stood on tiptoe, arched his spine, threw back his head, opened his mouth too wide, and hollered, "COOL IT!" so loudly the whole room rang like a cymbal.

Instant silence.

Highly gratified and showing it, Mike launched into whatever speech he settled on, but most unusually oddly. His mouth moved convincingly, his gestures seemed apt and well chosen, but no sound came out. This lasted for what would have been one and a half sentences, during which his face went through an amazing series of changes on the general theme of absolute dismay. Then he bent over, brought his lips as close to my ear as he could without exciting comment, and whispered tunelessly, "You tell them. I can't talk. Lost my voice." I was careful not to laugh.

So I got up on the table, waited for Michael to get down and some whispering to fade, and then with great solemnity said, "Laszlo Scott has finally gone and done it."

I told them about the invasion, playing Laszlo up and the lobsters down. They knew Laszlo, after all, and were ready to believe anything villainous of him, even to consorting with blue lobsters that they wouldn't've believed in otherwise. I dwelt at length on the horrible consequences of turning everybody on to the Reality Pill.

"Remember what happened last Saturday? Butterflies and chaos and confusion and the National Guard and what have you? Remember that? And that was just a handful of people high, less than a dozen. I mean, all it took was one cat from Texas to make all those butterflies!

"Now, what if Everyone was like that? The whole city of New York, ten million people, all of 'em high on Reality Pills at the same time. And it only took one cat to make all those butterflies. Think about that."

A few of them whistled approvingly at the notion, but then it sank in. They didn't like the idea any more than I did. It's nice to have friends who think the way you do.

Then I told them what the lobsters were planning to do, heavily stressing Laszlo's willing treason against the human race. I don't think I ever quite mentioned that the lobsters looked like lobsters. "Nonhumanoid blue aliens," is the closest I recall coming to a description of them, Laszlo or not, this particular audience might think that giant blue talking lobsters were a bit too much to be believed.

I was speaking quite rapidly, but very clearly and with great intensity, and I had the crowd in the palm of my hand all the way. Indeed, I was doing much better than I had any right to expect. Even Andrew Blake looked about to be convinced.

So I swung into a glowing peroration, saying—almost chanting—"And no one in the whole world knows what's happening but *us!* Nobody's hip enough to believe it but *us!* By the time anybody else can figure out what's happening it'll be too late for everyone.

"We're all alone with this thing, babies, and here is where it's at: We-Have-Got-To-Save-The-World-Ourselves! Us! Save the world from Laszlo Scott! Save . . ."

That's as far as I got. They were cheering and yelling and shouting things, and it didn't seem worth my while to go on. I'd been talking for under ten minutes.

I bent down and said, "Hey, Michael, voice back yet?"

"Just about." Actually, not quite. He could be heard, but his voice sounded tattered and shopworn.

"I didn't mean to get them all so excited," I said. "I just wanted to get enough volunteers to fill the bus. Now what'll we do?"

"Pick," his voice was really pitiful, "and choose. Tell the rest to alert the authorities."

"Groovy. That'll keep 'em hopping."

And that's the way we did it. When the noise died out, I recruited the mixed bag of warriors Mike and I had tried to phone a few hours back, sixteen head including ourselves, and sent the rest, some forty-five or fifty, jabbering hippies, out to warn the unsuspecting world.

And then it was five forty-five, ninety minutes till sunset and darkness.

"It's time, gentlemen, it's time," said Michael, beginning to regain some vocal strength. "Let's get moving." And off we went.

"Hey, Andy," Joe stopped me at the cash register. "Jeez, that was really Some Show you put on there, Andy. Honest to God."

"You liked it?"

"*Like* it? You was Great, Andy. Great. I ain't never heard nothin' like that in my whole life. Jesus Christ! You know what? You almost got Me believin' all that stuff. Honest to God!"

"Well, gee, Joe. I'm—well, I'm just Glad you liked it."

"Like it? Tell you what: you had a cuppa coffee, right? An' it's onna house. It's on me. *That's* how much I like it, see?"

And so I went off to the war feeling just a bit foolishly good about things.

20

I t wasn't until we'd pushed our way through a ring of gawking teenyboppers and boarded the much admired Tripsmobile that I stopped feeling foolishly good and started worrying properly once more. I realized, while Mike was warming up the motors and getting them in sync, while our unshielded air cushion side-blast was scattering tourists left and right like brightly colored shrieking leaves, while all this noise and busyness was happening . . . I realized that we'd now done everything we'd *planned,* back at the house, and that no one, least of all us, knew what to do next.

We were going to the Croton Reservoir. Sure. And there we were going to prevent Ktch and Laszlo and their buddies from pouring six hundred gallons of that fiendish reality drug into the city's drinking water. Sure.

It was all so simple until you wondered how. I was wondering how. Also with what. And worrying like a pro.

To begin with, we had our little army: sixteen standard Greenwich Village heads and hipsters of various kinds—except that there were two empty seats, so we had fourteen, not sixteen. We hadn't even started yet, but already we'd lost two men—which worried me—and I couldn't remember *which* two—which worried me more. And of the fourteen fighters we had left, one was Little Micky, who wasn't even on the list. That meant we'd lost *three* men, and I was thoroughly confused.

What an army. Besides Michael, Sean, Sativa, and myself, we had the rest of the band: lovable Stewart Fiske, a hundred pounds of muscle and ten pounds of hair on a six-foot-three-inch skeleton he must have bought at Sears and put together

146

in his spare time by himself, whose purple buckskin jacket was almost buried under buttons saying "End the War in Israel" *et al,* a less than awesome warrior whose gentleness was so complete we'd had to amplify his drums;

And playful Patrick Gerstein, an authentic human puppy wholly dedicated to romping—through pastures of cannabis, through female populations, through psychedelic fun houses and rock 'n' roll music rants—sturdy enough that he might be able to fight if he could want to, but impossible to imagine wanting to, a constant laughter without even a temper to lose—some warrior;

And Kevin Anderson, no kin of mine, who had the best furnished mind and longest kinkiest hair in Greenwich Village, plus a well-designed and carefully developed body, but whom I'd seen paralyzed with terror before a pugnacious twelve-year-old punk from New Jersey less than a week ago.

(While I was taking this worried inventory, the tourists and teenyboppers outside the Tripsmobile started jeering and making sarcastic cracks about windbags, beatniks and what have you, adding embarrassment to my worry, and a cop started walking toward us with clearly less-than-friendly intent. There were six motors, you see, and if they weren't properly synchronized, the bus would be, to say the least, unstable. And *this,* naturally, was the time Mike had to have trouble getting them in sync. All of this hassle just to save the world.)

I wasn't much of a fighter, either, and Michael—though I supposed he could if he had to—was basically more the undercover type. Any cover. Sativa, on the other hand, might actually be dangerous in a fight, if only because her gleaming nails were an inch and a half long.

Sean, being a Texan and all—healthy, strong, and all that jazz—was probably pretty good with his fists. Texas kids still tended to be sluggers in those days. But there were so many ways that he wasn't a typical Texan, who could be sure? Still, he might be a fighter.

Groovy. That's one.

(The cop was closer now, having trouble pushing through the crowd. Good old crowd. A ticket—the least I was prepared to expect from him—would cost us a good fifteen minutes, and we were running out of time. But Mike, cursing blandly, was adjusting the motors in a leisurely manner that threatened fair to overload my worry circuits.

(Then—BanG KlunK, ROAR—the motors suddenly meshed. The Tripsmobile rose its full eighteen inches from the pavement, the crowd cheered cynically, the cop looked disappointed, and we floated away up Sixth Avenue. But I continued to worry, of course.)

The band and Sean, alas, were the cream of our little army. The rest . . . words fail me. Look at them.

There was Andrew Blake, looking as though he weren't quite sure what he was doing in our company and most likely feeling the same. He might easily talk the lobsters to death, given time, or con them out of their evil scheme and everything else they owned, but he'd never impressed me as having any native gift for violence.

Karen Greenbaum, I decided, could be counted on to faint at the sight of almost any six-foot-tall blue lobster.

Little Micky was crazy enough to be, perhaps, pound for pound a real ferocious critter, but he didn't have pounds enough to matter much. I mean, he could doubtless lick anything his size, but he was only five feet tall and undernourished, and I couldn't offhand think of anything his size that needed licking.

Sanci Heller and Leo might be dangerous as a team, he being strong and wiry and she being a dancer, unless they happened to flip out, which they both tended to do from time to time, usually together. And if what she told me in The Garden ("Mutter jumble mutter garble Baby," with gestures) meant what I feared it might, the odds were she was pregnant and all bets were off.

(This catalog of worries didn't take as long to make as it's taking to tell. A moment's glance at each face was sufficient, and I'd ordinarily spare you all these personal details, but I think you ought to know what we had to work with. Why should I be discouraged all by myself when I can bring you along for company? And the action later on will much more nearly make sense if you know who's doing it, perhaps.)

But the thing that really worried me was this: as long as we had this busload of question marks to begin with, wherefore I was going into battle feeling more like a keeper than a general, why in God's personal name did our army have to include Gary the Frog and Harriet? Oh, I knew how we got them. Mike and I called them in on this out of habit, because we call them in on everything.

But Gary the Frog was anemic, full of parasites, extravagantly stupid, and a coward, and Harriet weighed more than three hundred pounds and had barely strength enough to climb a flight of stairs. This we needed?

Furthermore, Gary the Frog and Harriet *liked* Laszlo Scott (a chilling concept). In fact, they were even *friends* of his. He was one of their heroes. Ten to one they were on his side. I couldn't help thinking that, though there wasn't much they could do *for* us, if they wanted to help Laszlo, there was a hell of a lot they could do *to* us. What business did we have carrying Laszlo's spies into action with us?

I was runner-up last year in the World's Championship Worrying Contest at Poughkeepsie, but I think the winner cheated.

21

Michael," I said, taking care not to let the others hear me, "Michael, I'm worried."

"Swell." He was riding the controls like a cowpoke on a bronco, strenuously, almost fighting them. The two steering levers moved like willful live things trying to escape him. Mike struggled with them grimly. Sweat, a rare sight, stood in beads on his upper lip and brow, ready to pour down his face at any moment.

Groovy, said my worrying machine. Mike's having trouble keeping the bus under control. We're in trouble. Hell, we're doomed.

"What are you worried about?" He didn't look at me when he spoke—a bad sign.

"What's wrong with the bus?" I asked, neatly putting first things first.

"Nothing. Nothing at all. Running like a . . . like a bus. What makes you think there's something wrong with the bus?" He didn't sound concerned, but I was not deceived.

"Why do you have to fight so hard to keep it under control? What's wrong with it? C'mon, tell Uncle Chester."

"Fight?" Now he looked at me: one of his prime puzzled looks. Then, "Oh. I'm not fighting. Look."

He relaxed. The steering levers stopped having a life of their own. The bus continued to ride as smoothly as before. Oh yeah?

"Explain?" I said unpleasantly.

"I was just playing astronaut." He had the grace to grin sheepishly. "You know, landing the capsule and all that."

"Playing astronaut."

"I didn't realize it'd bother you. Sorry."

"Great."

"That what had you worried?"

"In part. Look . . ." I itemized our fighting crew's deficiencies in some poetic detail, devoting lots of extra fine rhetoric to the untrustworthiness of Gary the Frog. He listened to it all as politely as he could—intent sufficing for the deed—but devoted most of his attention to driving. We were in the midst of the usual traffic jam at 36th Street, and the bus was trying to mount the car ahead of us. This would've been impolitic. It was another police car. Our bus had amazingly strong preferences.

When I finished, Michael said, "Are you finished?" and I said I was.

"Swell. Now stop worrying." I started to object, but he went on. "Believe me," he said with galling patience, "I understand what you're worried about. I know why you're worried. But there's nothing to worry about, honestly. I've got it all figured out, really I do, and it doesn't much matter whether they can fight or not. As soon as we get out of this damn traffic I'll explain it to you, okay?"

I was dubious and said so.

"Why don't you go back and play your harpsichord?" he shrugged me off. "And don't worry about it."

There's not much can be done with Michael when he acts like that, so, trying hard not to worry, I shuffled to the back of the bus and sat down at my little solid state harpsichord.

En route, I collected another worry. We had nothing to fight *with*. No weapons. The closest thing to a weapon that we had, in fact, was my briefcase, which might be good to swing in a crowd but wasn't likely to make much of an impression on a hard-shelled blue lobster. But Mike had probably taken the lack of weapons into account, too. I carefully worried as little as I could and tried to play *The Carman's Whistle.*

(The trouble with letting Michael manage things is that three times out of five he takes everything into account, and two times out of five he doesn't, and there's no way to tell which he's done this time until things start to hit the fan. When his managing works, it works very very well, but when it doesn't, you notice. Boy, do you notice!)

The Carman's Whistle attracted Stu, Pat, and Kevin. They filtered back to the practice area, grabbed their axes, and wailed. We segued instantly into "Songwind," an incomprehensibly poetic, hyperromantic, hard-driving modal rock tune we were hoping to hit the charts with.

I played bass with my left hand and raga riffs with my right, Stu beat out something like a demented sixteen-stroke tala, Pat played poignant lead lines based on the *Kyrie cum Jubilo,* Kevin's twelve-string provided architectural solidity, I forgot to worry, and Sativa came back to sing.

> The lines cut into my life like poems,
> The changes howl at my defenses:
> All the winds of chance are humming daydreams
> And the cold year turns upon the wind.

We were deliberately being influenced by the *1 Ching* and Subud, a combination we thought singularly hip at the time.

By the end of the first verse, between 38th and 39th Streets, everyone but Mike was sitting cross-legged in a large semicircle around the band. Little Micky was muttering, "Oh wow! Dig it, baby! Wow! Oh, dig that, man!" under his breath as he usually did. Sean was watching Pat's left hand like a rabbit watching a snake. Lots of people were smiling and nodding in time, and Gary the Frog was lighting up a joint.

I thought next to nothing of this at the time. It didn't seem at all odd or out of place. People are always lighting joints at band rehearsals. I remember being a bit surprised that Gary the Frog had his own grass for a change, but I didn't think twice about the grass itself, and when the joint came to me, I took a good hearty toke before swinging into the second verse.

> The darkness has become a form of waiting.
> The wise dead men shall grow upon the wind
> of opening; the dead shall turn
> and bloom on the sundering wind.

Mike had somehow managed to get us to Broadway and 42nd, Times very own Square. It was early evening, clear, warm, and summer, so the Square was packed past endurance with all manner of machines and funny-looking people, and traffic was moving by appointment only and as seldom as the laws of chance allowed. And there we were, motionless and grooving, stuck in the very middle of it all.

We attracted a crowd instantly. Even when it's empty, the Tripsmobile gets a lot of staring at and gawking. With the band on board and playing, we were a free show, a very swinging free show, and everyone who could hear us—almost everyone—had suddenly nothing on his mind but getting close enough to *see* us, too.

And so the crowd gathered. I didn't mind. I like crowds— especially when I'm playing. I've often said that playing without an audience is just a form of aural masturbation. So I smiled at the people outside and they smiled back at me, they waved at me and I nodded at them, and I felt in general absolutely great.

Then somebody passed me the joint.

Once again my poor mind boggled under the strain. (Mind boggling was becoming a habit with me.) There in my right hand was an incredibly illegal marijuana cigarette. There, just a few feet away, were tens of thousands of strangers and countless cops—witnesses!—who had watched that criminal cigarette pass from hand to hand around the bus, to end up in my very own newly moist and lightly trembling paw. This was clearly not a healthy situation.

I knew better than to stop playing, or do anything else that might call outside attention to the seven-year sentence I had in my hand. Instead, I palmed the joint—burning my palm in the process—and staggered into the least sincere third verse I've ever played.

> The high wheel turned a stormwind and the wise
> Were powerful against it, and they died.
> Who could predict the new life tearing
> On the merciful claws of the wind?

We were still there. All those people were still there. The smoldering joint was still in my right hand. There didn't seem to be any way to get rid of the damned thing. If I dropped it, people would notice. If I just put it down on the top of my harpsichord, oh so very casually, it would be agressively visible for miles around. I didn't have any pockets loose enough to get into in the scant free time "Songwind" allowed my right hand. So I took the standard, traditional out—something I'd never had occasion to do before—and, with a gesture faster than snake tongues, I popped the joint into my mouth.

It was still burning. So was I, but I didn't dare show it. I extinguished the joint with saliva and undertook to swallow it, while the first verse reprise rolled past without my hearing it.

It seems that cigarettes aren't all that easy to swallow, not even little skinny marijuana cigarettes. It wouldn't go down whole, wouldn't dream of it, so I soaked it and chewed at it and broke it up fine. But a mouthful of loose pot isn't a snap to swallow, either. The stuff has—or this stuff had—the texture of rough sand, gritty and hard, with tiny sharp edges. No amount of saliva soaking seemed to soften it perceptibly, and my throat was reluctant to have anything to do with it, but by the time we'd finished "Songwind," I'd managed to get the stuff down and was able, aside from a convulsive racking cough, to breathe freely once again.

And then I saw Gary the incredible Frog getting ready to light yet another joint! He picked the damnedest times to be affluent.

"Gary," I said gently, "please put that away."

"Had enough?"

He was ready to say more, but I didn't let him. "I never have enough," I said, still gently, "but put that thing away just the same.

He stared at me as though I'd lost my entire mind, and made no move to put away the joint. By then he was the only person there who hadn't noticed what was happening. The silence of horror had frozen every tongue but his.

"If you don't want no more, that's cool," he gibbered, affronted, "but *I* want some more, if you don't mind."

I remained gentle. "Look around," I invited. He did, reluctantly. He looked around twice, in fact. At last it began, slowly, to dawn on him. His jaw dropped with an audible click.

"Now then," still very gently, "put that goddamn thing away before I shove my boot down your stupid throat. Understand?"

He panicked, of course, but he put the joint away. I didn't think his panic hurt us much. Gary the Frog's the kind of creep whose panics go unnoticed.

Then everybody started breathing. "Wow!" they all said, and went on talking. It sounded like lunchtime at your local junior high. I scurried to the front of the bus to relate the gory incident to Mike.

I needn't have bothered. He was having gory incidents of his own.

22

And what do you *call* this thing, now?" The Man was
standing tall and grim beside Mike's seat: an extravagantly
Irish cop just dying to arrest himself a whole truckload of
Us. (I've never really adjusted to policemen.)

"Right now?" Michael was being a wiseass, naturally. He
liked to get away with things. Any things.

"Oh, Michael," I cautioned softly.

The cop gave me a disapproving glance. The two cops
waiting on the steps gave me disapproving glances. The two or
three cops waiting outside made it unanimous. Cops make me
nervous.

The rest of the tribe hadn't noticed our uniformed visitors
yet, which was a blessing of sorts. They were all clustered about
Gary the Frog, telling him in redundant detail exactly how
uncool he was. Just a waste of redundant detail, that's all, but a
harmless enough pastime for the nonce.

"What *do* yez call this thing?" The Man rumbled.

"You mean the bus?"

"Oh, it's a bus, is it? You got a license to operate a bus?"

"License?" Mike hesitated. "But we just *call* it a bus, officer. I
mean, it isn't a *real* bus; it's more like a very big station wagon, if
you get what I mean. That is . . ." He ran down. The policeman
was unmoved.

The cops on the steps were committing the contents of
Michael's wallet to memory, which must have been interesting for
them, not to mention educational. Mike's wallet was always well
stocked with oddball ID—a National Association of Warlocks,
Conjurers, and Wizards membership card, for instance.

The outside cops were risking windburn for a look at the Tripsmobile's underside. Their hats went flying in our portable gale, and well-brought-up, clean-cut, healthy patriotic little kids caught them and brought them proudly back to be blown away again.

And the Irish cop inside had a larger-than-life-size expectant look that turned my central nervous system to silly putty. I became unhappily aware of a strong scent of pot smoke in the air.

"Doomed," I consoled myself. "Twice doomed. Gary the goddamm Frog is holding, and Laszlo and the lobsters are already waiting by the reservoir. So we're busted and we're dead. Groovy. Nothing else can possibly go wrong." I was being grateful for small comforts.

"Ah, Officer," Mike politely hinted, "could you tell me what we've done, please?"

"Done what?"

"I mean, why did you stop us? What've we done wrong?"

I could've mentioned a thing or two, but I left it up to The Man.

"Got 'is license there?" The Man asked The Men on the steps. One of them, the youngish spade, shook his head bewilderedly and passed The Man a bulging handful of paper.

"What's all *this* crap?"

"Them's his license, Sergeant."

"*All* of 'em?"

"Yes, sir. Every one."

"Hmmm." The sergeant didn't like it, but he accepted the wad of papers and started memorizing them. After each license, he granted Mike a glower of appalling sincerity.

"State of Hawaii operator's license."

"That's right, Officer. I used to live . . ."

"Delaware chauffeur's license?"

"You see, I had this job and . . ."

"Arizona private pilot's license, expired."

"That was when I . . ."

"*Two* New Hampshire motorcycle licenses?"

"I thought I lost . . ."

"What the hell is *this*?"

"Oh, that's my Russian driver's license. I was . . ."

"Russian, eh?"

"Yes, sir."

"Hmmm."

It struck me that Michael was cooking our goose with driver's licenses. The Man, frowning bitterly, seemed to agree.

"US Army driver's license, Indiana learner's permit, Wisconsin helicopter pilot's license . . . You move around a lot, don't you boy."

"Yes, sir, but I . . ."

"Jesus, Mary and Joseph! What's *this*? A New York ground-effect vehicle operator's license? Mother of God! And what in the name of God is a Ground-Effect Vehicle?"

"This is. Look . . ." Mike got up and led The Man outside for a short lecture on the ground effect. The remaining cops obviously expected me to make a break for it, but they were ready. I was something less than comfortable.

By now the rest of our brave little band was well aware of the men in blue. Gary the unspeakable Frog was gratifyingly pale, and the others were talking in half-whispers and avoiding rapid movements. The outside cops were clearing the crowd away, but the traffic didn't appear to be moving yet.

I noticed all this though a thick gray smog of quick, inevitable doom.

But Mike's lecture didn't really last forever, and when they came back in The Man was saying, "I still think I oughtta run the lot of yez in," which might be called encouraging, perhaps.

His argument for running the lot of us in was that our attendant hurricane was a clear and present traffic hazard. Michael, far more confident since his lecture, conceded this possibility, but pointed out that the bus was a duly licensed ground effect vehicle, claimed that the wind, being integral to the vehicle, was obviously implicit in the license and sanctioned by the issuance thereof. Michael had his moments.

The shaken Man's next argument was that he oughtta run us all in because we were funny-looking and suspicious characters. Mike countered by claiming that we were a professional rock 'n' roll band in full stage dress, en route to a gig, and that he was our manager (proving this by yet another weird document from his wallet). He was ready to go on, but:

"All right! All right!" The Man gave in. "All right! So get the hell outta here!" He showed clear signs of discontent.

"Right away, Sergeant," burbled Michael. "Thank you, Sergeant."

"Yeah. An' just make sure you keep your nose clean 'round here, you understand?"

Mike agreed to everything. The Man very gradually split, trailing admonitions in his wake. At last Mike closed the door. Traffic started moving. So did we.

"Oh wow!" said I to Michael, "what a copper-bottomed drag!" He grunted mild agreement.

"I thought for sure we'd had it that time. Wow!"

"The trouble with you, Chester, is that you're afraid of cops. You don't seem to understand: they're on *your* side. You lack faith, that's *your* problem. Like, what made you think that tired old sergeant was going to arrest us?"

"Well, for one thing, Gary the Frog's holding. Copiously. And some of it's been smoked—in plain sight of everyone in Times Square, mind you—and the whole bus reeks of burning marijuana. Why *didn't* he bust us. All he had to do was inhale."

"Like I said, Chester, you just lack faith. Here we have an old Irish cop in New York City. So there are two things you can count on his having: varicose veins and sinus trouble. Especially sinus trouble. He probably hasn't smelled a thing since 1933."

Mike's right. I don't have faith.

And there we were, moving fast up West Side Highway. The sun was sinking, time was growing short, but we were on our way at last. Maybe there was hope.

23

After exhaustively not settling the problems of battle plan and weapons—"Just have faith," was M. T. Bear's refrain—we reached the reservoir with less than fifteen minutes to spare—not to spare, rather: we still had to find out where the enemy was lurking.

It was twilight—blue shadows, red and name-it sky, little wisps of fog hovering gold above the water and tabby-gray under the trees—as pastoral a scene as you could ask. I suppose it was beautiful—it usually is—but I knew a bit too much to enjoy it properly.

"Hold on," Michael shouted. "Here we go!"

The bus angled steeply up the bank, bumped and tottered over the top, hurtled down the other side, then glided smooth and easy as you please across the water on beds of raging foam.

Al the chicks and Gary the unmentionable Frog screamed shrilly as we plunged over the bank. Patrick Gerstein hollered, "Yippee!" on the way down, and all of us said, "Oh wow!" when we floated out over the water.

"Now how do we find them?" I inquired respectfully. Mike was now officially in charge.

"Don't have to," highly pleased. "I know exactly where they are."

He piloted us mainly north, threading neatly through a cluster of inconsequential islands, while his look of smug self-confidence all but glowed.

"Back when I was in high school," he explained with somewhat indecent delight, "I had this plot to dose the reservoir with LSD." He almost never called it acid. "Never *did* get around to doing it, though. Got involved with some chick instead." Pause. "Hell! I've forgotten her name. How about that? She was my first girl, too, if you don't count my cousin Sheila—and you wouldn't if you knew her, believe me. And now I can't even remember her name. Let's see . . ."

He was quite capable of carrying on like that all night if no one stopped him, so I stopped him. "What about your acid plot?"

"Oh yeah, that. Well, the first thing I did, of course, was scout the reservoir for a base to" work from. I needed a place that was convenient to the road but well hidden—a wooded ravine or gully, say—with enough room for whatever equipment I might need, plus easy access to the water, like a sheltered beach or inlet. Found it, too. There's just one place hereabouts that's suitable for this kind of action, and we're headed straight toward it now."

It was getting dark, but I could see the place he meant ahead of us: a low beach leading into a willow-choked ravine.

Then, "Michael?" a bassoon implored. Andrew Blake had joined us.

"Yes, Andy?"

"We're nearly there."

"Right."

"Yes. I've been wondering."

"What about?" Mike reduced speed. The bus crawled toward the hostile beach.

"We're planning to, ah, Fight these creatures. Right?"

"Right."

"Yes. But how? We don't even have a gun." It was nice to see somebody else worrying about that.

"Don't need guns, believe me. We've got the perfect weapon, Andy. Just relax."

"What weapon?" We were getting closer to the shore. It looked deserted.

"Why am I the only person who can think around here?" Mike snapped. Andy recoiled in alarm. "Think, Andy, think! We already have the perfect weapon. You've seen it yourself. Now just think about it."

The odds were forty-nine to fifty-one that Michael's perfect weapon was essentially bull, quite unbeknownst to him, of course, but it was worth thinking about. I'd rather think about that than the withering tide of alien annihilation I expected to stream out at us from under those suspiciously innocent-looking willows. The perfect—Oh.

Andy had it, too, and stuck an index finger up to mark it. "Of course!" he said in wonder. "Of course!"

"Sure," I ratified. "The bus."

"What else?"

What else indeed? The bus could go almost everywhere, over almost any obstacle, and its down blast was strong enough to turn even the biggest lobster into sky-blue library paste. But somehow I couldn't feel as certain about it as Michael felt. A weapon, yes. Even a good weapon, yes. But perfect? Or even very good? I didn't know yet what they were, but I knew in my bones there were serious flaws to Michael's perfect weapon. At least one of these was that we didn't know what kind of weapons the lobsters were likely to use.

Besides, I'm just not built to put much trust in perfect anythings. The word *perfect* seems to turn me off somehow.

We were now just a few yards offshore, cruising slowly back and forth parallel to the beach. The whole scene still looked thoroughly deserted, and I entertained the possibility of Michael's having goofed.

The MacDougal Street Commandos had deserted their seats to bunch up at the shoreward windows, stampeding from one side to the other every time Mike turned the bus around. This complicated driving considerably, but Mike didn't say anything about it. Most unusual for him.

"I don't see nothing," from Gary the Frog. "You see anything, Harry?"

"Not a thing, sugar lump." God in heaven!

"Me too," says Brother Gerstein. All the rest chimed in.

Now that we were actually there, I found myself feeling uncomfortable in a different, more practical way. The trouble was, I couldn't *hear* anything. Nothing important, anyhow. Thanks to my absurd myopia (20/300), I've never been much of a visual cat. In fact, I'm more of an ear man, which is convenient, since I hear better than just about everyone I've ever met. But now my hearing was being sorely handicapped.

In our present situation, with night coming on strong and all, straining my eyes to see a hypothetical blue lobster in an almost black shadow didn't make much sense, but if I'd been able to hear properly, I'd've known in a minute if the lobsters were out there, and if they were, exactly where they were hiding. A muffled claw click, willow leaves brushing against a carapace— such tiny, all but inaudible noises would've told me all I needed to know.

But I couldn't hear. The mingled roars of the bus's props and engines drowned out everything but fairly loud talk inside the cabin. Right. So much for perfect weapons.

And it was now quite dark. Mike switched on the headlights and the movable high-powered spotlights and lashed the beach with strands of brightness. Still nothing to be seen.

"Hey, baby"—Little Micky speaking for the first time since Times Square—"we got, like, the wrong address. You dig? We . . ."

He froze with his eyes opened wider than his mouth, staring out the window behind me and beginning to shake just a little bit. As I was turning around, one of the girls—don't know which one—issued a staccato shriek that was a good bit more convincing than the customary sostenuto job. Someone else, also unidentified, keeled over with a sonorous thump.

Now I could see it, too, standing gold and scarlet there in unearthly power and brute splendor on the beach that just a clock-tick back was utterly deserted.

It was roughly twelve feet tall, essentially saurian, overwhelmingly carnivorous. But it had three toothy heads, all evil, each on its own long, muscular, sinuous neck, and at least six limbs—two big ones at the bottom, two slimmer but incredibly powerful-looking ones at the bottom of its rib cage if it had one, and two small and maybe not very strong short ones at the top, all ending in unusually large numbers of long, battle-sharp talons. It looked like a red Tyrannosaurus rex with lots of optional equipment.

I couldn't for the life of me figure out why and how it had three heads. I should think one would suffice, and be a full day's work to manage, too. But what kind of environment would favor multiple heads? None I'd willingly imagine.

With a liquid, terrifying motion, the beast aimed two of those heads at us. The third, held high, slowly turned from side to side, ignoring us completely. So: a built-in sentry.

One of the heads roared at us. Then another one joined in, not on the same pitch but a pretty good fifth above. The two roars merged in a subbass sonority that shook our bones. Then the third head joined the chorus and I fell down and blacked out. There are some disadvantages to being an ear man.

When I came to, we were cruising thirty yards offshore. The thing was gone.

"Don' know where he went to, baby," Little Micky reported. He just jumped straight up and forgot about the comedown, dig, it, man?"

Despite the air conditioning, the bus was growing warm. The beast's triple roar had powdered our windows.

Sandi and Harriet had fainted and were still out of it. Sativa was wandering blankly, saying, "Ohh." I wondered if she'd had second thoughts about her daily karma.

Gary the inevitable Frog seemed to have vanished. For a wild instant I thought he'd been devoured, and then I remembered where, knowing Gary, he must be. Sure enough, when I opened the toilet door, there he was, in a sadly unaesthetic condition from having reached the john an inch too late but otherwise undamaged.

Leo was hovering over Sandi, somehow clucking but unharmed. Andrew Blake was muttering to himself, or maybe God, or both, in execrable Latin. Karen was holding his hand. Apparently she hadn't fainted. Very odd.

Pat and Stu were as excited as kids at an earthquake and kept asking one another, "Did *you* see it, man? Did you *really* see it?" Kevin was serenely manufacturing quaint theories to explain the thing. Little Micky was at a window, waiting for the next event.

Everyone was basically all right, so I went forward to confer with Mike.

"Perfect weapon, Mike?" I teased unfairly.

"Hey, I thought you said these lobster men were nonviolent."

"They are. But they don't object to anything else's being violent, if that's its nature. And if something like that triple dinosaur happens to get violent at us, well, that's our affair—and the dinosaur's—and doesn't concern Ktch and company at all. That's how *they* explain it, anyhow."

"Oh."

"But I don't think they meant to let that creature hurt us any. You noticed that they got rid of it the instant it jumped. They just wanted to scare us, that's all."

"Swell. They sure know how to get what they want, don't they?"

"Generally."

From the rear floated treble snatches of, "Oh dear God! I *saw* it! Oh my!" which meant that Sandi was conscious again and functioning normally.

"How do you feel?" Mike almost whispered.

"Me? Scared."

"Me, too."

"Groovy. What do we do now?"

We thought about that for a while. Outside, the darkness thickened. There were no stars visible and no moon, though last night at this time the moon was halfway up and nearly full. The sky had been clear at sunset, too. Apparently the lobster gang wasn't taking any chances or missing any bets. I didn't mention this to Mike, though.

We were waiting, intensely waiting, all of us and everything, consciously, yearningly, terrifiedly waiting. It was a texture, this waiting, a pressure where pressure was impossible. The dull, scared taste of apprehension covered everything: I could almost hear it. I had to give Ktch credit; he was thorough.

"I don't know," Mike said a little shrilly. "I don't know what to do at all. I had something worked out before, but I've forgotten it." I'd never heard him sound afraid before. I didn't like it.

"Well, the first thing we've got to do," with fraudulent briskness, "is keep that beach as brightly lit as we can, to keep the lobster gang from pouring their reality drug into the reservoir. That's the important thing."

"Light? Why should that stop them?" He still sounded scared.

"Shame, Michael, unadulterated shame. The things they believe and the things they do are almost mutually exclusive, for one thing; and they seem to be compulsive rationalizers, for another; which leads me to think they have an overdeveloped sense of shame."

"Hey!" a bit less fear, "maybe we can work on their sense of shame!!"

"Not a chance. A sense of shame's not much use to anyone. They won't mind dosing our water, but they won't want to do it while we're watching, and that's all the benefit we can expect from their sense of shame. However . . ."

One of the troopers screamed like a sudden banshee. Mike nearly fainted. I ran back to see what was happening.

Nothing was happening.

"I don't know what got into me," Karen sobbed. "I just, you know, kept getting scareder and scareder, until I just had to let it out or do something horrible. I don't know!" She poured tears on Andrew's shoulder.

This was Ktch's waiting-and-apprehension game at work. I could feel it myself, though I wasn't paying much attention to it. But something had to be done. A mere glance at our formerly brave little band was enough to tell me that. They were all unnaturally pale, some had developed tics, more had taken to looking back over their shoulders nervously, as though some hellish Thing were lurking there, and none of them looked at all happy. Even Pat's grin, impossible to erase, had a rather hollow look to it.

"Listen to me, you guys," I ordered firmly and loudly. "This is just one of the lobster gang's tricks, this fear-and-waiting bit. That's all it is, just a trick. It's not real. Honestly it's not."

They looked half hopeful and a bit less credulous, which was an improvement, but not enough.

"Listen. We don't have to put up with this. We can make them stop it. Yes we can. *I* did it. I did it last night, and I did it again this morning, when they had me tied up in their loft. It's easy."

I moved back to the harpsichord, gesturing to the rest of the band to follow.

"All we have to do is sing at them. Really. That's all there is to it. We'll give 'em 'Love Sold in Doses,' right? That's the song *I* used, and it worked like a charm. Honestly! I think they're a little afraid of it. Everybody sing, you hear? If you don't know the words, hum something. Ready? Let's go!"

And Sativa and The Tripouts and the MacDougal Street Commandos swung into "Love Sold in Doses." It was pretty ragged at first, but it firmed up quickly, and by the end of the second verse we were doing right well by it. We were feeling better, too—all of us. You could tell it from the singing.

And then, suddenly, like a guitar string snapping, the waiting-and-apprehension business stopped. We all lit up like happy bulbs.

"Keep on singing!" I yelled. "Sing it again. Don't stop until I do. And sing louder! Let the lobster gang hear it like it is. Louder!"

Oh my, but they were loud! Gary the cacophonous Frog was the loudest of the lot, of course, and flat to boot, but this was no time for technical quibbles. I smiled encouragment at him and—*mirabile!*—he sang even louder.

Halfway through the second time, the sky began to lighten. When we started on the third time, it was perfectly clear, with stars all over and a big old full moon brighter than a streetlight, and we just went on singing.

At the end of the fifth performance, Laszlo Scott shuffled onto the beach waving a piece of white cloth. We gave them a sixth performance for luck, then quit. We were all a little hoarse, and some of us weren't as fond of "Love Sold in Doses" as we had been, but we'd won our first skirmish with the lobster gang and we all felt approximately wonderful.

"Head for shore, Mike," I yelled. "Loathsome Laszlo wants to talk."

24

He didn't have a lot to say, and he didn't say it very well, but that's Laszlo. We weren't expecting more.

We might as well forget the music gambit, he told us. All the lobsters were wearing protective suits now. I accepted this, but only because I could see lurking in the trees behind Laszlo two lobsters dressed in silvery blankets. Even so, I wasn't all that sure we couldn't make them feel at least a bit uncomfortable. We had a lot of energy going for us.

Ktch sent me his regards, said Laszlo, and promised that if my friends and I would agree to go home right now, he'd personally guarantee that we'd get away from the reservoir unharmed.

I gave Laszlo four detailed and imaginative things he and Ktch could do with that safe-conduct guarantee. Then I demanded that Ktch come out like a man or whatever and speak to me man to thing. In fact, I made quite a scene about it, a virtuoso tantrum, at the end of which Laszlo was huddled on the sand, sniveling, and the MacDougal Street Commandos were cheering.

No soap. Ktch stayed safely out of sight. Too busy, Laszlo claimed. Chicken, I replied.

Then Laszlo haltingly expressed Ktch's regret that our ill-advised stubbornness (those words gave Laszlo fits) forced him to take strong measures. If we still refused to leave, said Laszlo, Ktch couldn't even guarantee our lives.

Since we hadn't expected any such guarantee, I replied, not having it wouldn't seriously inconvenience us.

(I didn't feel half as cocksure as I sounded. The triple dinosaur was proof that Ktch could throw some pretty strong magic at us. But I knew that if we didn't win this fight, being alive afterward wasn't going to be a particularly advantageous condition. And there was always a possibility, albeit a misty one, that we might actually win.)

Because he so respected me, Laszlo choked out, Ktch was going to give us one last chance. He was going to show us what we'd be up against if we didn't go quietly home right now like good little cats and chicks.

Then we all screamed. Something was standing behind Laszlo. It was only a shadow, a big opaque black shadow, featureless and formless; but just looking at it turned my stomach, and when it moved a prophecy of pain crawled through my nervous system, a memory of agony to come. It wasn't just a shadow, it was Evil, a whole history of Evil, contradicting everything I loved in waves of future torment. That was bad. Oh, bad.

And then the thing was gone.

That was only one of the weapons Ktch could use against us, Laszlo chortled, and not the worst one, either. Surely we could see we had no chance. Why did we persist in this foolishness?

By then I wasn't too sure myself.

Perhaps, Ktch said through Laszlo, we were being so headstrong because we hadn't time to think the problem out. Or perhaps the group didn't agree with me as unanimously as I thought. Perhaps I wasn't as appropriate a spokesman for the group as they had formerly believed. Perhaps the group would like some time to discuss the situation, maybe even take a vote.

Therefore (another hard word for Laszlo) Ktch was giving us twenty minutes' grace before he loosed his arsenal against us. He instructed us to take the bus out a hundred feet from the shore and talk it over. He also apologized for putting guards around us, but surely we could understand his position? And he wished us wisdom in our deliberations. (Poor tongue-tied mindless Laszlo.) If we decided to go home, we had only to blink our lights and he'd have us escorted to the nearest road.

That ended our parley. Laszlo shut up, turned, and shuffled back into the willow thicket. Mike backed the bus off a hundred feet, as ordered, keeping the beach well lit all the while. Our guards were pretty bad—huge, luminous green swimming things with red eyes, lots of teeth, and tentacles—but they didn't even disturb us; not after the black shadow.

We were all thoughtful and quiet. When we spoke we didn't whisper, but our voices were low. No one even mentioned going home but Gary the customary Frog, and even he protended he was joking.

I found myself standing beside Sean, and felt a duty to apologize.

"This isn't what I expected last Saturday," I said softly. "No, it's not at all the way I expected things to go. Now I feel I should've sent you back to Fort Worth, or not taken you in, or something. I'm sorry I got you into this mess, Sean." We shook hands.

"Hell, man, *you* didn't get me into this. I done that myself. Me an' them damn butterflies. Shucks . . ."

"Butterflies!" I yelled, scaring everyone on board. "Butterflies! Yahoo!"

"Hey, man, cool it!" Sean thought I'd flipped, and, I *had*, too, but not that way.

"C'mon!" I grabbed him by the arm and dragged him toward the harpsichord. "Everybody!" I was shouting. "C'mere! On the double!"

Everybody, looking mighty puzzled, came running.

Butterflies indeed! And there under the harpsichord, where I'd left it hours ago, there was my briefcase. I pulled it out, set it on top of the harpsichord where everyone could see, and opened it.

And there they were, hundreds of thousands of pretty blue Reality Pills. We had our weapon!

Maybe.

Time was our only problem. We had something less than twenty minutes, and I had no idea how long it took the pills to get to work. Except for that one little hangup, we were saved.

Well, we had a chance.

"Everybody take at least five," I ordered, hoping superstitiously that the more we took, the faster they'd work. Considering what Ktch and company were planning to dump into the reservoir— ten billion doses—I wasn't seriously worried about overdoses, and it didn't really matter anyhow.

"Take at least five," I repeated. "The more the better."

I grabbed a handful of the pills, stuffed my mouth with them and started swallowing. The US Cavalry was on the way!

25

For a while we were too busy swallowing pills to talk. Adam's apples twitched, solemn faces grimaced, pills went slowly down, time passed. I learned that pill swallowing loses its charm after the twenty-fifth pill. You get to feeling like a sack of BB's—nothing like my favorite way to feel.

When all the pills were dealt with, I started talking. I told my loyal troops how to control the hallucinations they were going to have, time and lobsters willing.

"Concentrate on Fighting," I told them. "Remember, whatever you imagine will be real, no matter how kooky it may be. Imagine weapons: death rays, bombs, bigger and better killing machines. Think death!"

I had to stop. I was embarrassing myself. What kind of talk was this for a pacifist? Forget it. I went on.

"I don't know what they're gonna throw at us, but in general here's what to do:

"Kill anything that moves in your direction. Don't stop to ask questions. It won't be friendly.

"Kill lobsters. That's probably the only way to persuade them to give up.

"Above all, don't let anybody pour Anything into the water. The only reason we're here is to keep that from happening. If they get that stuff into the water, We've had it, no matter how the fighting goes.

"If you can avoid it, don't get killed.

"Also, if you can avoid it, please do *not* kill Laszlo. I have plans for that boy."

I couldn't think of anything more to say, so I sat down. Everyone looked solemn. Time passed.

Just plain waiting is a drag. Waiting for a pill to take effect is worse, and waiting for a battle to begin has nothing at all to recommend it. Put them all together, it's depressing. We sat quietly. Time passed.

Michael said, "Ten minutes." Everybody twitched.

"Ten minutes since or ten minutes till?" I wondered.

"Till."

"Groovy. Is anybody getting high yet? Even a little bit?"

Little Micky raised his hand. "I don't know, man," shrug, "but like . . ."

"Groovy."

We sat quietly. Time passed.

I was trying to think up something to say before the fireworks, something terse and memorable that would look good in a history book, but I couldn't seem to find the words. The best I could come up with was "54-40 or fight!" and "Don't give up the *glub*!" neither of which fit somehow, so I gave it up.

Time passed.

Little Micky was smiling ecstatically. That was encouraging. I too, was beginning to feel the first faint stirrings of euphoria. Groovy. And how about the rest of the gang?

Michael was expressing solemn dignity, which looked in his case like a banker breaking wind. Gary the ultimate Frog looked Garyish—or Froggy, if you like. Sean's left eyebrow was raised a full inch higher than his right one—a possibly hopeful sign, if you weren't too hard to please. The others just looked serious.

"Five minutes," Michael chimed.

Little Micky giggled. Sometimes being short and scrawny helps.

"Micky?" said I.

He giggled again.

"You may have to do a solo set at first. No one else is off yet."

"That's cool, baby." Further giggles.

"Can you do it? Seriously."

"I *said* it's cool, baby." Additional and prolonged giggling. I crossed my fingers.

Actually, I was starting to feel decidedly better. The hopelessness of our situation was beginning to amuse me. The fact that we fourteen ill-sorted nuts were sitting here waiting to get high enough to save the world was so outrageously absurd I couldn't help giggling a bit myself.

Little Micky politely giggled back at me.

"Two minutes," said Michael. "Let's go upstairs.'"

The Tripsmobile had a sun deck on the roof, planted with grass and dandelions. We'd intended to put a few lawn chairs up there, too, and a table with a parasol, but we never got around to it. And now we were going to use it for a battlefield. I giggled again. Little Micky joined me.

We took our places along the fence, ten of us facing the beach, four guarding the rear and flanks. Sean was now among the gigglers, and most of the others were smiling.

"One minute," Mike announced. "And before we begin, I have a request to make. Please try to avoid killing each other. Especially me."

"I agree," I said. "Don't blow your cool." Several people giggled.

There was nothing happening on the beach yet. It still had that deserted look. There was no trace of the lobster, gang, no sign of the war approaching. Only Laszlo's footprints on the sand suggested anything had ever happened there.

"Thirty seconds."

I tried to project a test hallucination, but I wasn't ready yet. I wished Little Micky'd run a test. I decided against suggesting it—he'd doubtless want an explanation, and I didn't feel up to it.

"Twenty."

Nothing happening yet. No more gigglers, either, but that might not signify: some heads never giggle. I, for instance, never giggle. But . . .

"Fifteen."

Nothing, not even a breeze in the willows.

"Ten. Get ready."

I hate countdowns. Always have. Michael, on the other hand, is passionately fond of countdowns. You never can tell.

"Five. Four. Three." Nothing on the beach. "Two. One. Zero!"

Nothing continued happening. Mike's face expressed innocence betrayed in exhaustive detail.

"Is it kosher to use negative numbers?" I inquired.

"Sloppy, that's what they are," said Michael. "Sloppy." He was really burned. "How do they expect to . . ."

Something was happening! The willows were shaking. Something was pushing its way through the willows. Something was . . .

It was a lobster in a silver blanket. Maybe even Ktch. He pushed the last layer of willow wands aside with his huge claws and stared out at us for maybe half a minute, making good and sure we were still there. Then he backed away into the thicket and we started breathing again.

"I hate an unpunctual lobster," Michael said, still peeved.

And the willows were rustling again, more vigorously, as though something larger than a lobster were forcing a way through them. They went on rustling for a painfully long time. Whatever was coming wasn't in a hurry. The willows' agitation mounted to frenzy. The last curtain of leaves was hurled aside as though by a gale.

Somebody moaned.

The black shadow moved slowly toward us down the beach.

26

L ittle Micky bracketed the shadow with odd-shaped, rapid-fire camions, but the shells passed through it like nothing at all, not bothering it a bit. I got the impression that the shadow didn't even notice the cannons and shells, that it was aware of nothing on this whole green planet but our shaggy selves. This was not an impression to treasure.

Little Micky switched to explosive shells. They revised the landscape pretty drastically, but failed to inconvenience the shadow.

The shadow, meanwhile, was projecting gross despair and future pain much more intensely than before, inconveniencing us no end.

Little Micky poised two flamethrowers above the shadow and smothered it in fire. The shadow noticed this. It absorbed the flames, and then the flamethrowers, doubled its height, and kept coming.

I was now officially up tight. This wasn't going according to the script at all. Of course, I hadn't expected the first assault to be the shadow, but there it was, and Little Micky didn't seem to be able to cope with it, and it didn't seem especially stoppable, and I didn't like anything that was happening.

Micky dropped bombs on the shadow—good, fat, healthy bombs—and the shadow didn't notice.

"No!" Micky yelled. He was losing his temper.

The shadow reached the water while Micky was working out his next move. The water drew away from the shadow, as though refusing to touch such a thing. Spooky. The water wouldn't come within a foot of the shadow, nor could I blame it. So the shadow moved toward us in the center of an absence of water. If I were superstitious . . .

"All right, you mother!" Micky had worked something out. "Take that!"

High-pressure hoses surrounded the shadow and shot iron-hard jets of water at it. The thought was good, but it didn't work. The twelve-inch limit still applied, and the jets were shattered and deflected upward in a spectacular fifty-foot-high fountain that soundly drenched us and accomplished nothing else.

"No!" Oh, but Micky was bugged. "You mother, you! Dig it: I'm gonna put a flippin' A-bomb right inside of you, you dig?"

Mike and I yelled, "Stop! Don't do that!" and similar phrases intended to stop Little Micky from setting off an A-bomb in our laps, but he ignored us. He was POed at that shadow.

There was a muffled, almost subsonic *Whump!* The shadow bulged out at the middle, then grew another twenty feet, changed from a black shadow to a black flame, and kept on coming.

Little Micky went berserk. He started jumping up and down and screaming unbelievable polyglot invective and abuse at the flame. He was extravagantly out of his mind.

I was nearly out of mine. The flame was thirty feet away and coming strong, and the only member of our team who wasn't helpless was throwing a temper tantrum. We were in trouble. I tried another test projection, and nothing happened again. I wasn't properly high yet, but I could tell it was only a matter of minutes now. So, unfortunately, was that black flame.

But Little Micky stopped screaming and jumping, stood trembling still, and whispered in the tone that panthers use for hissing, "You mother! I am digging you a Pit!"

A moment later the approaching darkness abruptly fell out of sight and was gone. The whole world suddenly felt better.

Little Micky laughed forever in the space of two minutes and was glorious.

"How did you do it?" I wanted to know.

"Easy, baby, easy. I just made this like Pit underneath that mother an', dig it, he fell right into some other dimension. Ain't that a bitch?"

Ktch hadn't expected to need a second act for us, so we enjoyed a ten-minute intermission while he assembled our next entertainment.

We needed those ten minutes. They gave the pills time to take general effect, giving us all a good jolt of euphoria, which always comes in handy, and curing our helplessness.

Ktch's unplanned intermission gave our dozen neophytes some time to get more or less used to the techniques of projection, and it gave Mike and me a chance to better our working conditions.

The darkness bothered me, so I scattered a dozen nuclear flood lamps around at five hundred feet and put on my shades. I tried to throw a spherical force field around the bus, too, but that didn't happen. So the pill *wasn't* unlimited after all. Force fields (I hoped) were probably too abstract for it.

(I also hoped I wasn't going to learn any more of the pill's limits under fire. That could be expensive.)

Our rooftop position was too vulnerable to suit Mike, so he hung an acre of wire netting twenty feet above our heads and clogged the water around us with barbed-wire emplacements. Our toothy guards had disappeared while we weren't looking.

And then it started.

Nameless things were charging us from all directions, screeching, mewling, roaring, howling, piping, yelping, making sounds inside our heads, and all with grossly malicious intent.

My particular concern at the beginning was a transparent flying thing built like a loose heap of dry-cleaners' plastic bags. It had taken a fancy to me for reasons I couldn't imagine and didn't care to learn. I broke it up with a well-conceived grenade, but the fragments were just as lively as the whole and shared the same fondness for me. They were too small to shoot at and too scattered to burn, so I gathered them up in a vacuum cleaner and burned *it*.

Then, there being nothing specifically after me at the moment, I took a brisk look around.

Andrew Blake and Karen, working together were coping with a swarm of what looked at first like long-tailed bees but turned out to be tiny flying serpents, no doubt ingeniously venomous. Being Andy and Karen, they were scooping the snapping beasties up in electrified butterfly nets. Each of them had on his shoulder a birdly creature with green angora fur and a huge appetite for such of the pests as managed to sneak past the nets.

Michael was being proficiently menaced by the front end of an orange and silver-striped centipedish horror, three feet thick and apparently quite long, overequipped with quick-moving needle claws and topped with a red and black face that was mostly mouth, and that mostly teeth. Naturally, Mike was using a sword to quell this monster. In fact, they were actually dueling—lunging and thrusting and parrying and all. The beast was down on points when I looked, with lots of open cuts oozing yellow and several arms lopped off. The thing made great soughing noises as it moved, like a very fat lady sinking into an armchair, and Mike was reciting something from *Cyrano*. Show-off!

Harriet, screaming like a dime on dry ice, was watching a large green lion with yellow spots devour something scarlet that *would* have been a lion if it had known how. The green one was obviously hers, and the screams were just embellishments.

Then Sean called for help. He had a squad of three large not-quite rats wearing blue capes and carrying weapons that looked like miniaturized stock goads attacking him with shrill cries from the left, and something I thought was a brown net but was really another flying thing clinging to his right arm in a hostile manner, and he'd panicked slightly.

On a hunch, I soaked the flying net with vinegar. It shrilled just within the audible range, fumed, shriveled, and fell off. Sean kicked it overboard.

The caped rats were a whole different thing. They were fast, smart, vicious, instinctive kamikazes, and their little stock goads were some kind of ultrapotent neural weapon. Even near-misses were painful, and I still limp a little from having been touched on the leg by one. Nasty. Our immediate project was to keep the rats at a comfortable distance, but there were three of them and only two of us, and by their standards we were pathetically awkward and slow. Using larger versions of their own weapons, we could keep any two of them at bay, but the third rat was impossible.

But we kept trying until I got stung on the leg. In that first intricate moment of pain, I realized how stupid it was to fight these things with their own weapons, so I dumped five gallons of rubber cement on them and left them for Sean to sweep overboard.

The pain in my leg also reminded me that I wanted to do something about the jolly lobsters who were providing all this healthful exercise. I coolly stole a military robot from some half-remembered science fiction story, made a few slight alterations, and planted a dozen of them in the ravine behind the beach. Then I resumed my look-around.

Gary the Frog and an ancient battle-ax were busily shortening the tentacles of a slimy gray water beast most of which was out of sight. The severed tentacles dripped a thin blue liquid that sizzled and evaporated as it fell, leading me to wonder where the beast came from and why. Oh, the tentacles had claws at their tips.

Gary seemed to enjoy his work. As he chopped, he loudly flatted "I Want to Hold Your Hand" to the rhythm of his battle-ax. Ah well: each man to his taste, I suppose, but I'd've used a laser.

We seemed to be in a minor lull. Oh, carnage was being dealt out left and right, with our side doing all the dealing, but there were three of us caught at the same time with nothing to do. I returned to my original post and took stock.

Our side seemed to be doing pretty well for itself. We'd beaten off all boarders so far, without casualties. But that was just holding our own. We were actually doing somewhat better than that. The sky, for example, was crowded with gleaming metal gadgets—probably Michael's—that were efficiently stopping most airborne attackers before they could get to us, so—the best battles being those you don't have to fight—we were pulling a bit ahead of the game.

Of course, Ktch's having bought his fighters at a rummage sale or whatever was to our advantage, too. It's a hell of a lot easier and safer to fight isolated members of a thousand races than a thousand members of one race. If Ktch'd mounted a concerted attack, we'd be in trouble, but this catch-as-catch-can stuff was fun—even for me, and I'm no fighter.

Furthermore . . .

"Hello?"

"Gah!" I had company. Lots of it. Only one animal, but big. And it Talked?

"Did you," I asked, "just say Hello to me?"

"I did."

"How 'bout that?" This one was a serpent by trade, complete with forked tongue and fangs. A hooded serpent. He was silver above, gold-green below, had an armlike pair of tentacles (or a tentacular set of arms) growing just below his hood, and would've been quite pretty if he hadn't been so huge. His head was larger than my body, and his tail was resting high up on the beach more than a hundred feet away. Big snake. And he could talk.

"You know, I've never been spoken to by a serpent before.

"I understand. Some of us are *excessively* secretive." Not speech, telepathy.

"If you'll pardon my asking, sir: why did *you* speak to me?"

"I wanted to know who you are. I *never* eat anyone I don't know. It's not safe." Okay, but snakes are easy.

"Are you intending to eat me?"

"One of you, maybe more. That's why I was brought here. But I don't know which ones yet. You see, I'm very *particular* about my food. Picky. I have to be. I'm really very—Sensitive."

Groovy. Ancient Village line, right? So I filled his inside and bathed his outside with liquid helium and watched him topple. Snakes are easy. Especially the sensitive ones.

But what was I thinking when the serpent interrupted? Oh yes, something had to be done about the lobster gang. With a mere shrug of the imagination, I established a dozen military robots in the willow grove behind the beach.

That minor lull was growing major. Kevin, for reasons of his own, was sprinkling salt and pepper on a giant amoeba. Stu was hurling balls of colored fire at a six-armed but otherwise humanoid horned giant who, with a weapon in each hand, was diligently trying to get at Stu. The giant's skin was the colors and texture of a Gila monster's, but Stu didn't seem to be in trouble. And Pat was off in a corner *singing* to some avant-garde crystalline life form that . . . Oh. The crystal shattered.

And that was all the action there was. The rest of the gang was just tossing ex-things and chunks thereof overboard—housecleaning.

Was it over? I still felt wildly manic, and I certainly hoped not. "Hey Michael," I yelled, "this is our chance." But maybe Ktch was only rounding up another team.

"Chance for what?"

I walked up to him and whispered, "Chance to attack."

"Attack who?" Stu yelled. He was at large, too. He'd left old six-arms slumped down on the grass like a pyramid and burning merrily.

"Hey, man," I reproached him, "I wish you wouldn't burn your things on the roof. It's bad for the grass. And what if the bus catches fire, hah?"

"Sorry 'bout that." The fire died away.

"Strategy meeting," Mike proclaimed. "Strategy meeting at this end of the roof. Meeting time."

So we gathered at that end of the roof, all but Little Micky, who wasn't interested in strategy and volunteered to stand watch at the other end.

"I've been thinking," said the Michael, "that now's the time for Us to attack Them."

I: *"You've* been thinking!"

Mike: "I don't claim to be the only one. All I said . . ."

Sativa: "For this kind of strategy, who needs a meeting?"

And then Little Micky made That Noise, the one that wakes me up some nights. High, thin, twist-tight, inhumanly sustained: I'd never heard anyone die like that before.

And there were Little Micky and this kid, this absolutely beautiful five-year-old American blond Kid—but Micky was dead and this Kid was pulling him apart and tossing the pieces overboard.

The kid looked up at us and grinned. There was blood on his chin. He threw a piece of Little Micky at us and yelled a treble war cry. A million shrill voices returned the cry, and the kids swarmed over the fence and charged. They were all beautiful children, all five-year-olds in pastel shorts, and they came at us yelling, with knives in their hands.

Our defense was pure instinct at first, hand- and footwork, dirty, minus intellect or any emotion but fear. Our minds hadn't functioned since Micky made That Noise.

Here's a little redhead coming at me, knife held low and pointed up. Kick him before he gets too close, kick him anywhere. Groin's good. Get him under the chin and break his neck, but he'll probably cut your leg before he does. And don't just hurt him, kill him. Pain doesn't stop these kids. Watch it! There's another.

They came in waves ten feet apart, and they didn't stop coming. Death was all they wanted—ours or theirs. Mortal wounds and broken bones only slowed them down a little. Kids' bodies lay heaped three feet high around us like a wall. All of us were bleeding. This went on and on.

And all this bitter time they yelled shrill ferocity in glasscracking, searing, mind-crushing, impossibly unending ultra-treble tones more agonizing than knives and more shuttering than fear—a million-throated irresistible loud cry of driving madness. Even their voices were weapons.

The first one to snap out of it was Harriet, our group's outstanding lover of children. Suddenly she remembered that we didn't *have* to do it this way. She swept the charging wave with submachine gun fire, and did it again and again. Her face was soaked with tears.

The rest of us remembered. Now we attacked with terrible weapons. And we got them all. We made darn sure of that.

But when it was finally over, we couldn't find Little Micky's body.

27

I threw the last small body overboard and it didn't splash. Our starboard corpse pile now rose well out of the water—quite impressive—and our portside pile rose even higher. I hadn't realized we pacifists could be such dangerous animals.

I rather *liked* being dangerous. A taste for it was growing in me.

The operation we'd just finished—the kindergarten kamikaze horror—had left the grass on the Tripsmobile roof in a sorry state. It was all bloody and scruffy, but especially bloody, and I wondered whether I should send the grass out to be dry-cleaned or just sit back and pray for rain. I mean, I was glad to know that the beautiful children we'd been slaughtering weren't Earth kids at all but two-hearted aliens with incomprehensible genitalia, but that didn't ease my bloody grass problem. And I'd always been so proud of The Tripouts' touring sun deck, too.

That nice warm chemical euphoria—quite depleted by the last campaign—was beginning to rise in me again.

Otherwise there wasn't much going on. That is, nothing was trying to kill us just then. On the other hand, Sean was making butterflies again, far superior to his Saturday productions, and Sativa was wreathing them in enriched and augmented rainbows, all of which spoke well of Sativa and Sean.

I wondered—this was a time for wondering—what was going to become of our heaps of unearthly cadavers. Not a chance in the world they'd escape being noticed, jutting bizarrely up in the middle of what ought to be a plain, uncluttered New York City reservoir. And the moment anyone at all saw just what kind of bodies we'd collected in these monster midden heaps of ours, every breed of entertaining hell would pop loose from Manhattan to Helsinki—a prospect I looked forward to with blandly anarchistic glee. (All of which was based upon the rattletrap assumption that the lobster gang would not complete Phase Two.)

And then I regrettably wondered what effect this interstellar carrion was having on our water. Some days it just don't pay to wonder.

Michael the Theodore Bear and the rest of our jolly band were nervously trying to reconvene the interrupted strategy meeting. Michael was peevishly enduring mild administrative hangups.

"Sean," he sighed, "Sativa: can't you let that wail till we get home?"

I thought they were rather pretty, but I guess Michael was right. The Reality Pill seemed to have some unexpected aphrodisiac effects.

"Gary," with theatrical patience, "what the hell do you think you're doing?"

"Fishing?"

"I'd rather you didn't. In fact I . . . Andy! How in God's name can you *sleep* at a time like this?"

"Sleep? I wasn't asleep. I was only . . ."

". . . resting your eyes," Mike completed wearily.

I might as well join the party. "Dear friends and fellow killers," I proclaimed hoarsely, "henceforth the only water I shall drink is bottled spring water. This city water's just too rich for my blood. Otherwise, what's happening?"

Michael shrugged. "Nobody's attacking us," he conceded.

"Groovy! Let's attack."

And so much for strategy meetings.

Mike pulled the bus up on the beach and cut the motors. Hush! Suddenly the world was a very quiet place. I had forgotten quiet.

I could feel my ears stretching out to catch the nice, informative little noises they had been deprived of for so long. From the poleaxed look on Kevin's face, I gathered that the stretching effect was moderately visible.

"What are *you* staring at," I inquired pro forma.

"Me? Oh—nothing. I'm not staring at your . . . I'm not staring. Honestly!"

"Bigot."

The beach had undergone some monumental changes. It had been brutally plowed over by countless extraterrestrial catastrophes. The tail of my quick-frozen friend, the Sensitive telepathic snake, cut diagonally across it to pass out of sight among the battered willows. Little Micky's forgotten cannons had churned the sand up with too many pounds of futile high explosives. Ktch's grab bag E.T. army had decorated the beach with scattered chunks of totally inexplicable litter. Unimaginable violence had scrawled its complex signature on what, a mere few hours ago, had been a paper-smooth and more or less deserted little beach, leaving it looking very like the children's sandbox in Washington Square.

And Michael, like a mother hen in master sergeant's clothing, was trying to maneuver our courageous band of flipped-out volunteers into something approximating orthodox platoon formation. But chemicals euphoria was having comically disastrous effects on martial discipline.

Everyone was suddenly exclusively concerned with his own Thing. (Come to think of it, so was Mike.) Andrew Blake had conjured up what could pass for the ghost of Henry James—barring unsuspected gaps in Andy's memory—and was trying to get it to teach him how to write dirty books in pure 1890's florid high style; but the ghost of maybe Henry James, concerned more with the subject than the style, insisted on asking blunt, unflorid questions that made Andy blush from beard to brow and rendered him extravagantly useless for Mike's purposes.

Gary the cupiditous Frog and Harriet were happily projecting millions of enormous diamonds—but Gary's looked suspiciously like paste. Consistency is such a charming accident!

Sativa was walking insecurely fifteen feet up in the air and looking unsure whether to enjoy the sport or cry. Karen was building a scale model of the Pyramid of Cheops in vanilla halvah. Sandi was assembling separate but equal layettes in dusty pink and blue, suggesting she might well be pregnant after all.

Leo was also constructing a scale model, Rodin's "The Kiss," out of a greenish-brown substance that looked like Persian hashish. Pat and Stu were removing gobs of this strange substance just a bit less quickly than Leo could put it on, while arguing in unknown tongues both seemed to understand.

Sean and Kevin were playing a lively game of anti-anti-missile missile, using genuine miniature anti-antimissile missiles, with the score, while I watched them, pretty loudly tied.

What the hell? I put up a double of the Wanamaker organ and tossed- off a few bright choruses of *The Carman's Whistle.* Like they say: if you can't run your tongue across them, merge with them.

None of this sat noticeably well with Brother Michael. His face was trying to register so many different disapprovals simultaneously it seemed frozen in a disbelieving blank. He was trying to shout, too, but he couldn't make up his mind what to shout first, and nothing came out but a vaguely well-bred gurgle.

I could understand a lot of what Mike must be feeling. After all, we really weren't in anything like fighting trim just then. A pair of moderately irritated nuns could've wiped us out one-handed. To test this thesis, I projected a pair of moderately irritated nuns, but they just sniffed disdainfully, rattled their beads, and strode off into the woods. Nevertheless, we *were* pretty grossly ignoring out mission, and something certainly ought to be done. I hoped Mike could figure out something to do.

But he didn't have to. Three vulgarly well-armed military robots clanked out of the thicket, Sativa fell to the sand with a tentative squeal and an alarmingly tactile thump, and all our maniac fun and games evaporated.

Well, nearly all. My mighty Wanamaker organ didn't seem to want to go. The robots ground to a halt amd made it overwhelmingly clear that they were waiting for me to get rid of my overdone playtoy before they'd state their transcendentally important business. This was terribly embarrassing.

I unimagined my music box in painstaking detail and nothing worth mentioning happened. The robots, chugging softly, continued to wait. Mike's face found a single expression it could maintain, but not one I enjoyed. The rest of the gang stared at me as though the whole thing were all *my* fault.

I carefully wished the organ off to the deepest pit of hell, where it might even do some good. It tootled derisively and stayed put.

"All right, you guys," I sneered. "Who's the wise guy put a hex on me?"

Nobody giggled, not even the robots. Most of my erstwhile friends gave me the kind of smile you're supposed to use only when visiting elderly relatives in mental wards. Michael's left nostril twitched in Morse.

"Aw come *on!*" I was running out of temper. The last time that'd happened to me, I gave the Old Empire State Building such a punishing kick I had to walk on crutches for a week. Recalling that mistake, I gave the musical monster—that forty-nine-ton albatross—an experimental tap with my right boot.

PoP! like the emperor of soap suds. It was gone. Someone was unkind enough to cheer.

"Now are you satisfied?" I asked the air a few yards to the left of the lead robot. They all three hopped to pots-and-pans attention, and the one in front threw me a bell-like salute so crisp it would have turned a West Point kay-det mauve.

"T-X two-three beta, sir. Are you Galactic Grand High Marshal Anderson?"

I floated him a return for his salute, said, "At ease, things," and allowed as how I might well be the institution he was seeking. I almost remembered having vaguely considered conjuring up some such gadgets to keep the lobsters occupied a few hours back, but I couldn't even pretend to remember having *done* it; and besides, any hallucination of mine would've known I'm just too modest to put up with such inflated titles.

Still, "What can I do for you, gadget?" I asked kindly, not wanting to hurt the poor thing's ferric feelings.

"Begging to report, sir. Armored details Toggle-Xylophone and Marshmallow-Buggywhip" (I could hear the military Michael gagging somewhere to my left, but I ignored him. Why should I use someone else's secondhand phonetic alphabet?) "engaged units of the enemy at 2100 hours, killing three aliens and capturing nine, plus one humanoid associated with the enemy, sustaining only superficial damage and no casualties, sir."

He shot off another of those tool-and-die salutes, which I alertly fielded and returned. "Well done, device," I said, "well done," in a warm and well-oiled tone calculated to win me the instant love of my troops. "Please bring in the prisoners."

After another volley of precisely machined salutes, the three gleaming golems snapped about face and returned to the woods.

"Chester?" Michael, fatally wounded, implored.

"I don't know any more about it than you do," I assured him. "Maybe less."

"I certainly hope so," just short of a sob.

One thing was relatively sure: either those machines were programmed by some unidentified subversive over-poweringly disrespectful of our hallowed military traditions, or I programmed them myself and was in desperate need of psychiatric care. Imagine, as didn't I dare, the anguish those boiler-plate parodies were inflicting on poor Michael. I felt a sinking certainty he'd never forgive me for this.

Our gang—impressed, overawed, or otherwise incapable of free expression—shuffled feet, beat twitchy rhythms on thighs, uttered fractional whispers, and displayed other symptoms of uncomprehending restlessness. An exaggerated red, white, and bluely chauvinistic butterfly glided by within a half inch of my nose.

"Cool it," I suggested. "I think we've got it licked now." I was careful riot to define my terms.

Then the mechanical marines returned—a good two dozen of them—riding herd on nine psychotically depressed blue lobsters and one ambiguously frantic Laszlo Scott. The cockles of my heart—whatever they might be—warmed to an instant ruby glow at the sight. (But where in hell did two whole dozen robots come from?)

"Hiya, Lasz!" bleated Gary the compulsive Frog. Laszlo didn't respond.

The metallic militia lined the wilted prisoners up before me, took a uniform giant step back, discharged a barrage of salutes clearly audible halfway to Fort Mudge, then aimed a complete assortment of semiportable artillery at the prisoners and stood as still as robots standing still.

And there I was, staring at the first honest-to-God real enemies I'd ever honest-to-God really defeated—and I discovered that I didn't know what to do with them. Nothing my previous experience had prepared me for this situation.

"Okay," I asked the world at large, *"now* what am I supposed to do?"

"Why," somebody started, "don't you just . . ." and faded out. Right. Nobody said anything for a while.

Then, "I suppose there ought to be a trial," I supposed. "That's what they did last time. Nuremberg. It seems to be traditional."

The courtroom was. dark, but the darkness illuminated it. The lobsters were standing on separate round raised platforms in bulletproof glass cylinders. Laszlo was similarly housed, but at some distance from the others.

The ceiling, dark and glowing, rose powerfully to meet the wall some forty-five feet above the judge's bench, from which point a flag—a glowing spiral nebula against a field of light-absorbant black in depth—hung down almost to the floor.

The judge's bench was a plain white table with an inset display screen, and a white straight-back chair.

The judge wore vibrant gray robes that perfectly concealed the shape of his body, and he was some three feet taller than you'd expect a man to be; but his face was acceptably human— longer than ours and narrower, more angular, considerably wise, hairless, and bright yellow: not Homo sap., but human all the way.

I didn't know who was responsible for it, but I surely did admire that set.

"Pay heed to the court," a deep and sourceless voice admonished.

"An unaffiliated group of native Terrans now bring cause against one non-Terran, Ktch, and against his coracialists and their superiors, if any, for the crimes of felonious trespass, inciting to warfare, intent to practice genocide, and conspiracy to enslave. Cause is also brought against one Terran, Laszlo Scott, for voluntary participation in crimes against his species, for conspiracy to enslave, and for racial treason," the judge read solemnly from his display screen. "Are you people ready? Come on, now. Let's not take all day."

We stepped up to the bench, all a little overawed.

"These bastards are as guilty as sin," the judge said. "What's it worth? Want 'em killed?"

Pause.

"No," Mike said quietly. "That doesn't fit, somehow."

"Okay. Then how about expulsion and sanctions?"

I wasn't quite sure what that meant, but it sounded right to me, and I said so.

"Right. Offender Ktch, give heed. You—by which are also meant and included your coracialists and superiors, if any— stand convicted of each charge. It is the order of this court that you shall withdraw from Terra and adjacent space no later than one local hour after the end of the present trial. You are further ordered to abstain henceforth from the practice of conquest and colonization, and to abandon all colonies no older than the oldest living member of your race, under pain of termination. If we catch you at this racket one more time, you've had it.

"Now what about the other one?"

This I'd made plans for. I'd been five years gathering recipes for Laszlo's just deserts. I knew to the erg how to pay him back for all the Laszlo tricks he'd played. Elaborate visions of quaint retribution were a minor mainstay of my fantasy life. But now all these schemes felt inappropriate.

"How about sending him off with the others?" That had a certain humorous appeal.

"Quite poetic," the judge smiled (sideways, by our reckoning). "All beings present and attending now bear witness," he intoned. "Offender Laszlo Scott stands convicted of each charge, accusers urging clemency. Therefore this court declares and redefines said Laszlo Scott coracial in perpetuity to offender of the first cause, in full and equal membership and subject to the sanctions of this court. Wherefore the present cause is now closed and this body is dismissed.

"All right, you people, you have an hour. Start hopping."

Which put us all on battle beach again. I'd've blamed the whole thing on the pill, except that the lobsters were scurrying and Laszlo was complaining, "Hey, man, Cool it! That ain't fair! What're you picking on Me for? I mean, what'd I Do, man? What'd I Do? Hey, baby, No!"

I hadn't counted on that: Laszlo in voluble distress, myself in empathy. Very depressing. I felt sad and righteous, a brand-new combination for me. And I pitied Laszlo, which I also hadn't counted on.

Not all of us experienced this hangup.

"Please don't let 'em do it to me, baby. Man! I won't ever see real people anymore!"

"Don't sweat it, Laszlo," Kevin said. "You probably won't even notice the difference.

The lobsters' ship—a conventional saucer model with a highly polished mirror finish—was concealed in a dune just a few yards away from the beach. They had it cleared and ready to fly in under twenty minutes.

Laszlo was still in his glass cage, screaming, "I don't wanna go away! Oh wow, man, I'm like scared, man. Somebody help me!" He was falling apart unprettily.

"Hey, baby," Patrick comforted, "just think of all them groovy things you're gonna see. Wow, and all those far-out planets and like that. Hey, man, what a gas!"

"No! No, don' wanna! No!"

Ktch very shyly sought me out.

"I must apologize, Mister Spy," he abased himself. "We misjudged you. I am sorry."

Not sorry for trying to conquer us and all. Sorry he'd insulted us by underestimating us. This wasn't a way I could ever think, but even so I had to give him credit: Ktch had class.

I forgave him everything he thought needed it, and we parted on technically friendly terms half an hour ahead of schedule.

"Please!" Laszlo shrieked prayers as the lobsters carried him to the ship. "Nonono I'm *Sorry*! No! Please! I'm Really sorry! I'll be good, I promise! No! Don't put me out in the dark! I won't do it anymore! Don't make me all alone! Please! I'll be Good!" Then the ship's lock closed and no one ever heard the voice of Laszlo Scott again.

I could feel the day at last begin to curve in toward a close. A day full of years. Mortal fear, mortal combat, victory, justice, and repentance: suddenly and all at once that day I had encountered concepts that I'd always thought were mythical, and they just weren't what they'd been cracked up to be.

The ship rose above my nuclear lamps and out of sight. A few minutes later we all heard a pop like prepubescent thunder and I knew they were gone.

"Swell," Mike privately rejoiced, then, louder, "Okay, everybody. Let's pack it up and hit the road."

Silently—the trial and its aftermath had put us in a collective thoughtful mood—we dismantled our imaginary artifacts and boarded the tripsmobile.

Mike had to get us home somehow without the benefit of my expert worrying. I fell asleep the minute I sat down.

28

nd that, we all naively thought was that.

The world was saved to a fare-thee-well and only slightly battered. Laszlo and the lobster gang were gloriously out of it for real. The papers were hilarious with mad and earnest speculation on the curious corpses we'd abandoned in the reservoir. Sean'd bought me a bottle of spring water. And I had a practically inexhaustible supply of Reality Pills for Halloween, saturnalia, and bar mitzvahs.

There was, of course, a skinny outside chance that somebody might want Little Micky's absence explained, but it wasn't bloody likely. Micky'd been one of the hundreds of Villagers *in vacuo:* no family, no relations, no hometown, no background, no pad, no chick, no past, little present and let's don't have any morbid talk about the future. Out of the nothing, into the here and away— just one of the hundreds. It didn't seem reasonable to expect Little Micky to have more kinfolk dead than he did alive; and, barring that acute unlikelihood, we didn't have a problem to our names.

But all day Thursday afternoon I kept finding random little things I wanted right there underneath my hand, which wasn't really consonant with my established way of life.

And the first tweet of the vidiphone brought me Andrew Blake saying, "Chester! God in heaven help me, it's Happening again!" as openers for a half-hour lamentation on his new, improved, four-color Art Nouveau psychedelic Carnaby Street halo.

And Sandi phoned a little after that and did nothing but giggle uncontrollably for seven minutes.

And after that, when I was donning my gaudiest celebratory threads for work, I happened to look out my bedroom window and see in the courtyard below a perfectly lovely small quiescent steam calliope all garlanded with improbable blossoms.

And then Mike's malty, dry, let's-explore-the-obvious voice tiptoed into my room, saying, "Know what, Chester? I've been thinking," and I braced myself.

"And what have you been thinking, O Michael?" I dreaded, entering the living room. Sean, looking rurally concerned, was already there.

"I've been thinking that we dropped a god-awful lot of those Reality Pills last night." Michael was standing on his head, feet and buttocks braced against the west wall. He'd never done anything remotely like that before. My spirit or something trembled.

"Go on."

"And an awful lot of Very Strange Things have been happening to everybody all day long. And somehow I've acquired this irrational conviction that we're never ever coming down."

He looked good, standing on his head. It *became* him, somehow. I piously wished that I didn't believe him.

But Sean, that puppy, hollered, "GrOOvy!" and hallucinated an intense silver and scarlet butterfly with, printed across its wings in some invisible color our eyes could real like electricity, the magic words:

THE END

But it wasn't, really.

Not at all.

Oh my, no!